# TERROR OF THE INNOCENT

A John Deacon Action Adventure

# Mike Boshier

# VIP Reader's Mailing List

To join our VIP Readers Mailing List and receive updates about new books and freebies, please go to the end section of this book.

# Books

High Seas Hijack

The Jaws of Revenge

Terror of the Innocent

Crossing a Line

Copyright © 2017 Mike Boshier
All rights reserved.
ISBN: 978-0-473-39854-5
www.mikeboshier.com

# Acknowledgements

I would like to take this opportunity to thank the people who greatly helped in the coming together of this book, from its original inception to the finished piece. Whether it was just comments and suggestions through to proofreading and corrections, I am deeply indebted to you all. They include my wife, Walter Hunt, Simon Helyar, Steve Lowndes, Peter Cook, Andre Mouradian, and, last but certainly not least, Sandra van Eekeren.

**If you liked reading this book, please leave feedback on whatever system you purchased this from.**

Check out the rear pages of this book for details of other releases, information and free stuff.

# Chapter 1

## Iraq - 2003

Captain Ammar Muhammad Hamoodi didn't want to die. Had he known the consequence to answering the phone he would have ignored it and let its staccato noise continue echoing through the darkened house.

But he was a good soldier, and he reached for the handset.

The call that started the end of his life was brief. It ordered him to be at the offices of the Special Republican Guard at 06:30 that morning. It left no room for discussion.

Then the call ended.

Sighing he dressed quickly. Looking around his sparse apartment, he kissed his pregnant wife and sleeping son goodbye before heading downstairs. He could feel his heart beating faster and his blood pressure building as he drove his dented Toyota to the SPG headquarters through the already heavy early morning traffic.

Captain Hamoodi was a loyal soldier. He'd been in the Army all his adult life, following in his father's footsteps. From university, he'd joined as an officer candidate, and his skill at organising had placed him in logistics. After good and steady progress and some promotion, he'd finally been promoted to Captain in charge of a transport division, which was where he was likely to remain.

Unfortunately, war was coming. Iraqi television and radio constantly berated the West about their military build-up in Kuwait. War was coming, and America was leading it. Officially Ammar only listened to Iraqi radio and TV, but all the channels from around the Gulf were easily received, including Al-Jazeera from Qatar. He knew the build-up was happening and he knew 'Dubya' wouldn't stop until he'd taken Baghdad this time. Ammar also knew first-hand war was coming. Being in charge of a 12 fleet division of Mercedes trucks in the Army Logistics Corp based at Al-Taji, the largest tank maintenance facility in Iraq, for the past two months he and his men had been moving stores, weapons and men nearer to the borders.

He was worried this time. He wanted no part of the fight now he had a family to protect. Twelve years ago, he'd met and fallen in love with Nadira. They'd married the following year, and four years later she had presented him with the finest gift a man could have. His son. Wissam Abed Hamoodi. He was a beautiful boy, already seven and growing up fast. Soon he'd be a man and Ammar couldn't be prouder. Nadira was expecting again, and she thought life was as good as it was possible to get, living in the strictly controlled regime of Saddam Hussein. Luxury goods were hard to get, but her husband's military rank did open a few doors.

Ammar parked and walked nervously to the gate. Showing his ID, he was searched and made to hand over his sidearm before being escorted by two guards and marched directly to the Colonel. There was no small talk. He stood to attention while his new orders were spat at him.

"Captain. You and your men are now under my command. You report directly to me. These orders are from his Supreme President himself. You will not discuss this with anyone. Understood?" the Colonel barked as he thrust a large envelope towards Ammar.

Without waiting for any response, he was dismissed and escorted back out of the office.

Over the next eight weeks, Captain Ammar Hamoodi and his team of twenty-four men hardly had a chance to

2

get back home or to their barracks. They would arrive in convoy at various locations throughout Iraq, most of them army bases such as the mega-site Muthanna State Establishment and Al-Taji itself, as well as various storage facilities, but also some factories and company buildings, where they would load the twelve trucks before heading for the Syrian border. Each truck had a driver and a driver's mate, both Ammar's men, as well as two fully armed SPG soldiers on board at any time.

The loads would consist of new weapons in crates, stripped down radar equipment, missiles ranging in size from hand-held to full Scud warheads, anti-tank weapons and support gear. They also transported hundreds of oil drum sized containers of chemicals, as well as yellow plastic barrels, all displaying chemical or biological hazard symbols, many with skull and crossbones painted on them. Some of the shipments included enormous amounts of laboratory equipment, computers, servers, printers, air scrubbers and cleaning equipment.

They would drive towards the Syrian border then wait for confirmation to continue. The local Iraq border guards would leave and other Special Republican Guards would man the Iraqi side of the border. The Syrian border guards would also be replaced by Syrian Special Forces who would then escort the trucks through to their destinations in Al-Safira, Homs, Hama, Latakia, & Palmyra, wait while they were unloaded, then escort them back to Iraqi territory.

Finally, in the middle of March, their work was completed. Home leave had been cancelled due to the expected imminent invasion of coalition forces, and Captain Ammar Hamoodi and his team of men were finally stood down in the quiet desert area south of the country near Shu'aiba, close to Basra.

The Colonel had been under strict orders direct from Saddam Hussein to ensure all those involved in this project be silenced. Knowing coalition forces were intercepting all radio traffic, he radioed various locations using an old cypher known to have been broken by the U.S., claiming the twelve trucks at that particular location were there to distribute gas and support weapons to the front line troops.

War commenced at 05:34 am 20th March 2003.

At 06:12 am on that morning three British Tornado GR1 strike attack aircraft carrying laser-guided bombs were directed to Captain Hamoodi's standing column of 12 trucks 20km behind enemy lines by U.S. AWACS, having previously decoded the message.

From more than five miles away the Tornado's 'painted' their targets with ultra-violet encoded pulsed laser. The laser-guided bombs dropped clear of their restraining brackets tailfins working furiously to steer and target the devices before self-arming when within ten seconds to impact.

The bombings were completely successful. All vehicles and contents were totally destroyed.

There were no survivors.

On 26th March, having not yet been informed of her husband's death, Nadira was shopping at a local market in the Al-Shaab district of central Baghdad, while her son was attending daily school. Above the general noise of the market and the sounds of the local cars and trucks, the engine noise of a fast-approaching, low-flying jet aircraft with U.S. markings was briefly heard moments before two loud explosions.

Western journalists, who were on the scene within minutes, said they had counted at least 15 bodies being hauled from the carnage.

One of the bodies was the heavily pregnant Nadira.

# Chapter 2

## Iraq - 2016

Cheryl Thompson, Michelle and Laura Williams, Emily Baker and Debbie Morgan had all majored in social and humanitarian studies at UCLA. Cheryl, Michelle and Laura were from the Pacific Palisades region of Los Angeles, while Emily was from Inglewood and Debbie from Sherman Oaks. All came from privileged backgrounds, owned their own cars and had never suffered any hardships in life. Studying the same courses and sharing the same dorms, they had all become friends and spent free time together as well.

UCLA had hosted a number of gala evenings where companies and organisations presented to the students, trying to entice them to join. One such evening was organised on behalf of the International Aid Committee & Rescue Charity (IACRC) - a global humanitarian aid relief charity supplying emergency relief aid and long-term assistance to refugees and those affected by war, persecution or natural disaster.

Currently recruiting for additional support people in the safe Kurdish regions of northern Iraq and south-eastern Turkey, all five girls were excited at the prospect of joining for a twelve-month overseas adventure before possibly settling down. Routed through Paris, they would be volunteering for work in the relatively safe Kurdish cities in northern Iraq particularly in and around Dohuk. Protected by heavily armed Kurdish Peshmerga soldiers, the girls would visit local villages offering aid and support, usually in the form of assisting the medical staff of Médecins Sans Frontières (MSF). The support included treating, comforting and feeding the many displaced individuals and even entire families who having escaped the ravages of war had sought refuge in the area. Local villages would include Zawita, Daristan, Bagera and Sarke, and they would be housed and live in a fully guarded armed compound close to Dohuk High School. There would not be any salary, but all costs including flights would be covered by the charity.

Realising the enormity of what they were trying to do, Cheryl and Michelle organised a meeting with all of the girls' parents, the girls themselves, and representatives from IACRC to satisfy everyone and provide as much information as possible to gain the support of their parents.

There was some reticence mainly from their mothers, but the videos, photos and general information provided from IACRC gradually won the parents over; and when Emily Baker's mother said she and her husband would fly to Paris with them as a start to a much-needed vacation, the remaining doubters folded.

With much excitement and celebration, the contracts were finally signed, and it was agreed the girls would fly out two weeks later.

For the following twelve days, it became a manic rush for the girls to buy what they needed for the trip, say goodbye to friends, and generally to come to terms with the fact that for the next twelve months they would be away from the 'West'. They would only have limited email and phone contact and likely no access to social media - the staple diet of so many teenagers today.

After what seemed to little time they were saying their final goodbyes to family and friends and boarding the U.S. Airways flight to Paris, where they stopped overnight, before an onward flight to Ankara, Turkey, the following day. Sat as one group on the flight they were buzzing with excitement as they watched the views change through the aircraft windows from the urbanised lush green areas of Western Europe to the less populated regions of Serbia and Bulgaria before changing again to the drier, dustier landscape of central Turkey as they finally approached Ankara. There they were met by Stefan, the local representative of IACRC before they continued travelling overland to the small town of Habur Sinir Kapisi on the Turkish-Iraq border.

The border crossing took over three hours with their suitcases and personal belongings being closely inspected and examined by the slovenly dressed border guards. The Kurdish tribesmen on the Iraq side of the border leered at the girls with one of the tribesmen laughing while holding up some of their underwear before grabbing Debbie's buttocks. She screamed and slapped his hand away.

"Hey, keep your hands to yourself," she shouted. "Fuck off."

Immediately two of the other tribesmen stepped back and raised their rifles. The next few minutes seemed like an age with a lot of angry shouting, raised voices and hand gesturing by both Stefan as well as the tribesmen before order was finally restored and they were allowed to repack their belongings.

"It is the way of the Kurds," Stefan murmured. "Women here are subservient to men. Men own them like they own cattle or weapons. You must not shout at a Kurd. It is very disrespectful to them."

"Grabbing my ass is disrespectful to me, dirty little fuck," Debbie said. "Tell him if he does it again I'll slap his goddam face."

Stefan spoke some more words in Kurmanji, the local Kurdish dialect, to the men before hustling the girls onto

8

the waiting minibus for the last fifty-kilometre drive to their final destination of Duhok.

Talking quietly in the back of the minibus the girls discussed what had happened. The only one who stayed ominously silent was Laura, secretly thrilled at the possible attention her golden blonde hair, well-endowed chest and long legs might bring her.

Arriving at their compound close to the Dohuk High School, they stepped down onto the dusty ground.

"Well it sure ain't the Hilton," Michelle said looking around.

The outsides of the buildings were filthy; mainly plain concrete and covered with graffiti. Some of the windows looked intact, but many were broken or missing glass entirely. Everything was the same dirty grey sand colour, and the courtyard was covered with a layer of dirt, sand and stones. Walking in through the entrance door they stopped as a rat scurried away, causing one of them to emit a small scream.

"Your room is upstairs," Stefan said. "It's a dormitory room for all of you."

"What, we all sleep in the same room? I thought we all had our own rooms?" Debbie said.

"Not here," Stefan explained. "Here you all sleep in one area. It's much safer that way. There is only one way into and out of this building, and it will be guarded night and day. I will introduce you to the guards later."

"Guards? Why do we need guards?" Emily asked with a look of concern on her face.

"It's just to make sure you are safe, and no harm comes to you. It's quite normal and nothing to worry about."

Trying to ignore the looks of panic on the girls' faces, he then showed them the laundry, the kitchen and what he called 'the lounge' all located downstairs, then walking upstairs he introduced them to their bedroom dormitory. Each girl had a cot bed with a metal cabinet next to it and a small metal wardrobe next to that. There were bug nets over the windows, and each bed had a dirty, unwashed mosquito net hanging over it. At the end of the dormitory was a washroom and toilet block containing four old sinks, two showers and two toilets in cubicles. The girls looked at one another as they inspected the filthy sanitation. Two of the toilets were conventional western pedestal, but two were the local 'hole-in-the-ground type.

With her nose wrinkled in disgust, Debbie said, "Well, I for one am not baring my backside to THAT! God, it stinks!"

"And just look at the dirt in the showers."

"Yuck! It's like living in the Flintstones house," Debbie added.

Gathering them around him in a group, Stefan said, "Ladies, I know it's not what you were expecting, and we're hoping that we can move you to better accommodation soon, but in the meantime, this is the best we can offer. This is an old school converted for basic living. There isn't any air-conditioning — ."

"What? No air con?"

"As I was saying, there isn't any air-conditioning and electricity is only on for a few hours a day, water the same. However, there's dry and tinned food in the kitchen, and fresh food will be delivered when available. I know it's not great, but it's the best we can do for now."

Looking around the girls were less than impressed. The building was dirty, and there was evidence of rat or mice droppings on the floor. What little paint was left on the walls was flaking off, and there were cobwebs along the ceiling.

Having paused for emphasis, Stefan continued, "Okay, now for the rules. You must not go outside the compound without a guard at all. No exceptions! Understood? It can be dangerous out there, and I don't want any of you getting hurt. However, you are all safe in here, and there will be guards on duty day and night." Moving around the room as he talked, he said, "There are rechargeable lanterns over there. Keep them plugged in, so they recharge when power is on. Use them wisely otherwise you may have to use candles. Bugs are a problem, particularly mosquitos. Always pull your net over you at night, or you'll be eaten alive. Some of the bugs are big and nasty, and their stings can really hurt. There is bug spray in the cupboard, but I suggest you don't walk around barefoot. And always wear shoes outside in the compound as there are lots of sharp stones and broken glass within the sand, and there are many scorpions just waiting for a lovely white foot to stand on them. I know we gave you a list of suggested items to bring so did you all bring sturdy boots?"

Gaining a few nods from them, he continued, "Flip Flops and open shoes are not a good idea outside. Cuts to feet have a nasty habit of becoming infected really quickly, so I suggest you only wear boots. OK, now the bad news —."

At which stage Emily interrupted, saying, "Bad news? You mean that was all the good news? Haven't you given us enough bad news already?"

Smiling and trying to keep them encouraged Stefan said, "Our day starts at 06:00 due to the heat. The same minibus and driver will drive you to various villages around here where you will work with other support staff in giving aid to the locals. There are a lot of sicknesses here and many families missing one or both parents. You'll help feed babies, change simple dressings and generally do as requested by the other support staff."

In answer to their groans at the thought of starting work at 06:00, Stefan continued, "Please do not wear jewellery or carry money. In fact, don't carry anything of value. Your clothes must cover you from neck to ankles at all times and all of your arms down to your hands. You must not show any skin at any time."

Cheryl looked aghast. With tears in her eyes, she said, "So all my clothes I've brought with me I can't wear. You want us to walk around here looking like nuns?"

"Please ladies, remember this is a Muslim country. Women here are virtually fully covered. You must blend in the same. Do you understand?"

Gaining nods and shoulder shrugs from everyone, he said, "You should wear scarves as well to cover your hair. As you've already discovered women are seen as the possessions of men here. They have no rights. The locals here are strict Muslims and don't understand our Western ways and don't understand that women in the West and in America particularly have the same rights as men. What little Western television has been seen here will have been porn so as far as the local people are concerned all white women are just prostitutes and will have sex with anyone. Hence, you never go anywhere alone without a guard. Okay?" he said.

"You'll tell us next we can't wear make-up and nail varnish?"

"Well, your choice, but I would suggest not. You are here to work and help not to parade around. Now one final point. Please don't photograph the locals - they don't like it, and again, let me re-iterate ... never, ever, wander off alone or away from the group. This is vital to keep you safe. Do I make myself clear?" Stefan said, looking at each of them, in turn, to ensure they understood.

"Okay, enough talk. Your two guards are your drivers as well. One of them will always be on duty. You've already met Abduhla Almani and your guard and driver tomorrow is Masoud Saadi. Get yourselves settled, have something to eat and get a good sleep. I'll see you in the morning at 06:00 sharp," he said.

After he'd left the girls sat down on their beds, two of them sobbing. Debbie put her arm around one of them saying, "C'mon girls, at least we're all together. I know it's rough, but we did all volunteer. Maybe it won't be so bad."

That evening, after a meal of beans, bread and tinned meat, they all retired to bed exhausted from the long journey.

Over the following week, the girls became accustomed to the long hours and hard work. It was hot and dusty however all felt they were doing a great job helping out those displaced and tormented by the ongoing war that northern Iraq had been suffering from for as long as anyone could remember. They'd rise at 05:00 and wash and shower before eating breakfast. Picked up at 06:00 they'd be driven to that day's location, often an hour or two's distance away before starting work with the medical staff of MSF. Initially, they only fed babies and changed nappies, but gradually they also began providing a basic level of first aid such as cleaning simple wounds and changing dressings.

Laura, in particular, looked forward to the days Masoud Saadi was the guard and driver. She found him attractive and would often lay awake at night fantasising of romantic horse rides out into the desert with her handsome stud. He in turn just thought of her as a blonde whore with big tits but would bring her little gifts of some almonds or a small wooden stick figure he'd made.

Occasionally she would touch his hand or arm as a way of saying thanks. Once she had even kissed him on the cheek for a flower, he had given her.

Laura's sister Michelle worried about the budding relationship between them kept telling Laura of her concerns. She was unhappy with Laura showing Masoud all her photos from her phone, of her sitting close to him, and letting their knees touch when she sat in the front passenger seat of the minibus, and of her constantly glancing and smiling at him. However, it all fell on deaf ears. Laura was too smitten to see the dangers.

# Chapter 3

## Somerset - UK

They were behind schedule due to the weather. Four weeks had been allocated, and it was already halfway through the second. It had rained almost continuously throughout April, and the ground had become sodden. Luckily the organisers had laid gravel over some of the main access tracks a few years previously so the heavy trucks could still enter. Also because there were now so many stages some of the main frameworks were left up all year long, but they still had to be thoroughly inspected, and every fastening checked for tightness before this year's coverings could be applied. And the rain hadn't helped.

Now with a prolonged spell of drier weather and sunshine, they could crack on and catch up. The almost 900 acres of fields usually contained 400 plus cows to keep the grasses short, and they had already been moved to new pastures. Stand-style seating had been delivered and was being assembled. Power lines were being safety checked and additional feeds installed. The mobile operator, Vodafone, always set up a number of temporary repeater towers for the event and they were scheduled to commence work the following week. Engineers from the BBC were also onsite installing over 40 miles of power and camera cabling.

Portable toilets and showers would also arrive during the next week. One of the complaints of attendees previously had been about the lack of ablution facilities, so the organisers had invested thousands in the building of six permanent washing and sanitation blocks, but they would still need over 4,000 additional portable toilets for the 5-day event. The event would also support almost 1,000 small stalls selling everything from blankets to beef burgers, many of which were already arriving to add to the chaos.

Some of the 8.5 miles of perimeter security fencing, including the recently installed 'superfencing', had been damaged in the early spring gales that had swept in from the Atlantic and caused so much damage to the south of the UK. The severe low pressure had created sustained winds of more than 130mph and many towns and villages along the English Channel coastline had suffered damage. The winds had also funnelled north along the Bristol Channel, and the low-lying grasslands of Somerset had caught the full unabated force. This year to stop hangers-on outside viewing the event for free new opaque covers had been ordered and were being installed on every section of the twelve-foot-high fence. However, organisers had not allowed enough time for this labour-intensive job. Hence they were now behind schedule.

Lighting equipment and sound systems would be the last to be installed and tested just a few days before the start of the event on the 22nd June. Thousands of security personnel would also be employed for the 5-day period, and recruitment adverts had already been placed on websites and at employment agencies. Most would be from large private security firms, but many would be just individuals who could pass the security vetting. Guards from previous years would receive priority placement.

As events of this size and complexity often seem when viewed from outside, the maelstrom of activity and chaos would run at full speed until miraculously everything would be ready on the opening day.

# Chapter 4

## Al Qayarah Airfield - Iraq

Lieutenant John Deacon checked his map again as he looked through his binoculars. Deacon and his men had been sent, along with over four-hundred other U.S. troops, to 'assist' the Iraqis' in preparing for war and to help the Iraqi Prime Minister, Haider al-Abadi.

Late in 2015 al-Abadi had publically stated "2016 will be the year of the big and final victory when Daesh's presence in Iraq will be terminated," in a speech broadcast on state television.

"We are coming to liberate Mosul, and it will be the fatal and final blow to Daesh," he'd added, using the derogatory Arabic acronym for ISIS, the Islamic State in Iraq and Syria.

It had all sounded good, but the Iraq Army just wasn't prepared to attack the well-defended city of Mosul yet. The first stage was to secure Al Qayarah airbase located about seventy kilometres south of Mosul then using the airbase as a staging post build up strength for a concerted push into Mosul itself.

The U.S. President had pledged support to al-Abadi and sent U.S. troops to help train, support and motivate the Iraqis. Publically the President had stated the troops were there only in an 'advisory, planning and training' role and would not actually be involved in combat. After the fall of Al Qayarah airbase, the Americans would send five hundred additional troops to assist in the planning and build-up towards the final push to retake Mosul later in 2016.

Well, that was what the American people believed, Deacon mused.

The U.S. had some of the finest information gathering capability in the world. Between intelligence gathering flights of AWACS coupled with real-time satellite and drone imagery, Deacon and his four-man SEAL team had a real-time 'God' view of the airbase. What didn't help though Deacon thought while looking through binoculars were hopelessly optimistic Iraqi officers stating they had men on the ground in specific positions when the imagery and his own eyes proved otherwise. The Iraqi Forces had been trained, but their level of discipline was nowhere near as strict as western forces. To that end, most of the Americans were happy to work with the Iraqi's but wouldn't trust them not to turn and run if the fighting got tough.

Cursing quietly, he turned to his colleague, Petty Officer Hancock.

"Go get their friggin' General to mark again on the map where he thinks his front line troops are, will you? Then show him these aerials and see what he says of where they actually are compared to where he thinks. I'll keep a lookout," he said.

As Petty Officer Hancock moved off, Deacon thought, 'Shit. Two weeks ago I was sailing in the warm waters off San Diego, and here I am now back up to my ass in the sand again.'

As he blew the dust off the lenses and kept watch through his binoculars, he thought back to the sunny southern Californian breezes he'd recently left behind.

Deacon's upbringing had been slightly unconventional. Born in '81 and raised in Norfolk Virginia, his life had always centred around the Navy. His mother was an Accountant, his father a U.S. Navy attack submarine Commander, both now retired. His father had been away

18

weeks or even occasionally months at a time, so Deacon had become the 'man of the house' at a far younger age than wanted. The middle of three children, both sisters were now happily married with the elder having two boys who adored their adventurous uncle.

He'd grown tall and muscular and had always been extremely fit, playing American football at college and in the High School swimming team. Graduating Columbia University with degrees in Political Science and Mechanical Engineering, he'd chosen the Navy specifically with the SEALs in mind. He'd finished high in each of the rankings, particularly in swimming, unarmed combat and planning. He was equally at ease talking with an Admiral or a canteen worker and was always willing to push himself to extremes. He had a wry sense of humour and was 100% dependable.

At a little over six foot tall and with short dark hair he'd never considered himself particularly good looking, especially with the scar across his chin - the result of falling off a motorbike he'd been trying to repair when he was fifteen, but women didn't seem to agree. Slightly rugged and with dark brown eyes he always found it easy to have a lady on his arm when it suited.

Growing up he'd always been very protective of his sisters often getting into fights and scuffles when older boys at school had tried to hit on them or were overheard making disparaging comments about them. He treated women overall as the fairer sex, inasmuch as he would open a door for them or offer them a seat - not that they couldn't manage on their own, but it was the gentlemanly thing to do. He knew from the fights the three of them had when they were young that girls could punch as hard as boys could and fight dirtier, but he'd always been taught to treat everyone with respect, to be a gentleman and to be honourable to men and women alike. His father had taught him that when he was six or seven and Deacon felt it was still a good code to live by.

Deacon had always enjoyed messing about on boats. Stationed in Coronado as part of SEAL Team Three, a few years back he'd found Abbot's Boatyard, an old fairly run-down place a few miles from his base. It was much smaller than the shiny new marinas springing up everywhere, but it had a cosy 'old-world' feel about it. He'd often go along and just sit near one of the yard pontoons to enjoy the ambience. He'd struck up conversations many times with the owner, Jesse Abbot. Old and partially crippled by arthritis but with a mind as sharp as a razor, Jesse had story after story to tell, usually when sharing a fifth of Bourbon with Deacon, and what Jesse didn't know about boats wasn't worth knowing.

Back in 2012 Deacon had been stationed overseas for quite a period and then had gotten his left hand injured when in the Canary Islands. In fact, the knife going in had done some damage, but Deacon pulling it out quickly had done more. However, it had been life or death at that time. The damage had been to some of the nerves and Deacon needed a number of microsurgery operations to get full mobility and sensations back. During that time he'd been stationed back at Coronado and had heard that old Jesse Abbot had finally passed away and his daughter, Melanie, had taken over the business. Going along one afternoon to introduce himself he parked and walked to the entrance, passing two flashy motorbikes parked outside. There were two guys wearing bikers leathers at the counter talking to a slim, pretty woman whom Deacon assumed was Melanie. Not wanting to interrupt, Deacon wandered around looking at the various racks of sailboat and yacht items for sale.

Glancing over, Deacon could see the two guys were leaning over, pushing into the woman's personal space.

They were talking hard with an aggressive tone, and she was by the register, back arched away by an equal amount. The guy's leathers had some sort of logo or markings on the rear. Deacon couldn't see their faces clearly, but they looked pretty scruffy, long-haired and unshaven. They also had a number of nose and ear piercings and tattoos. Not the usual clientele he'd expect in a place like this. The one on the left was banging his fist on the counter, showing how easy it would be to break it. Finally, the guy on the right tapped his watch and, as they turned to leave, trailed his hand along the counter and knocked over a small display scattering the contents over the floor. Deacon watched them leave, mount their bikes and ride off and then he looked back to see the woman knelt down picking up the spillages.

Walking over he bent down next to her. "Are you OK?" he asked.

"Y..Yes, I'm fine, thank you," she said.

"My name's John Deacon. I knew your father. He was a friend. You must be Melanie. When are they coming back?"

"Oh, Mister Deacon. My father often spoke about you. Please, it's nothing, nothing for you to be concerned about."

"The names John. Tell me. When are they coming back and how much do they want?" Deacon asked again.

"Just after I close at six," she said her eyes full of tears. "And they want $500 a week going up to $750 when the place picks up. Dad was paying $500, but it was crippling him financially. I don't know how I'll manage. Maybe I'll just sell the place and let someone else worry about it."

"Your father said he was leaving this place to you. I can't ignore a friend's last wish. Do you have a permanent marker pen?"

Opening a drawer she searched through until finding what she wanted.

"Here you go. What do you want it for?" she asked.

"Do you have someplace else you can go for the next couple of hours?" Deacon asked. "Why don't you lock up at five and go home. Come in tomorrow as normal," he said.

Walking back outside, Deacon walked around the boatyard until he found an empty bench overlooking the water and settled down to wait.

His SEALs training had reinforced his view of not to be afraid of anyone. He wasn't the sort of person who would walk away from danger, and he wasn't the type of man who would allow a grieving daughter to be taken advantage of.

He pulled his SEAL trident insignia out of his pocket. Scaring away these two thugs was easy, but keeping them away was tougher. Standing up for Melanie's rights was all well and good, but he knew he couldn't be around all the time. What these thugs needed was to know he had a bigger group supporting him.

At two minutes before six Deacon moved back towards the entrance leaning on the wall with his hands in his pockets. At five after, he heard the muffled roar of two motorbikes approaching, and they wheeled in by him and parked a few feet away. As they dismounted, both pulled baseball bats from inside their long jackets and walked towards the entrance.

Pushing himself off the wall, he faced them.

"Guys, let's go round the back," he said.

Close up they looked mean. They were in their mid to late twenties and solidly built with muscle. They had tattoos covering most of their skin with numerous piercings, were unwashed and smelled of body odour.

"Who the fuck are you?" the one on the left demanded.

Deacon glanced at him and ignored the question.

"I said 'Who the fuck are you?' asshole."

"I'm the guy with the money," Deacon said.

"You got all of it?"

"Of course. All $500. Let's go around the back and sort this out," Deacon said, walking away and around the corner.

Deacon sensed them follow him. Once around the back he turned and faced them. Completely out of sight of anyone from the road out front, Deacon beckoned them to come closer. They'd already glanced around to make sure Deacon didn't have a group of colleagues waiting, and realising it was just the three of them they relaxed slightly with the biker on the left tapping his baseball bat against his lower leg while his pal on the right held his at both ends behind his head.

"So where's the money, asshole?"

"Look, guys, the lady's just trying to make a living. Why don't you leave her alone and hassle someone else," Deacon said.

"You what? Maybe you wanna pay us both on your knees instead, asshole before we go and make the bitch pay the same way," said biker number one, rubbing his crotch.

"Well, I tried," Deacon said, moving a little closer then turning his body slightly as if to reach into his pocket. Then he sprang at the one on the left hitting him with all the force he could muster with the heel of his hand to the side of the head and just below his ear. With all Deacon's weight and muscle power behind it, it was as if he'd hit him with a wooden club. He saw the biker's eyes glaze over and the bat begin to slip from his fingers as his muscles relaxed and his knees began to buckle. Deacon followed up with a knee to the groin and as the biker's head snapped forward, and he bent double Deacon got both hands behind the biker's head and forced it down hard onto his rising knee. With a loud crack the biker's nose fractured and with a broken nose and dislocated jaw, a crushed groin and an almighty blow to the head, the first biker was already only semi-conscious.

The second biker was quick off the mark, loosening his right-hand grip on his bat but he still had to swing it out from behind his head. Deacon leapt in quickly and head-butted him high on the brow on the bridge of his nose at the same time bringing his knee up into the groin. Between gasping for breath and his eyes filling with tears, the biker's grip on the swinging bat loosened. Deacon easily grabbed it left-handed and pulled it free. Grabbing it by the shaft, he poked it hard into the biker's stomach. Moving slightly right, Deacon quickly changed grip to the handle and swung it sharply lower down. The crack of the full force of his swing onto the guy's patella was drowned out by the biker's scream. As the biker's leg collapsed and he sprawled onto the ground, Deacon had a final hit with the bat onto the biker's right hand breaking at least two of his knuckles.

With both of them down, one unconscious and the other barely moving, it was easy to go through their pockets. There was a total of just over $1,800 cash, which Deacon took along with a flick-knife. Leaning heavily on the chest of the second biker and putting pressure on his groin, Deacon looked him in his watering eyes.

"What gang are you from?"

"Fighting Scarabs. You're fucking dead, man."

"Is that so? Well, we've got a message for you pussies in the Fighting Scarabs. Game over. Now keep still."

Getting the permanent marker out of his pocket and pressing the point of the open flick-knife up into the soft skin under the biker's chin until it drew blood, Deacon wrote across the thug's forehead Abbot's Boatyard is protected.

Getting off he moved to the first barely conscious biker and wrote the same across his forehead.

The second guy decided to have the last word and spat at Deacon.

"You're so fucking dead, man," he said.

"Well I wasn't going to do this but if you insist ..." Deacon said as he yanked the small skull and crossbones nose ring from the guy's nose, as the thug screamed in pain.

Pulling the thug to his feet, he told him to help his colleague up and get out of there. Facing them and looking into their eyes Deacon could still see a look of defiance.

"Don't even think about it. Get lost and don't come back. Ever. Abbot's Boatyard is under my protection, and I've got a lot of friends. I suggest you find someone else to hassle. Got it?"

He sat back and watched them slowly stagger to their bikes and ride off.

The following morning he was back at the boatyard when Melanie arrived.

"Hey, you can rest easy. They've gone and won't be back. They've even realised their mistake and donated $1,800 to your success," he said handing over the money much to her amazement.

"But where did this come from?" she asked.

"Well, let's just say they realise the error of their ways and this is to cover you for any inconvenience," Deacon said, smiling.

Since then the boatyard had improved year on year and even started a sailboat charter division. To express her gratitude Deacon could take any sailboat out for as long as he wanted, as he'd done two weeks ago. But usually, he would still just visit to sit by one of the pontoons and enjoy the ambience.

# Chapter 5

Distant gunfire brought Deacon back to the present. He turned just in time to see Petty Officer Hancock returning.

"Boss, the General has updated the map. I think we're on the same page now."

Glancing at the roughly drawn markings on the map, Deacon tended to agree. The men now were placed where Deacon and his colleagues had advised they should be for maximum effect.

Overall the fighting in and around Al Qayarah was intense with a large number of suicide attacks from ISIS, both by individuals and in vehicles, although these were relatively easily defeated. The U.S. contingent was keeping back and allowing the Iraqis to do all the fighting. They were merely advising and recommending although would obviously fire back if directly attacked. The Iraqi Army had previously been completely overwhelmed back in 2003, and all of their weapons were eventually surrendered to the American-led coalition forces. Once peace, or the resemblance of peace, had been restored and a new government put in place the Army had been re-equipped and now had some of the most modern weaponry including some of the latest anti-tank shoulder-launched missiles. A suicide attacker driving a car or truck didn't stand much of a chance against an anti-tank missile or rocket-propelled grenade.

The airbase was approximately ten miles south-west of Al Qayarah city - a local ISIS stronghold. Although heavily defended, most ISIS positions had been identified and already targeted and destroyed by a mixture of drone and U.S. Navy aircraft attacks, followed up by Iraqi Special Forces, supported by the conventional Iraqi Army. ISIS had very few pilots and what few aircraft they'd seized had already been destroyed early in 'the push', with many ISIS fighters withdrawing either to the local Al Qayarah city or further back to Mosul. Between the U.S. air superiority and local Iraqi tanks and ground forces, it was a relatively straightforward attack with eventual victory guaranteed due to superior firepower and numbers. ISIS had already destroyed much of the airfield, runway and facilities to render the airfield unusable to the attacking forces, but Deacon knew from experience just how quickly U.S. construction forces working with local contractors could turn a barren wasteland of desert into a front-line working airbase again.

Knowing the eventual fall of Al Qayarah airbase was inevitable, and that the Iraqis would use it as a springboard for their planned attacks later on Mosul, local ISIS leader Abu Nayef Al-Jaheishi ordered the use of chemical weapons to hold the airbase for as long as possible.

Iraq had used chemical weapons in Iran during the war in the 1980s, and also used mustard gas and nerve agents against Kurdish residents of Halabja, in Northern Iraq, in 1988, so was no stranger to the effects and effectiveness of gassing combatants.

The first volley of shells fired from three 130mm field guns located over nine miles away and missed in the initial U.S. led airstrikes exploded far to the rear of Deacon's position. Alarms quickly sounded that gas was present, but luckily the shells had over-ranged, and the prevailing wind was blowing to the east dispersing the gas cloud over a mostly empty desert, although one convoy of Iraqi soldiers moving to the front line was affected with many succumbing to its effects before they could put on protective clothing.

A Boeing E-3 Sentry AWAC flying high over Iraq detected the field guns and directed four U.S. Navy F/A-18 Hornet strike fighters from the Carrier Battle Group USS George HW Bush in the Gulf to intercept using 500-pound laser-guided bombs to destroy the targets. Adjacent to the guns was an arsenal of gas shells that exploded causing additional deaths and injuries to ISIS fighters close by much to the cheering of the Iraqi government forces.

The battles continued for many more days, but the outcome was inevitable.

Al Qayarah airfield was eventually taken by Iraqi government forces in June 2016.

# Chapter 6

## Dohuk - Iraq

The girls driven by Abduhla had returned from Bagera late today at almost six o'clock. Usually, they finished around two just before the hottest part of the day but today had been busier than normal, and it was already getting dark. More refugees had arrived, and the staff of Médecins Sans Frontières had been kept busy checking their overall health. There was always a worry for diseases to break out, particularly typhus or dysentery due to the poor hygiene of most of the population but the doctors felt they had everything under control. The girls had been busy feeding the children after they'd been checked over.

As they stepped down from the minibus, Masoud walked from around the corner with two other figures. As one moved towards the main compound entrance, Masoud raised his pistol and shot Abduhla in the head from close range. The girls screamed and tried to run, but Masoud fired again into the air.

"Stop," he shouted, "I shoot. Get in minibus. NOW!"

Terrified and crying, the girls clambered back into the minibus as Abduhla's body was pulled free through the door, a trail of blood and brain matter dripping from his shoulders.

Masoud climbed into the driver's seat and started the engine while his second gunman squeezed into the rear gap between the girls. As the minibus slowed near the compound entrance, the third gunman jumped into the front and sat facing the rear with a pistol in his hand. As they pulled away, the girls could see the body of the entrance guard lying face down in the dust, blood covering the rear of his head.

"Sit. No talks. No sound. Okay?" he shouted to the crying girls, "No talks."

With the darkening sky and little traffic now on the dusty roads, the minibus sped out onto the main road and turned south onto Route 2 towards Bajerke Fadiye and on towards Mosul seventy-five kilometres further south.

"You must stop and let us go," a terrified Emily gasped, tears flowing down her cheeks. "We won't tell anyo––," as the guard in the rear slapped her hard across her face, raising his hand to do so again. Masoud muttered a few words in Arabic, and the guard lowered his hand slowly, leaving Emily and the other sobbing girls in no doubt he would strike again unless they kept quiet.

Just over two hours later they arrived near the outskirts of Mosul having been stopped over a dozen times at armed ISIS roadblocks. Each time Masoud had spoken and shown paperwork and they'd been allowed to pass, the guards leering eagerly at the light coloured flesh of the girls.

From here on in they were escorted by jeering and shouting ISIS troops in accompanying vehicles, some firing their weapons into the air. Eventually, after crossing the river into the old centre of Mosul and following a requisitioned American Hummer in through various quiet and filthy back streets, Masoud finally stopped and switched off the engine. Hustling them out into the hot, dusty night two of them fell to the ground.

"Get up American whores. Get up and look me in the face," Abu Nayef Al-Jaheishi, the leader of ISIS in Mosul commanded in clear English.

"You are now mine. You will do as you are instructed. If you do well, great happiness awaits you as a bride to one of our brave fighters. If you fail you will be treated like the whores you Americans are, and you will satisfy many men," he continued.

Michelle, a little braver than the others, raised her head fully. Looking him in the eye, she said, "What if we refuse? We are Americans. We demand to be taken to the nearest U.S. embassy. We don't need to do what you say."

"If that is your choice, so be it," Abu Nayef replied, "You will be given to my finest soldiers for their pleasure and then beheaded at dawn with the videos being sent to your parents. Then your bodies will be left in the desert for the wild dogs and rats."

With a terrified gasp, Michelle's bladder relaxed, and a warm stream of urine ran down her leg.

Turning, Abu Nayef spoke in Arabic and out of the shadows a group of old women, dressed entirely in black abayas, grabbed the girls and hustled them towards one of the many buildings.

Sobbing and stumbling, the girls were shepherded in through a small doorway, continuously being beaten and whipped by the long bamboo sticks carried by the women.

Turning to Masoud, Abu Nayef said in Arabic, "You have done well, my brother. These whores are a prize from Allah himself. You will be paid one thousand U.S. dollars for each girl. Now they are here, you and your colleagues will continue to guard them. Today is a great day, Allahu Akbar."

Over the following days, the girls slowly became used to their daily chores. They lived in a tiny dusty room below ground level and slept on reed mats. They were all imprisoned in one room, which was kept locked. A single naked light bulb provided dim lighting when power was on as the only natural light came from two small windows high up. There was no glass but wire netting across the opening. With so many power cuts during the day, the girls' existed in a dark slum environment. They only came out into daylight to use the toilet, a hole-in-the-ground type surrounded by flies, bugs and cockroaches and shielded by a weathered old blanket offering them little privacy. It was located close to the courtyard wall and in direct line-of-sight where the guard near the gate could see and leer at them. Against one wall was a tap for washing, but the guards would stare and afforded them no privacy so the girls would fill jugs and a basin and take them down below. The building was a mixture of old brick and concrete and was within a small compound surrounded by an eight-foot high wall with barbed wire along the top. The large wooden entrance gate was kept closed with an armed guard constantly on patrol. The women in black, or 'crows' as the girls called them, didn't speak any English and would point and mutter in Arabic, with a swift thwack of a cane if the girls hesitated to do the cooking or cleaning as instructed. Bullied and beaten they were tired and dirty with sanitation being somewhat basic and the chance of a warm shower a pipe dream. However, they hadn't yet been assaulted or separated.

Even this treatment didn't deter Laura and convinced in her own mind of their love for each other. Still, she smiled and touched Masoud's arm or hand when she could. A smile here, a finger brush there. She even felt Masoud must love her when he rubbed her backside once and even briefly cupped her breast.

<><><>

Unknown to the girls, their capture had been videoed along with their arrival and the videos passed to Al Jazeera News along with a $60 million release fee.

# Chapter 7

## Iraq

Over the next two weeks after the fall of Al Qayarah airfield, senior U.S. and Iraq commanders met to expand and confirm the plans for how and when they would attack Mosul.

Mosul is the largest urban centre under the militants' control and had a pre-war population of nearly 2 million. Its fall would mark the effective defeat of ISIS in Iraq according to the Iraqi Prime Minister, Haider al-Abadi, who had previously stated his aims to retake the city this year.

It was being estimated that over 1.4 million additional refugees would leave Mosul once fighting intensified in the region. Many would flee to Jordan and Turkey and would remain there, but many more would attempt to escape to Europe.

The plan has been under discussion for many weeks, but finally, both the U.S. President and the Iraqi Prime Minister agreed on the details.

"In consultation with the Government of Iraq, the U.S. is prepared to provide an additional 500 plus U.S. military personnel to train and advise the Iraqis as the planning for the Mosul campaign intensifies," a U.S. Government official said. "U.S. troops will be in harm's way and likely to be placed closer to the combat area than previously, but will not be stationed on the front line. All front line attacking troops will be Iraqi, Kurdish Peshmerga soldiers and possibly Turkish Forces."

Iraq began immediately building up its forces along the airfield with a plan to begin the offensive during October, and the Iraqi military commenced a full training program.

Iraqi aircraft began regular flights over Mosul dropping paper pamphlets advising the locals to leave. Any locals caught doing so by ISIS militia were rounded up and usually executed at public meeting places.
Executions were also videoed and placed on the internet to deter others.

Iraq television and news channels also started reporting about the impending government-led attack on Mosul, which was quickly taken up and repeated by other Gulf television and news outlets.

# Chapter 8

## Washington

Online video emerged of ISIS leader Abu Nayef Al-Jaheishi parading Cheryl Thompson, Michelle and Laura Williams, Emily Baker and Debbie Morgan through the back streets of Mosul. The girls were wearing their Arabic clothing and although clearly upset looked to be in good health. They were being shepherded by armed guards. Over the backdrop of the video Abu Nayef's voice was clearly heard first in Arabic then English, stating, "In the event of any attack on Mosul the girls will be executed in public, their bodies strapped to tanks to fend off the attackers."

Within minutes these videos were being watched around the world.

In Washington, the first calls to the White House from an angry and enraged public started minutes later.

The American President called one of many emergency briefings in the situation room underneath the White House. Sitting around the conference table were representatives from around half of the U.S. Intelligence Services.

"Gentlemen," the President stormed, "I don't know how we've gotten into this cluster fuck, but I can't be seen supporting some goddam A-rab attack in a country we already goddam invaded and secured years back, with the lives of five young American girls in the balance. It's a friggin' election year, my ratings have plummeted, and I'm seen as a 'has-been' President. Every goddam channel is showing this video, and the phones have gone mad. I will not leave office and be remembered as the President who let five American girls be sold into slavery or murdered live on television. I want answers on where they are and how we're going to get them out. We are the strongest country in the world, and we will not be held to ransom by some half-arsed camel-jockeys. Get me some fucking answers and get me them today. Understood? Dismissed!" as he slammed his fist on the desk before storming out.

General Ulysses P. Mansfield, the Joint Chief of Staff, was first to speak, "Gentlemen, you heard the President. We need to find those girls and rescue them. The longer this goes on, the bigger laughing-stock we become." Turning to the CIA Director, he continued, "Doesn't the CIA have anything?"

"We're working furiously to find any information. IACRC had assured us the girls would be safe. They've housed over forty groups in the last two years, and none have had a problem before. I've got Shane Walker and his team in Baghdad working non-stop to get something," the CIA Director said.

Simon Clark, the Director of the FBI, said, "We're checking into IACRC both here and at their headquarters in Geneva. We're monitoring their email systems and trying to discover if anyone working there has terrorist connections. The Swiss Federal Intelligence Services are being supportive, but they don't like us monitoring IACRC. However, they have agreed to investigate, and we are sharing information.

Finally, Admiral Douglas Carter, the uncompromising Chief of Naval Operations stood up and addressed the audience.

"Gentlemen. We will find them, and we will rescue them. I've got two teams of SEALs stationed at Al Qayarah and another team on the George Bush Carrier Group in the Gulf. I don't have the answers yet, but we will get them. As always, the Navy will come through."

The discussions around the table carried on for another fifteen minutes or so but just covered the same ground before the meeting broke up.

# Chapter 9

## Mosul - Iraq

After extensive tracking and a series of missed opportunities in early 2015 a lucky U.S. drone strike just north of Mosul had killed Abu Malik the original chief chemical expert working for Saddam Hussein from the 1990s through to 2003. He was targeted due to the growing worry ISIS was acquiring chemical and biological weapons for use in Iraq, Syria and potentially for attacks on the West. It was already known that after the fall of Iraq, Abu Malik had been selling his skills to Al-Qaeda and more recently had become an avid supporter of ISIS.

Unknown to U.S. intelligence, Abu Malik had set up operations a number of years ago directly under Al-Qaeda. More recently he'd moved to ISIS control reporting to the overall leader of ISIS, Abu Bakr al-Baghdadi, also known as Caliph Abu Bakr - the supreme leader of ISIS.

Working for Abu Malik was Sleiman Daoud al-Afari. Together they'd specialised in chemical and biological weapons at Saddam Hussein's Military Industrialization Authority at Muthanna State Establishment, 60 miles north of Baghdad. Also working for him was Faisel Husseini, a brilliant up-and-coming young student. After the fall of Iraq in 2003, the team had ceased working on military weapons, instead being employed at Mosul University and its laboratories in a teaching capacity. With the rise of al-Qaeda, Malik and his team had begun again to experiment and offered their skills and expertise to help 'The Leader' defeat the new Western-led puppet government of Iraq. After the demise of Osama bin Laden and the rise of ISIS, Malik's loyalties progressed, and he became a keen supporter of Caliph Abu Bakr. The laboratories of Mosul University fell into ISIS hands in June 2014 providing the needed facilities with him and his team providing the knowledge and skills to make and produce mustard agent.

Although quite deadly and extremely effective, mustard gas agent like many similar basic chemical or biological weapons is not a complex chemical to produce by anyone with a chemistry degree.

After the sudden death of Abu Malik the remaining colleagues and supporters, except Faisel Husseini, moved to the relative safety of the large ISIS-held city in northern Syria, Raqqa. There they met and joined forces with other disgruntled Syrian scientists and chemical experts utilising the remains of Iraqi chemicals and weapons previously moved to Syria in early 2003.

Faisel Husseini was excited and proud. He'd been working on this new idea for over six months, and now he'd finally cracked it. Requesting a meeting with Abu Nayef Al-Jaheishi, he waited eagerly to explain what he'd built.

Three hours later escorted by his heavily armed guards the Mosul ISIS leader Abu Nayef Al-Jaheishi finally arrived.

After the customary greetings and after Faisel had been searched for any weapons he was carrying they both sat on large cushions.

"Excellency, I have great news," Faisel began. "May I ask what your esteemed Excellency knows of VX Agent?"

"I know it can be lethal, my son. But consider my knowledge in this subject as minimal. Inform me, my son. Let me gain great knowledge," he said.

"Excellency, VX Agent is quite deadly compared to Mustard Gas. Mustard Gas causes blistering of the lungs and eyes. Sufferers have trouble breathing, and it blinds them. But it takes a few hours to work and can be treated quite effectively. Only ten percent of people infected will actually die. It is heavier than air, so settles on the ground, but being a gas, it can disperse quickly in the wind. In World War I, it was used on the battlefields of France, and it was most effective because it would often be trapped in the shell holes where troops were hiding, but on the open battlefield, it's nowhere near as deadly. VX Agent, however, is different. It's not a gas, it's a liquid. My colleagues and I had a small amount left from Saddam's days, and I have been working on methods to improve it. It is extremely deadly - if I placed just a minute drop on your skin, you would be dead within minutes. It is quickly absorbed through the skin, and within a few seconds, you begin to succumb. You have trouble breathing, and you suffocate and drown on your own body fluids. There is a cure but only if it's administered very quickly - almost at exposure stage. After that it's too late as your lungs have already collapsed," he said.

"So if it does this already, what is your news?"

"This is an awesome weapon, Excellency, but too deadly too quickly. Because people succumb very quickly, others can see the effects and put on protective clothing. What I have done is combine it with another chemical to delay its action. I have combined it with a polymer coating which does a number of things. It coats each minute particle of VX Agent into a globule with a protective covering. Standard VX can also be diluted in water, and its effects are thereby reduced. This new protective coating stops VX being watered down and diluted, rather it allows the potency of each VX globule to remain as powerful as before, but it can now be carried by water. Also, it stops the VX Agent being absorbed into the bloodstream immediately after penetrating the skin - rather it works with a delaying action before being released some hours later. This makes it especially dangerous as being odourless and tasteless it can be distributed as an aerosol. If we were to spray our enemies from the air the symptoms wouldn't occur for a number of hours, meaning we would be able to infect many more before they detected it," he said.

Steepling his fingers together, touching them to his lips and bowing his head slightly, after holding up a hand for silence, Al-Jaheishi sat thinking for some minutes. After what seemed an age to Faisel, he raised his head again.

"Hmm, you have done well, brother. There is much possibility here. How much have you made?" the leader asked.

"Only a small amount so far, Excellency. I only had a small amount of VX Agent to work with here as most of the stockpile has been moved to Syria."

"But if I move you to Raqqa and you are supplied with more VX, can you produce more of this coating?"

"Certainly, Excellency. Now I know how to do it I can easily produce more. I just need the right equipment and a bigger laboratory."

"That, brother, is something you shall have. Praise be to Allah, Allahu Akbar," Abu Nayef replied.

# Chapter 10

## Raqqa - Syria

Abu Bakr al-Baghdadi, known by his followers as Caliph Abu Bakr, commander of the faithful, current leader of ISIS - Islamic State in Iraq and Syria - and falsely stated as having been killed in a U.S. airstrike was in regular contact by ultra-secure radio with Abu Nayef Al-Jaheishi - ISIS leader of Mosul. Extremely anti-American having been captured by U.S. Forces near Fallujah in 2004 and then forcibly held and tortured at Al-Ghraib prison under his name Ibrahim Awad Ibrahim al-Badr, he was finally released in 2009.

After his eventual release, he was elected overall head of ISI - Islamic State of Iraq - and was responsible for many atrocities and attacks in Iraq. Finally, in 2013 when ISI expanded into Syria he announced the formation of the Islamic State of Iraq and the Levant (ISIL) – alternatively translated from the Arabic as the Islamic State in Iraq and Syria (ISIS), and claimed to be the new leader of ISIL and its Caliph.

Informed of Husseini's success with the VX Agent, al-Baghdadi called for 'Saif the Palestinian', currently working with Hamas in the Gaza Strip to come to Raqqa and meet with him.

Saif, whose full name was Saif Mohammed Khan was born in Iran in 1968 but moved to the U.S. as a child where he grew up. His parents were both Iranian sleeper agents and were located in New York, close to the UN, their cover being owners of a rug and carpet import business and a restaurant. Saif grew up as a typical

American boy, changing his name to Steve Caan and joining the U.S. Navy in 1987. A quick learner with a sharp mind, he was fast track promoted to the role of Lieutenant and was stationed aboard the USS Sides, a guided-missile frigate. Specialising in intelligence and surface warfare, he became an excellent planner and tactician. He was very highly rated within the U.S. Navy and was heavily involved in setting up Navy tactics and planning Special Forces operations and incursions. He slowly became disenchanted with the way America treated Muslims and was affected badly after 9/11 when his mother was raped and his father beaten during mob retaliation in New York. When increased security checks identified his parents as being of Iranian birth with suspicious loyalties against the USA, his prospects for promotion within the Navy ceased. Utterly disillusioned with the West's attitude and in particular America's towards Muslims he dedicated himself to working harder and harder against the USA by actively supporting al-Qaeda and Iran. He excelled in planning numerous smart attacks against the West, including the nearly devastating tsunami attack against the U.S. in 2012.

Since 2013 he had been working extensively with Hamas, the Taliban and the remaining members of al-Qaeda in Afghanistan and Yemen in devising new ways to attack their enemies. He had proposed and been extremely pro-active in the recruiting and converting locals to the 'lone wolf' approach against the West, where lonely and disenfranchised individuals could be turned and used to commit localised atrocities. Still in regular contact with his superiors in Iran, particularly Rear Admiral Behbahan of the Islamic Republic of Iran Navy IRIN, who originally supported him and had since continued to provide excellent cover and funding. While working with a number of the Palestinian militant

Islamist groups, his loyalties to Palestine were never questioned, and he became known as Saif the Palestinian.

Arriving in Raqqa via Turkey, Saif Khan was checked for weapons, then hooded and taken to the secret headquarters of Abu Bakr al-Baghdadi deep underground in the central city. The rooms Abu Bakr was using were adjacent to the underground sewage system. The entrance was through a number of disused but heavily armed buildings and then down four sets of metal steps. Unable to see and with his arms clasped by the guards as he stumbled down the last set, Saif slipped and would have fallen heavily against the railings had one of the guards not held him. In his stumble, his hood moved enough for him to see where he was walking, but all he could see was the wet and dirty walls and floor. The smell from the sewers was overpowering, and he was glad when they moved along further corridors and through various closed doorways before coming to a large room set up with desks, computers, screens and telephones. The smell was still present but not as overwhelming as before.

"Salam alaikum, Oh, mighty exalted leader, I am humbled in your presence and honoured your Excellency," Khan said, blinking in the sudden glare after his arms had been released and hood removed.

"Wa alaikum al salaam," came the reply. "I have heard many good things about you. Come, sit and drink. Refresh yourself then tell me what work you do to make the mighty Americans fear us so."

Rubbing his eyes, he saw an outstretched hand of greeting. He quickly took the hand, and gripping it firmly, shook it gently. Sitting down on cushions, they observed the traditional Arabic ritual of drinking sweet tea and eating small sweet cakes.

"Master, I have been working on new ideas. For the past few years, I have been building a network of what the Americans call 'lone wolf' soldiers based in the West. These are people who feel the West has betrayed them. Most have no jobs and no future. When I started this project, I thought I would find some, but Allah has been merciful, and I have found many hundreds in many countries."

"How do you recruit them?" Abu Bakr asked.

"Usually the first contact comes from the local Imams who know these people. They meet and talk to them at daily prayers. If the person is seeking help or the Imam believes he is open to persuasion, I get their contact details passed to me. I then either get other local trusted brothers to meet them or I contact them carefully through their email. Once they have been recruited and committed to our ways, I call them 'my followers'."

"But surely much email is monitored by the West's security services?" Abu Bakr said.

"Correct, Excellency, but usually only if the person is already known to the West as what they call a 'radical'. Most of the people I contact are totally invisible to their authorities. They have usually kept all their worries and thoughts to themselves. I approach them very carefully and introduce them to other, like-minded, brothers. Together, we groom these new recruits, almost hypnotise them, some of whom will travel and join Hamas or ISIS in their fight, but many we convince to stay quiet, mix with their locals and strike when the time is right. Because they are unknown to the authorities each attack, when it happens, has much more impact and their police and authorities look fools when they have to admit to not detecting these people before."

"And how successful have you been, my brother?"

"Very master. Over eleven attacks in the U.S. with more than 65 killed and 140 injured and many more in France and Germany. The attacks in Brussels airport in

March were instigated by me using followers in Belgium. Before that, I arranged the execution in Copenhagen in February of a cartoonist who defiled the mighty Prophet Mohammed. Another was of senior people at the Charlie Hebdo magazine in Paris last year, who also defiled Islam and mocked our beloved Prophet Mohammed. In November I arranged with various followers for them to attack a number of locations in Paris. Over 130 non-believers were killed, from the Stade de France stadium to many restaurants and the Bataclan Theatre. That was my most successful use of them so far, Excellency. Of course, some attacks do fail, usually because of nervousness by the recruits or by carelessness, but most are successful. From a terror perspective, lone wolf attacks are the most frightening as people don't know whom to trust. Even if they are caught and questioned, there are no leads back to me." Khan said.

"Do you have more planned?"

"Yes, master, many. The next big attack will be in France on their Bastille Day. It will occur in Nice, and the impact shall be felt around the world, Insha' Allah."

"Well my friend, I have asked you here for another task. You have been blessed with great planning and foresight, and I want you to use these skills Allah has bestowed on you to present me with a plan using this new information I've received," Abu Bakr said. "You will stay as my esteemed guest and if you need anything, just ask."

"Master, I am honoured to be of service to you. Please, tell me of this new information." Khan said as they moved towards another quieter room. This one was adorned with rugs, cushions and chairs. There, the two of them sat in comfort while Abu Bakr discussed the conversations he'd had with Abu Nayef about Husseini's achievement.

<> <> <>

Within a week, Saif had devised and developed a plan to use the VX Agent and, having already received approval from Rear Admiral Behbahan, presented it to Abu Bakr al-Baghdadi and his senior ISIS leaders.

Saif knew the Islamic Republic of Iran, a Shia-majority regime, officially supported President Assad in Syria and Prime Minister Haider al-Abadi in Iraq, both also Shia majority regimes, against the extremist Sunni regime ISIS; but he also knew Iran had always been adept at playing both sides. Officially anti-ISIS, Iran has been purchasing cheap oil from ISIS in exchange for supplying them weapons. Iran saw an advantage in wanting to destabilise what it saw as the whole western influenced region of Iraq, Afghanistan, Jordan and Syria, as well as the rich major oil and gas producing countries such as Kuwait, Qatar, Saudi Arabia, and the UAE. Iran continued to try and tie-up and harm USA and British interests in the region, hence its continuing support and funding for various terrorist organisations such as Hamas and for causing destabilisation in the area.

To great interest and applause, Saif detailed his plan to the waiting audience.

"Brothers. Praise be to Allah the greatest. Saif the Palestinian has great words and this attack will surely be Satan's downfall, Insha' Allah," Abu Bakr said after hearing the complete detailed plan. "This is truly a great day, and we shall see the fall of the mighty U.S. and its puppet, Great Britain. Join me in congratulating Saif. Victories shall be ours, Insha'Allah!"

After the initial congratulations had subsided, Abu Bakr again took the floor.

"My brother, your plan is good and very detailed, but I ask one question. You plan to run both the UK and U.S. operations yourself with support from local 'lone wolves' you have recruited, correct?" he said.

"Yes Excellency, that is my plan. Does it trouble you?" Saif said.

"Brother, I think it exposes you too much and risks your discovery. I recommend you run the U.S. end of the operation and we use a trusted colleague in the UK to run the UK attack. I already have the person in mind.

"In late 2002 and early 2003, I was still a Colonel in the Special Republican Guard. Under direct orders from our leader His Excellency, Saddam Hussein, I ordered the movements of multiple shipments from various locations in and around Iraq to secret and secure locations in Syria. This task was to be completed before the American invasion and was given to a Captain I chose for this role. He and his men did an excellent job, but they were terminated on orders direct from His Excellency to keep the operation secret in the event of any of them being captured by the U.S. invading force. I had them deliberately targeted at the outbreak of the war by a British airstrike. Unfortunately just a few days later the Captain's wife, Nadira, was also killed at the Al-Shaab market when a lone U.S. fighter-bomber dropped bombs killing and injuring almost 60 civilians. The Captain's son, Wissam Hamoodi, was informed of the British and American airstrikes and he became very anti-Western. I helped reinforce his hatred and arranged for him to move to the UK under a new name of William Hammond where he has become a trusted agent for me. I require you to use him to control your UK operation," Abu Bakr said.

"As you command, Excellency," Saif replied.

"Then it is agreed. Funds will be made available and transferred. This is truly a great day and success will be yours, Insha'Allah!" Abu Bakr said.

# Chapter 11

## The Pentagon - Washington

Admiral Douglas Carter was feeling particularly depressed this morning. As Chief of Naval Operations, he'd been part of the team the President had called into the White House and tasked with the problem of how to rescue the girls out of Mosul before Iraqi action starts, and so far, he was stymied. In control of the world's largest navy and some of the toughest fighters on the planet, he still couldn't see a quick and easy answer without knowing exactly where the girls were.

He'd ordered additional drone flights and real-time satellite imagery over Mosul, but the girls' whereabouts were still unknown. Even the CIA was apparently still in the dark. Usually, before any attack or potential hostilities, the CIA had assets on the ground feeding them information, but the iron grip ISIS held over the locals, along with the savage consequences they bestowed on anyone they suspected of dissent, deterred most individuals from doing anything other than submit to total obedience.

Lieutenant Mitchell 'Mitch' Stringer knocked on the door and walked into the Admiral's office carrying two cups of coffee.

"Good morning, Admiral. Did you sleep well?" Mitch asked as he handed one over.

"No, I friggin' didn't, Mitch. Too many goddam problems and no friggin' answers," the Admiral said between slurps of coffee. "Still, that's what I'm paid for, I guess. What's the threat board look like this morning?"

Putting his drink down, Mitch moved towards the electronic wall display. The Threat Board originated in WWII and was the daily briefing for the President and his Generals of all the current threats and issues. Since then each military division has copied the idea. The President still received a daily overview of current threats against the U.S., but these have usually been compiled by staff members of the heads of the various agencies working for him including Admiral Carter. The Threat Board discussion Mitch was about to have with the Admiral was different. Mitch was short-listing all the compiled raw data disseminated from various intelligence agency sources, all being recognised by their 3-letter acronyms, including the CIA, NSA, NRO, DNI, FBI, and DIA.

Turning to the screen, Mitch began, "Sir, overnight just a few incidents. We've had some Chinese pilots flying too close to our carriers in the South China Sea. The Ronald Reagan was buzzed by a couple of Chinese Shenyang J-11 and Xian JH-7 warplanes flying aggressive action against the Reagan's F/A 18 Hornets. They came within 98 miles of the Reagan before withdrawing. The Reagan's Captain had already issued an ultimatum to the Chinese pilots they'd be shot down at 100 miles, but they were just probing. However, the Hornets did get a radar lock on the Chinese and made it clear they were ready to fire before the Chinese withdrew. The Captain feels their aggressive action will likely trigger an accidental release soon, so he's reissued orders to his flight team to only fire on his explicit command. The Nimitz is joining the Reagan later today, and we are ensuring all military U.S. ships and aircraft remain in international waters and airspace, but the Chinese are constantly pushing," he said.

Changing screens, he continued, "The Nimitz has come close in past Hughes Reef in the Spratly's, and various U.S. craft were lit up with missile radars from

Chinese ships with a number 'locking-on'. No shots were actually fired, and State has already issued complaints at the highest level against continued Chinese build-up in what is seen as international waters. The Nimitz and her fleet have now moved north away from Hughes Reef in preparedness of joining the Reagan for the joint exercises off Taiwan, so everyone is keeping alert but hopefully keeping calm as well. The rest of the board looks much the same as yesterday. Normal issues elsewhere - Iran sabre rattling sending a few of their torpedo boats out towards the George Bush but then turning away before they come within distance, North Korea threatening more missile launches - they're all listed here in the printed briefing, sir," Mitch said, as he handed over a folder.

Banging his almost empty mug down on his desk and spilling the small amount of coffee remaining, the Admiral drew a breath and started cursing, "Goddam President with no balls … the U.S. has the biggest and most powerful navy in the world being humiliated by those slant-eyed fuckers … namby-pamby President too fucking scared to push back ... too worried about trade deals ... not interested as it's an election year ..." he cursed.

Deciding there was a time for talk and a time for silence, Mitch stayed by the desk while Admiral Carter vented his rage.

Eventually, after a minute or two, the Admiral had calmed enough, so Mitch handed him an envelope.

"Sir, this was delivered to you by hand this morning. It's cleared X-ray."

Opening the envelope, Admiral Carter read a brief note while holding up two tickets.

"Hmm, it seems Mrs Carter and I shall be attending Swan Lake tonight. Can you get her for me on the phone?" the Admiral said, showing Mitch the note.

It said attached were two tickets to the American Ballet Theatre showing Swan Lake at the Kennedy Centre tonight for the Admiral and his wife, from Gideon Shem Tov working directly for Major General Yaacob Ayish at the Israeli Embassy in Washington.

"Sir, I've not come across Major General Ayish. Who is he?" Mitch asked.

"Officially, he's the military attaché, and Shem Tov is his deputy, but he's actually a senior officer in Mossad. He must want to talk but not officially," the Admiral replied.

Exiting his government limousine, the Admiral walked with his wife in through the entrance to the Kennedy Centre. Due to Carter's political position, a number of other attendees recognised him and bade him and his wife greetings. Leaving his security bodyguard at the rear, Admiral Carter guided his wife to their seats. Picking up the programme from their pre-allocated seats, a small square of paper slipped out onto his lap. The message was typed and was brief. Rear steps 20:15. The lights dimmed on time, and the Admiral enjoyed the first thirty minutes or so before excusing himself saying he is going to the bathroom. His wife, used to these often-interrupted events and sudden clandestine meetings, just smiled and kissed his hand.

"Don't be too long, darling," she said as he moved back along the rows to collect his bodyguard.

At the rear steps, a black sedan with the engine idling was waiting. A blacked-out rear window lowered, and Shem Tov smiled and opened the door. Getting in, the car quickly drove off.

"Admiral, it is a pleasure to see you again. I trust you and your wife are well? The Major General expresses his apologies for not being here in person but felt there was information you should have. He hopes your wife will enjoy Swan Lake while we talk," Shem Tov said.

"I am sure she will. So what can you tell me?" the Admiral asked.

"We can't be seen talking openly, but Israel has a source, Hakim Gerbali, in Mosul who thinks he is working for the Jordanians but is actually working for us. He is based in Mosul University as an administrator with Faisel Husseini, and he knows that Husseini and ISIS have increased and stepped up their VX nerve agent programme after using and deploying chlorine and mustard gas at Al Qayarah recently. It seems this Husseini has made some sort of breakthrough and is very excited about it. Gerbali reports Husseini recently had a meeting with senior ISIS members and has told Gerbali that he will be joining Sleiman Daoud al-Afari in Raqqa, Syria shortly under direct orders from Abu Baghdadi. This al-Afari is a senior researcher and chemist and has been involved in the manufacture of mustard gas and of the arming of shells with it. It will be a disaster for the region if ISIS starts using VX Agent against its enemies."

"Does your source know where this Faisel Husseini is now? Does he know when he leaves and how he will get to Syria?" the Admiral asked.

"He believes so, Admiral, but as I'm sure you can imagine communications with him is not easy. But more importantly, I understand, he also claims to know where the five U.S. girl hostages are being kept."

Together they spoke for another thirty minutes or so before the sedan returned and dropped Admiral Carter back at the Kennedy Centre in time for him to catch the last act.

# Chapter 12

## Washington

On arriving home, Admiral Carter contacted the White House Chief of Staff for a one-on-one call with the President as soon as possible.

At eleven thirty that evening Admiral Carter was put through to the President.

"Mr President. We may have a lead at last on the whereabouts of the five girls. We believe we know within a hundred yards radius of where they are being held within Mosul. Earlier this evening I met with Gideon Shem Tov who works directly for Major General Yaacob Ayish, one of the most senior Mossad directors. They have a trusted source in Mosul. We are getting secondary confirmation of this, and my team have already been working on a plan to extricate them," the Admiral said.

"That's excellent news, Admiral. When can you show me a final plan?"

"Now we believe we know where they are, Mr President, we can put the final touches to the plan we have been working on. I should have it ready for you by 18:00 tomorrow, sir."

"Sooner if you can, Admiral. Sooner if you can," he said as he hung up.

Shane Walker was the head of intelligence gathering stationed at the palatial US$750 million U.S. Embassy in Baghdad. Relocated there from Dubai, Shane missed the freedom he enjoyed daily in the UAE where he'd been free to move around at will. He used to enjoy a daily run along the beach promenade, and there were so many cafes and restaurants he rarely ate at his apartment. On days off he would indulge in some of the many water sports available on the nearby beaches as although being a Muslim country the UAE is extremely tourist friendly.

Unfortunately having moved to Baghdad, he found the differences quite extreme. One of almost 1,400 government employees stationed there, at least Shane's role took him outside, while virtually all of his colleagues stayed permanently within the Embassy's blast-proof walls.

Completely self-contained the Embassy generates all its own power, has numerous water supply wells, a sewage waste plant, indoor swimming pools, and outdoor sports facilities. Covering an area greater than the Vatican City it contains food courts, a shopping mall, basketball courts, a gym, and fully self-contained apartment blocks protected by bullet-proof glass.

Shane's title was Captain, and his role was Military Attaché, but he was actually CIA Head of Station. Usually driving around in various old battered and unmarked cars he stayed as much below the radar as possible while running a number of sources in the new Iraqi Government and generally keeping an eye on anything the CIA found interesting.

With the latest information from the Israelis, Shane was now trying to verify it through various other sources he had throughout Baghdad, some even within parts of ISIS. Working closely with Mitch Stringer in devising a basic operation plan to extract the girls, Shane was also involved in agreeing if any payments for information or access were needed. He was also trying to gain as much background information on Hakim Gerbali as possible.

Lieutenant John Deacon and his men, being one of two SEAL teams currently located at Al Qayarah, had already been alerted and were ordered to come up with a rescue plan, either on their own or as part of a bigger force.

Deacon, Mitch, Shem Tov and Admiral Carter finally agreed on a basic plan. It had already been confirmed this mission would be extremely dangerous as any U.S. personnel captured by ISIS would be a big public relations boost for them, and no one wanted to guess at the potential fate a captured U.S. Navy SEAL would have to endure.

Aware that ISIS knew Mosul was next on the list for the Iraqi Army to attack and therefore had built heavily dug-in defences in the general direction of the expected attack, only some form of pinpoint insertion and escape would be likely to succeed.

Mossad confirmed again the girls were in an unmarked guarded building a half mile or so from Al Noree Al Kabar Mosque in the central old-town area of Mosul, the roads and paths having no name as the whole area is part of the old shanty town. Impossible to attack in force as hundreds of local ISIS supporters reside around there, it was decided it would need to be a small covert operation. Although with luck, and working alongside Hakim Gerbali, they might be able to get a small team in undetected, the main issue would be in extracting them safely after they'd rescued the girls.

By four o'clock the following afternoon Admiral Carter, along with Mitchell Stringer and Gideon Shem Tov were in the situation room below the White House. Also present were the others heads of services and agencies brought in previously, as well as the President. Deacon and his men were connected by secure video conference at Al Qayarah airfield.

Admiral Carter took the floor and began, "Mr President, colleagues. We now have confirmation of approximately where the girls are being held. They are in the old area of downtown Mosul and are under twenty-four-hour guard. The Mossad local source Hakim Gerbali has agreed to work with us in rescuing the girls and will complete a single pass of the suspected building later today to confirm its exact location. Bearing in mind none of these pathways and tracks in the centre has names, he will place a locator beacon as near to the building as possible. This will aid identification of the exact building from the air and also help lead a team in."

"Can't we just chopper a SEAL team in, rescue the girls and fly them straight back out?" the President asked.

"No sir, far too risky. The whole area is crowded, and the noise of a chopper will bring everyone out into the streets. We know ISIS have heavy weapons including hundreds of MANPAD portable ground-to-air shoulder-launched missiles as well as possibly thousands of RPG's. Even with Apaches flying close cover, it's far too risky. One lucky shot by ISIS and we could have a rerun of Blackhawk Down. No, sir, the only possibility of success is by doing it covertly, Mr President," the Admiral said.

"Understood. Go on," the President said.

"I would now like to pass over to Lieutenant Deacon. He will be leading the rescue attempt. Lieutenant! "

"Wait, where do I know that name from?" the President asked.

"Mr President," Deacon said, "You met me almost four years ago sir. After I cleared up some trouble in the Canary Islands."

"Aha, now I remember. Stopped us getting our feet wet, didn't you? Well if you're leading this then my confidence level has just skyrocketed."

"Thank you, Mr President. Kind words, sir. We won't let you down. Shall I continue?"

Having received a nod, Deacon switched his screen to a map layout and started running through the plan.

"A team of four, Hancock, Martock and Dawkins, led by myself, will deploy from higher up the Tigris River by High Altitude High Opening parachute jump. This will be from a height of thirty-two thousand feet and at three-hundred knots and we will 'chute in and land immediately next to the Tigris in farmland. We will then swim the eight point five miles to the meeting place 0.6 miles upriver from Alshohada Bridge, where Hakim Gerbali will be waiting with a truck and extra clothes. We will change out of our wetsuits and journey into Mosul with Hakim, carrying just small weapons and rifles. Hakim will lead us to the right building where we will overpower the guards and extricate the girls, before retreating back to the truck and then drive north. Once away from the front line along Route 1 we turn left just after Badosh Prison and head three miles out into the desert." Deacon said while pointing to the screen.

"On demand, a Seahawk will fly in to rescue us while two Apaches will provide close-in support, with four Super Hornet's from the George Bush Carrier Battle Group, currently patrolling in the Gulf, supplying high-level protection. We will be dropped off back at Al Qayarah airbase where a flight will be waiting to transport the girls on to Ramstein airbase in Germany for medical checks before being repatriated home. During the operation, a Predator drone will be stationed overhead with live video back to Al Qayarah and the Pentagon and will provide us local voice comms and will also be monitoring the buildings locator beacon."

"Sir's, the operation is planned to commence at 18:00 Bravo UTC tomorrow," he continued, looking around the room, "does anyone have any questions?"

Having gained nods and general agreement around the meeting forum, Deacon then spent the next thirty minutes or so further expanding some of the details.

# Chapter 13

## England

William Hammond rubbed his neck and stretched his shoulders as he alighted from his car. He'd been driving for over four hours through heavy traffic up the busy M1 motorway towards Leeds before stopping at the Roadchef services at Tibshelf for a quick evening meal before continuing on towards Bradford.

Hammond lived in Reading, just outside London. He kept himself very private and rarely spoke with neighbours, only having done so initially to set up a 'legend'. Locals believed he was a salesperson for an office equipment company covering West London and the Home Counties, which would explain his often early morning or late evening journeys. Born Wissam Abed Hamoodi, he'd grown up initially in Iraq until his father, a Captain in Saddam Hussein's Army, had been killed by the British on the first day of the 2003 war against Iraq. His mother and unborn sister had also been killed in a U.S. airstrike a few days later, and he'd become an orphan. Friends of his father had looked after him during the U.S. led occupying period, sending him to the UK to finish his studies and changing his name to the more western William Hammond. Fervently anti-British and anti-American, he was one of the most successful sleeper agents for ISIS, usually working at stirring up hatred and aggression against the British in the heavily Muslim dominated areas of Slough, Tower Hamlets, Newham, and Luton.

Finishing his meal, he paid cash and then continued his journey towards Bradford, taking the M62, and then the A650 through the town to the suburb of Manningham just as the heavy rain had begun. Parking his car in a quiet back-alley, he stood for a few moments looking around, confident he hadn't been followed. Slipping a flick-knife into his right hand, he began walking along the darkened pathway, out onto wet empty back roads. After a half-mile or so, changing direction a number of times to foil anyone following him, he came to the required road. Turning left he kept to the shadows before going through the far door of an Arabic food shop entrance, past the counter and straight out through the back entrance before then climbing the dark stairs to his left and entering the darkened room, his knife at the ready.

"Salam aleikum, brothers," Hammond murmured quietly, "Allahu Akbar."

"Wa aleikum as salaam," they replied. "We are pleased that you are here, Insha'Allah!"

Looking around the dimly lit room he confirmed it was just the three of them. Relaxing slightly he introduced himself as Mr Green as he pocketed his knife.

The two youths introduced themselves. Jamal Aboud was stockily built with a typical straggly Arabic beard and long hair. He was working as a trainee mechanic at his uncle's small garage repair workshop. Amjad Wazir was smarter dressed and clean shaven and worked as a shelf stacker at a local Supermarket. Both were British-born Pakistanis and regularly prayed at the small mosque in the backstreet of Springstone Road, one of the twenty-seven mosques in and around this area of Bradford.

Both knew each other from school having grown up locally, and the two of them had shown interest in learning more about their past and their religion. Jamal Aboud's parents were strict Muslims, and his upbringing had been ruled by the culture of Islam. Amjad Wazir's family were more relaxed about religion and although followed some of the Islamic doctrines, had become more westernised. Both Aboud and Wazir had mentioned a number of times to their local Imam their want and willingness to join and fight for ISIS. The Imam would regularly pass those details through to his superiors.

Messages from Imam to Imam were usually based on verbal communication passed directly one-to-one, or by small encrypted notes passed by hand. Occasionally messages of higher importance were sent over an ultra-secure digital network directly to the Inter-Services Intelligence organisation (ISI) of Pakistan.

Estimated to be one of the world's best and strongest intelligence agencies, ISI had devised and built an ultra-secret communication protocol, jokingly nicknamed ImamNet by the CIA. It was designed and operated jointly between ISI and MOIS - the Ministry of Intelligence and Security in Iran, the ISI equivalent in Iran and the post-revolutionary successor to the SAVAK secret police and primary intelligence agency of the Islamic Republic of Iran.

Certain data is regularly shared between these organisations, including specific feedback from Imams worldwide who are instructed to provide names and details of those followers who are more likely to follow extremist views. Sometimes operating in reverse, a call will go out to all the Imams instructing them to ask their followers for certain pieces of information.

This data is then stored until needed by the various organisations that make up the terrorist community and can pay the asking price.

The CIA knew of ImamNet but had yet to intercept and decode it.

Hammond spent the rest of the evening speaking in whispers with Wazir and Aboud instructing them on what was needed. He advised them that they would be able to join and fight with ISIS and this first mission was crucial to ISIS. They were never to discuss this with anyone, but they needed to be ready to do as Allah willed, and they must be ready to leave at a moment's notice. They needed to pack a bag each with what they would need over in Iraq and Syria and have it ready to go. Aboud needed to shave his beard and shorten his hair for this first mission so as to blend in better with others.

Finally, after being with them for over an hour, and only referring to himself as Mr Green, Hammond left. He walked away from the food shop changing direction a number of times before stopping at a bus stop and waiting. Looking around he couldn't see any evidence of being followed, so he backtracked before eventually returning to his vehicle and heading south towards London.

# Chapter 14

## Al Qayarah Airbase - Iraq

The Rolls-Royce AE 2100 D3 turboprops screamed as full power was applied and the C-130J Super Hercules began rolling down the runway at exactly 18:00 Bravo UTC. Flying light today with just four Navy SEALs onboard as cargo, it flew south-west away from the front line while quickly climbing to its final cruising altitude then turning and taking a route out eastwards towards Iran before turning 180 degrees again just before it overflew the Iranian border. Now on a similar flight path and altitude to standard Tehran to Ankara European flight routes, it was safe from ISIS attack with their ground-to-air missiles.

Deacon and his team sat quietly on the canvas and aluminium framed seats, each weighted down with gear and each deep in thought. Every operation was dangerous some more than others, but every trip behind enemy lines contained risk. The key to success, Deacon agreed, was training, training and more training. You cover every possible eventuality with your team so many times that everything becomes second nature. You know without having to think what your colleague's actions will be and they know yours. If and when things happen you collectively think as one. You rely on them, and they rely on you. You have each other's back. It was German Field Marshall Helmuth von Moltke who, in World War One, famously said: 'No battle plan survives first contact with the enemy'. He was right. Everything is open to change.

But with the right training, you know your team will think as one, and everything is possible, Deacon thought.

The Flight-Sergeant came back to speak with him.

Plugging in his headset, he said, "Sir, fifteen minutes to the drop zone. Wind is a little less than first estimated at nine knots north-west. We're steady at thirty-two thousand feet and will slow to three-hundred knots one minute before greenlight. There is thin cloud at five thousand feet and all looking good."

Thanking him, Deacon motioned for the men to stand and start final preparations for the drop. Each of them would connect and test their own oxygen equipment before turning and getting the person behind them to double-check. Diving out of an aeroplane at thirty-two thousand feet is not conducive to good health. At that altitude, the air is too thin to breathe, and the temperature is almost minus sixty degrees Fahrenheit. If any of their equipment or clothing failed, they would be dead within minutes either of hypothermia or cerebral hypoxia. Even a small area of exposed skin would result in severe frostbite with possibly fatal consequences. Therefore every team member checked and rechecked their own and their colleague's equipment.

At two minutes to the drop zone, the red lamp was illuminated, the depressurisation light came on, and the alarm sounded.

At one minute to the drop zone, they could feel the aircraft noticeably slow as the engine noise reduced. Moments later the rear ramp began to open, and Deacon was thankful that the close-fitting helmet reduced the screaming wind noise to an almost acceptable level.

At ten seconds to the drop zone, the red lamp began flashing.

Then the red lamp extinguished, and the green burned brightly as Deacon followed closely by his team walked off the end of the ramp.

The first thing Deacon always noticed when doing these jumps was the sudden silence as you fell away from the aircraft. Looking briefly up he could see the tail ramp already closing and although he couldn't hear, he knew the engine revs were again increasing to bring the craft back up to cruising speed. This C-130 was going on to Incirlik airbase in Turkey before returning to Al Qayarah tomorrow.

Deacon had already heard in his earpiece that the other three were falling well. Moments later at twenty-five thousand feet their darkened 'chutes automatically deployed. These parachutes were modified to provide a high level of steering and were also oversized to minimise dropping speed and maximise flight distance. Having been dropped upwind the nine knots of north-west flow would help them quickly cover the twenty-three miles of lateral distance to their GPS coordinated landing point just over eight miles upriver from Mosul. Keeping in a close group, they came in low and fast directly from the north clearing the sewage treatment plant at less than five-hundred feet. Approaching the Tigris, they all turned collectively sharp right to head into wind as they touched down on the northern salt banks of the river with yards to spare.

Hitting the quick release buckle Deacon and Martock quickly took up defensive positions weapons drawn while Hancock and Dawkins gathered the collapsed 'chutes. A dog barked in the distance, but otherwise, everything was quiet. With Deacon and Martock still on guard, Hancock and Dawkins dug shallow holes and buried the 'chutes, helmets and protective clothing.

Pressing his thumb switch Deacon radioed over the encrypted network, "Anvil One down and secure."

Not waiting for an answer from the super-high-frequency secure burst transmission, Deacon and his team moved towards the water's edge wearing their dark wetsuits while donning fins, closed-circuit rebreathers and non-reflective facemasks.

Although cold by normal standards, the Tigris felt warm after the icy wind of the jump, each team member moved quickly into deeper water. Each was carrying a suppressed M4A1 Assault Rifle, a suppressed 9mm SIG-Sauer handgun, and a KA-BAR combat knife, with both weapons wrapped in a protective waterproof anti-rustle covering. Each member also had waterproof night vision goggles and a waterproof throat microphone and fully encrypted earpiece radio comms connecting them to each other, Al Qayarah and also back to Washington. Finally, each member also had their dive board containing a compass, a depth gauge and a chronometer.

The river was soundless and what buildings they passed were unlit. The evening was very still with just occasional dogs barking in the distance. Floating just below the surface the team made rapid progress downriver hidden amongst a large amount of flotsam caught in the medium flowing waters. Deacon ordered they drift out into deeper water to keep the furthest from any light sources on the embankment. As they neared the city of Mosul itself, the embankments got busier with lighting and some activity of voices being heard from afar. As they made the last major course change just over two miles to their landing point, Dawkins radioed he could see a powerful launch using a searchlight patrolling back and forth, the searchlight beam piercing the water with its loom reflecting almost to the far bank.

Well out of range of the light Deacon signalled to submerge and drift-swim past. All four dropped below the surface with barely a ripple, re-merging almost 100 feet downriver from the patrol boat six minutes later. They continued to swim and drift downriver until slowly approaching the bank landing point. Lying in the shallows, Deacon spent almost fifteen minutes looking through his night vision goggles just observing the landing area, checking for any traces of people or movement, or for anything that shouldn't be there. To the right was a truck with the engine cover raised and a figure stooped over, looking into the engine bay. Deacon quietly exited the river and moving silently towards the person, raised his weapon and from ten feet away, whispered: "The night is dark, my friend". The correct reply of "But the stars are shining" came back and Deacon quickly approached the figure.

It was 23:45 local time.

# Chapter 15

## Mosul - Iraq

Four weeks after being kidnapped the five girls, Cheryl Thompson, sisters Michelle and Laura Williams, Emily Baker and Debbie Morgan had slowly come to terms with their situation.

Since being paraded and filmed alongside Abu Bakr Baghdadi and told of their fate should they refuse, life had settled into a daily routine of cooking and cleaning and trying to minimise the beatings the 'crows' gave them across their backs if they were slow to do what they were instructed. They'd made their basement room as comfortable as possible, cleaning and scrubbing the rattan mats and washing the dirt encrusted blankets in between their chores. Only allowed into the courtyard under guard, they had daily washing, cleaning and cooking chores to complete. Kept as one group, they'd not been allowed further out of the locked courtyard, raw food being brought in by the 'crows' for them to prepare. Surrounded by other run-down buildings and with the stench of raw sewage constantly in the air, Emily and Michelle had quickly succumbed to stomach upsets and depression. Masoud Saadi was still guarding them and would still touch and grope Laura when he could. Laura being the youngest and still finding Masoud quite handsome was slowly falling in love with him and would even become quite aroused at his groping.

A psychologist would recognise her symptoms as Stockholm Syndrome - a phenomenon first described in 1973 in which hostages express empathy and sympathy and have positive feelings toward their captors, sometimes to the point of defending and identifying with the captors. Unfortunately, with the tension and depression within the group, there was no-one to talk to, and her condition and feelings grew.

All five girls slept together on blankets on the floor in the basement room with always two guards on duty - one outside the door and the other covering the courtyard.

Masoud was feeling more and more sexually frustrated. He groped Laura whenever he could considering her a cheap American whore but being constantly aroused decided it was time to take things further with her and convinced the other guard for them to take Laura to another room to have some fun.

Him first, then his brother-in-arms after he was done with her.

Later that evening, Masoud quietly opened the basement room door and crept in towards a sleeping Laura. Putting a hand over her mouth, he smiled at her and whispered in Arabic as she awoke in a panic. He nuzzled her neck and began kissing her while he slid his hands up under her blouse and began gently caressing her breasts. Feeling her nipples harden he began to squeeze harder and as she felt herself becoming aroused she quietly stood up and willingly took his hand as she followed him back outside.

# Chapter 16

The man turned and looked fully at Deacon as he approached. Recognising him from photos in the dim green light of his NVG's, Deacon offered an outstretched hand.

"My friend. Welcome to Mosul," Hakim Gerbali said, slightly taken aback at this tall figure all in black and dripping water.

Keeping a sharp lookout Deacon replied. "Hakim, it is good to meet you. Is this area secure?"

"It is now, my friend. I arrived twenty minutes ago but found a guard here. I offered him a cigarette, and we talked. He was off-duty so no one will be looking for him. His body is in the reeds now. There is no one else here."

"Were shots fired?" Deacon asked.

"No, my friend. I used a knife. It was very quick. Had shots been fired this place would be like your New York Times Square by now. ISIS soldiers are everywhere, but they are lazy. They are only tough when in groups. By now most will be dozing or fully asleep. They are just lazy bullies."

Beckoning to his team to exit the river, Deacon radioed "Anvil One. Liaison achieved."

Quickly changing into the Arabic clothing Hakim brought, they hid their wetsuits and swim gear in the reeds before climbing into the truck; Hancock, Martock and Dawkins in the rear, Deacon alongside Hakim.

"There is not actually a curfew, but ISIS doesn't allow celebrating, so everything shuts early and everyone stays home in safety," Hakim said. "We can drive to about 3/4 of a mile from where the girls are being held, but then we will have to approach silently on foot, as any vehicle at night in this part of the city will be suspicious."

Taking a circuitous route and stopping a number of times to check if they were being followed, they approached Nabi Jorjis St and found a quiet area to park the truck down a side alley.

Once parked they travelled on foot with their handguns, knives and assault rifles completely hidden, but ready for immediate action from under their long flowing Arabic clothes, their faces and skin darkened with brown dye.

Leaving Dawkins concealed in the shadows to watch the truck, Hakim led Deacon and the two others into the densely crowded Al Makkawi area.

This part of Mosul is like many thousands of other backstreet areas within this region. The buildings, mostly generations old, were built from a mixture of concrete, wood and even mud and plaster. It was a labyrinth of small paths, buildings close together and small alleyways. The ground was just sandy dirt and gravel. Many of the walls were bullet-pocked and were covered in ISIS praising graffiti, while the dustty ground was littered with broken bottles and discarded rubbish. There were a couple of burnt-out vehicles left abandoned, and the overall atmosphere was one of poverty. Deacon had seen hundreds of alleys like this from Fallujah to Tikrit, Kirkuk to Ramadi when he and his colleagues had been tasked to secure the areas when around every corner was a possible suicide bomber waiting, and every package of rubbish on the ground could be an IED. At least that wasn't the case here, he thought.

It was almost pitch black, the only dim lighting coming from the few stars and moon glowing on the low cloud, but the night vision goggles gave everything a bright green glow. Deacon had passed a spare pair to Hakim and the four of them made good progress through the dark, deserted alleys being careful not to kick discarded cans and stopping at every corner to check the way ahead was clear.

Hancock used a small spray can at every corner or junction to put markings on the wall. Invisible to the naked eye or in daylight, this showed brightly through their NVGs, making it easy for them to retrace their steps.

Three times they stopped because of voices or dogs barking, but the voices were from behind closed compounds, with the smell of tobacco smoke from old men having their last nightly fixes hanging heavy in the air.

Finally, creeping down yet another alley, Hakim whispered they'd arrived and pointed at one particular door.

The thought had crossed Deacon's mind that Hakim could be leading them into a trap, so he ordered Hancock and Martock to cover point. He'd already briefed his team that if that was the case, then the first bullet was for Hakim and for them to take as many others down with them as they could.

Quietly listening just outside the door he thought he could hear gentle snoring, so he carefully raised the latch and quietly opened the door a fraction. With his suppressed SIG-Sauer in his hands, his NVGs showed a sleeping guard in his early twenties, unshaven and dirty. His AK-47 rifle was leaning against the wall next to him, and Deacon could smell his body odour.

Moving in a little more, worried in case the hinges should creak, Deacon looked around the courtyard making out a building with dim lights in two rooms and a doorway leading down to what appeared to be a basement.

Creeping over to the guard, Deacon hit him once, hard, under the ear with the butt of his weapon. The guard slumped out cold for hours as Deacon whispered to his men to come in. Looking through the dimly lit windows, Deacon could see two men sat in one room while the other room was empty. Leaving Hakim hidden in shadow in the courtyard and Hancock guarding the gate with orders to shoot the two men if they came out, Deacon and Martock crept silently down the steps to the basement towards a doorway and darkened corridor.

The chair outside one of the doors was empty, but a key was still in the door lock. Quietly turning the key Deacon silently opened the basement door to find four girls asleep on rugs. Deacon and Martock put their hands over two girls' mouths each, whispering to them to wake up and not make a noise. One of the girls tried to inhale ready to scream. Deacon pressed his hand harder.

"Sshhh. We're U.S. Navy come to get you out. Quiet!" he whispered, "Who is missing? There should be five of you?"

Looking around Michelle gasped, "Laura. Where's Laura?"

Promising to find her while Martock took the other four quietly upstairs, Deacon moved silently further along the corridor.

Hearing a muffled wail of "No", Deacon moved further into the darkness, a small slit of light showing from under a closed door. Pushing open the door he entered into a dimly lit dirty room with an old blanket on the floor. Laura was on her back with her skirt pulled up and one man facing him near her head, grinning through toothless gums while pinning both her arms together with one hand and groping her breasts with his other. Another man was knelt between her open thighs with his filthy undershorts around his ankles and holding his full erection in one hand as he was leaning forward about to enter her.

# Chapter 17

Leaping forward, Deacon aimed and fired one suppressed round into the forehead of the man holding Laura's hands down. As the one about to rape her began to look up and turn his head, Deacon clubbed him with his pistol while kicking him off the girl.

"You sick fuck," he said as he fired two quick rounds into Masoud's chest.

"Laura, I'm U.S. Navy come to get you out. You're safe now," he said.

"No, no, you've killed him. I love him. You murderer," she cried.

"But he was about to rape you!"

"I love him. Murderer!" she cried, her wails beginning to get louder and louder, trying to move over to his body.

Urging her to keep quiet Deacon dragged her to her feet and pulled her clothes straight. Turning on him she began to pummel his chest as she gulped in air ready to scream.

"Shut the fuck up, or we'll all be dead," Deacon hissed, as he tried to put a hand over her mouth as her cries got louder.

Eventually, after running out of options Deacon resorted to the only thing he could think of. He quickly turned her around and put her in a sleep hold. Within seconds she collapsed, and he slung her over his left shoulder as he retraced his steps back up to the courtyard.

By now Hancock, Martock and Hakim had the other girls ready to go. Deacon passed the unconscious Laura over to Martock whispering to the other girls that she was fine and had just fainted. He quickly explained to Martock what he'd done and ordered them to start off back to the truck.

"Let Hakim lead you all back to the truck. I need to see what's going on in those lit rooms. I'll be just a few minutes behind you. Go on, get going," Deacon whispered before radioing "Anvil One. Packages retrieved, departing location."

Looking through the shuttered window, he could see the body outlines of two men talking. Due to the shuttering, he could only see parts of their faces. Both were speaking Arabic although one was speaking more rapidly than the other. Through his radio comms, he whispered for added gain and recording to be turned up and removed his throat mic before gently pressing it against the window glass. The glass worked like a large sounding board, and the faint scratchy voices would be better heard and recorded.

Not recognising them from photos as senior ISIS members, Deacon was about to burst in and dispatch them for kidnapping the girls when an urgent message from Martock came over his earpiece. His team had just seen two trucks driving through the shanty town in Deacon's general direction. The team and the girls hadn't been detected, but Deacon had better get away quickly before it's too late. Washington also came on the line and told him they could see from the Predator drone feed two trucks driving towards his direction.

He never knew what alerted the two men inside just as he removed the microphone from the glass. Maybe it was a faint noise or his shadow on the window. Maybe just a sixth sense, but suddenly the shutter was pulled back, and Deacon found himself staring straight into a face.

As he turned and ran, he thought he heard the face say "Fuck, he's white" in English. Quickly exiting the courtyard, he could see the loom of the truck lights approaching from just around the corner. Running the opposite way he quickly pulled his night vision goggles in place and ran as fast as he could through the inky black alleys, weaving left and right down as many alleyways as he could to throw off pursuit, amidst random gunfire and mass Arabic shouting. Although some lights came on, most people preferred to keep indoors and not get involved. ISIS were known to be extremely violent to the locals they controlled, and most times ignorance and non-involvement were deemed a blessing.

Eventually, after at least a mile, Deacon slowed and ducked in behind some large metal rubbish bins while he sorted out his bearings.

"Anvil Team, sitrep," Deacon radioed.

"Team in view, just approaching the truck," Dawkins answered. "New pick up point due west on Al Shaziani Street. Pick up in 15."

Carefully choosing his route and with Washington seeing his position in real-time through drone imagery and directing him which way to go, Deacon made as much speed as possible.

Eventually exiting the maze of the shanty buildings on to the larger Al Shaziani St, he could see the truck driving slowly away from him further down the street.

Dawkins saw Deacon in the passenger mirror and ordered Hakim to slow the truck as he watched Deacon racing down the darkened road after him, Dishdasha flapping in the breeze.

As Dawkins helped pull Deacon up into the cab, he shouted, "Hakim, Go. Go. Go."

Turning to face a flush faced Deacon, Dawkins said, "Welcome back boss, but we've got trouble".

# Chapter 18

As the first of the two trucks pulled up to the gate of the courtyard and ISIS soldiers rushed after Deacon, Saif Khan grabbed Faisel Husseini by the throat and questioned him.

"By all that is sacred, we are undone. You assured me this house was safe?" Khan said.

"Brother, this house was safe. It held the American girls and has guards. Who was that man?" Faisel asked.

"That, I don't know, but he was white, and the girls have gone. For your sake keep quiet and let me do the talking," Khan said, as the ISIS leader of Mosul, Abu Nayef Al-Jaheishi, arrived with his guards.

"Brother, you are unharmed?" Abu Nayef said.

"Yes, Excellency. The western dogs have released the girls, but brother Husseini and I are unharmed," Khan said.

"Has the plan been compromised?"

"No, Excellency, the plan is still intact," Khan said.

"It was unwise for you to come here," Abu Nayef said.

"Yes, Excellency, but I had to meet Faisel to fully understand what he has achieved. But you are correct, oh wise one. Allah the merciful and almighty has protected us. Allahu Akbar," Khan said.

Fuming that the girls had escaped, Abu Nayef stormed downstairs to see the two dead guards. Kicking the half-naked body of Masoud, he returned to the courtyard.

"Bring him to me!" he commanded.

The now conscious gate guard was dragged in front of Abu Nayef.

"Tell me you fought them. Tell me, in the name of Allah, you fought them until you could fight no more?"

"Master, I tried to fight," the guard blubbered, "I tried to fight them, master, but there were too many of them. In the name of Allah I trie —."

"LIAR," Abu Nayef screamed. "Your weapon is where you left it. You were sleeping, you lying dog. Hold him."

Removing a jewel-encrusted dagger from the scabbard in his waistband, Abu Nayef drew the razor sharp blade across the guards' face a number of times, slicing his eyelids off in pieces.

"You are no good to me, coward. Go to Allah, insolent dog, and beg his forgiveness," Abu Nayef said, as he slashed across the screaming guard's stomach, intestines spilling out onto the filthy ground as he kicked him backwards.

Leaving the guard to slowly bleed to death trying to push the blue and red tubes of his stomach back together, Abu Nayef turned back to Khan and Faisel Husseini. He ordered them to leave along with a team of his most trusted warriors as escort for Raqqa in Syria immediately, before turning and screaming at his men to stop the escapees.

# Chapter 19

Quickly getting his breath back, Deacon looked around as they sped south along Al Shaziani Street.

"Tell me!" he ordered.

"Boss, Washington has just said they can see increased activity around the roadblocks. Washington's just confirmed the Predator has picked up increased radio traffic now that ISIS is alerted. Images show extra roadblocks are being put in place and they're stopping all vehicles to get the girls back. They may not know we aren't on foot, but they're taking no chances. We should be reasonably safe for the next ten minutes or so unless accidently seen, but all roads out of Mosul are being blocked. It'll be impossible to get out on Route 1 as planned. Apart from Hakim, there are no known friendlies who would risk torture and murder by ISIS to help us."

"Hakim, turn around and head back the way you've come. They won't expect that, and we're less likely to be stopped heading towards the crime scene than away from it," Deacon ordered, just as the raid warning siren began to sound across Mosul.

Looking through the dividing curtain into the back of the truck Deacon could hear Laura, awake now, crying that she loved Masoud, that he'd been murdered and that she'll tell everyone back home what happened and how she wants to stay with ISIS. The other girls looked aghast though, terrified of being captured again. Washington came on the radio confirming the ISIS front line now looked to be on full alert, all ground-to-air radars were up and active, and people carrying weapons were swarming out onto the streets.

Deacon knew ISIS had triggered the raid siren as a call-to-arms for their men and knew that within minutes the streets would be full of them. He also knew that even if they could get to the planned pick-up point, it would be too risky now that ISIS was on full alert to jeopardise the lives of the helicopter pilots coming to rescue them.

Grabbing his map from a leg pocket, Deacon spent a few minutes thinking, while Hakim drove them back towards the shanty town centre.

"Hakim, two questions: first, can you get us back to the riverside pick-up point without being seen? Secondly, can you then dispose of the truck and get home safely without being caught?"

"Of course, my friend. Now the alarm is sounding the streets will become busy. I, as a good ISIS supporter, can come out and help. No one will know what to do because Abu Nayef will not want it known that the girls have been rescued. He will be saying something about attackers. The girls' rescue will be a loss of face for him. I can have you back at the river in five minutes," he said, accelerating and turning east.

Getting on the radio back to Washington and Admiral Carter while being driven back to the river, Deacon rapidly explained his plan to a more and more incredulous Admiral.

"Son, you sure do come up with some crazy ideas. Do you think it'll work?" the Admiral said looking at an equally surprised Mitch Stringer.

"I think it's our best chance, Admiral," Deacon replied. "In fact, I believe that it's our only chance."

"Well, Lieutenant. Mitch will put things in place at our end. Good luck, son, you'll need it," the Admiral replied before signing off.

Arriving back at the original pick-up point, Deacon and his men hastily got everyone out of the truck and removed any evidence of them having being there. Thanking Hakim for all he'd done and shaking his hand, Hakim assured him he would be safe. Climbing back on board the truck Hakim drove off towards some open farmland north of the city. The few local farmers living around there were used to seeing ISIS vehicles so would likely take no notice and not report it.

Hancock, Dawkins and Deacon quickly found their hidden dive gear and put it back on. Assigning Martock to stay hidden with the girls on the riverbank, Laura had started crying louder again. Grabbing her by the shoulders, he pushed his face right in close to hers.

"If you don't shut the fuck up I'll push you in the river myself and let the crocs get you. We're all getting out of here, and I don't give a fuck what you tell people when you get home, but we're all going home together. What do you think they'll do to you and your friends if they catch us? Now shut up!" he hissed.

Leaving Laura quietly sobbing, Hancock, Dawkins and Deacon swam out towards the middle of the river, holding their rifles just clear of the water. The launch they spotted earlier was still cruising up and down with its searchlight scanning the river. Separating from his men, Deacon started splashing the water and shouting. Even from 400 metres away, the boat crew could see something was wrong. With a roar of increased engine revs, the launch turned towards him, the searchlight sweeping back and forth trying to locate the source of the noise. With the light edging closer to Deacon and the machine gun in the bow already chattering away the water close to him began exploding from the impact of the 20mm rounds as he dived for the river bed.

# Chapter 20

As the launch came closer Deacon looked and could see the outline of the craft on the surface lit up by the flashes of machine gun fire and the loom from the searchlight as it motored over his position. Bracing himself for the expected assault by grenades, suddenly the forward movement of the boat slowed. Kicking his fins hard, he surfaced just to the rear of the two large outboard engines, weapon at the ready and watched his fellow SEALs, each 50 metres away on either side of the launch, expertly take out the machine gunner and the loader with headshots, having already shot the helmsman and his lookout. Moments later Deacon was climbing over the stern rail as his colleagues swam up.

"Nice shooting guys," he said, heaving the dead bodies overboard.

With the searchlight extinguished Deacon manned the controls and motored the craft towards the bank, gently nudging it to a stop just as Martock brought the girls to the water's edge.

Reversing back out into deeper water Deacon looked through the dead guard's holdalls aboard the craft for any anything of interest. Finding some blankets, food and drink in a couple of them, he passed them to the girls and advised them to eat something, then to lie down on the floor and keep quiet. In the meantime, he and his colleagues re-donned their Arabic clothes to better blend in from a distance.

Putting his Keffiyeh back over his head and holding it in place with an Agal, the black rope that is used to grip it to your head, Deacon then placed his night goggles back over his eyes as he turned the craft and headed downriver at medium speed.

"Anvil One. All afloat. We're coming home," he radioed.

Five bridges cross the Tigris, and they would have to pass under each one. As they headed downriver, they could see more activity on the embankments and roads close by.

Trying not to draw attention Deacon kept the speed to medium and remained in the middle of the river to be as far away as possible from anyone looking.

Having passed under the first three bridges without a problem Deacon breathed a sigh of relief. With three down and only two to go, he began to think that maybe they would make it after all.

Approaching Al Jamhuriya bridge, two searchlights suddenly came on and illuminated them, and a loudspeaker hailed them. Glancing down, Deacon could see the girls were covered by blankets, and he and his men looked like locals in their Arabic clothing over their wetsuits. Knowing there would be fingers itching on triggers, but they would be unlikely to shoot first, Deacon held to his course. The loudspeaker roared again, the voice louder and angrier this time. Deacon murmured, "A few more seconds then we will be passed … Just stay down—" when Laura leapt to her feet screaming "Help, Help, save me!"

Deacon pushed the throttles to the stops, and the bow rose like a horse rearing to gallop as the engine revs increased instantly and the propellers bit into the water. Hancock and Dawkins pulled their Dishdashas aside and, taking their places in the stern, shot out both searchlights, the stern being the most stable area of a speeding boat to fire from. Martock grabbed Laura, smacked her hard once across her face and stuck the barrel of his assault rifle up under her chin.

"You fucking keep quiet, or I'll shoot you myself, you stupid bitch!" he snarled, before pushing her back to the floor and taking a shooting position near Deacon and the controls.

As they accelerated down river leaving a glowing effervescent trail behind them another identical launch joined them from a side jetty. Quickly accelerating it slowly began to close the distance between them. Deacon concentrated on steering a weaving course while the three other SEALs focussed all their efforts on shooting out the searchlight and the gunner.

The last bridge to pass under was a four-lane motorway usually empty at that time of the morning, but now two trucks screeched to a stop, and armed men scrambled to the rails. Deacon glanced up to see one man fire an RPG at them while others were throwing grenades or shooting down on them. Yanking the wheel hard to the left the craft skipped sideways just as the RPG grenade hit the water where they would have been with the blast of the explosion almost overturning the boat and soaking them with spray. The high level 'CHUG CHUG CHUG' of the 20mm machine gun on the chasing launch firing at them was almost drowned out by the rhythmic chatter of the AK-47's firing down from the bridge. It was only the constant fierce weaving, and corkscrewing motion Deacon was putting the craft through that stopped them from getting hit.

A half mile further downstream Deacon could make out a line of white water stretching across the river and a number of small islands to the left.

"Rapids. Hold tight," he yelled as he again turned hard to port at full speed almost losing Martock over the side. The only choice now was to weave in between the islands and the shallows when eventually one of Hancock's shots paid off.

The turn, stable now for more than a few seconds instead of the back-and-forth weaving Deacon had been forced to perform, finally allowed Hancock to get a steady bearing on the chase boat. With two quick shots one of Hancock's rounds finally hit the gunner in the face, and with half his head blown off, he fell sideways his finger still on the trigger.

"Hooyah got the fucker— Fuck. Fuck. Fuck!" he said as the other craft's gun swung down from the weight of the barrel, the rounds keeping coming when two shots hit the starboard outboard engine with a third just missing Hancock's head before punching a fist-sized hole through the edge of the hull. With the engine spluttering and coughing smoke, Deacon had no choice but to throttle back, but by now they were amongst the islands and mostly hidden from view. Turning again suddenly into the shallows behind a high sand bank and pulling the throttles to idle, Deacon shouted, "We'll finish this here."

As the chase launch came past the sandbank, Deacon flattened both throttles again to the stops, and with a roar, both engines went from idle to full speed. The bow rose, and they leapt forward up almost alongside the chase launch. Caught in the sudden glare of Deacon's searchlight while trying to steer and reload their 20mm machine gun, they never stood a chance against the accurate automatic rifle fire from Hancock, Martock and Dawkins.

Within seconds it was all over as flames began to lick around their engines. With a deft nudge from Deacon's bow, the chase launch headed over towards the riverbank before flames finally turned it into a funeral pyre.

Deacon powered down his bullet-damaged engine as it was now belching smoke and making strange noises. Moving everyone to the port side to lift the starboard side slightly out of the water and keep the hole in the hull clear of the water, Deacon eased the port engine back up to maximum power, and they hurtled further away downstream towards safety. With Hancock and Dawkins in the stern still watching for pursuers, Deacon stood at the controls, his Arabic Keffiyeh headgear flapping in the breeze, only held in place by the Agal, looking for all the world like an ancient Arabian horseman heading into battle - the smile on Deacon's face saying it all.

Past the airport and Qiz Fahkri but before the next small riverbank town was a place Deacon and the Admiral had scoped out as a possible pick-up point. As Deacon swung their small craft towards the riverbank, he could hear the engine note of the approaching AH-60 Seahawk and could see the two AH-64 Apaches holding formation. Within two minutes they were aboard and were climbing away to safety all lights off and weapons hot.

Flying fast and low with the Apaches and Super Hornet's protecting them they arrived back at Al Qayarah airfield twenty minutes later.

# Chapter 21

## Al Qayarah Airfield - Iraq

Showered and wearing clean BDUs, Deacon and his team were sat in front of the encrypted video system.

"Admiral, although it was risky I don't believe we had a choice after the alarm was raised. There was no way we could exit by road and any 'copter flying north of Mosul would have been at high risk. The only thing I could think of was getting the girls out safely and getting somewhere safe enough for the Seahawk to pick us up. Nothing like a little boat trip when you're in the desert, sir," Deacon said.

"Well, your quick thinking saved the day, Lieutenant. Again. All five girls have been seen by army medics and deemed fit to travel. They are all sleeping now courtesy of your adventures with them and some sleeping pills the medics gave them. Tomorrow they fly at 08:00 local direct to Ramstein for full medical check-ups and debriefing, before flying home later that afternoon to be reunited with their parents," the Admiral said.

"CNN is already breaking news of their release, so well done again," Admiral Carter continued.

"What of the recording, sir. Did it come out?" Deacon asked.

"Yeah, it's a bit scratchy and not too clear, but it's been sent off for improvement and analysis. I'll let you know if anything comes of it. Anything else?" the Admiral said.

"Just that we'd have been stuck without Hakim. I hope he stays safe."

"My hope as well, Lieutenant. I would like the full mission debrief tomorrow."

Finishing the call, Deacon and his team walked towards the mess tent for an early breakfast, before sitting down and completing the entire mission report, his teammates having taken to calling him Lawrence after Martock had joked that he looked like 'Lawrence of fucking Arabia' while skippering the launch.

# Chapter 22

## England

William Hammond parked in a different part of town this time and was wearing different clothes as well as a hat and glasses. The rule to not getting caught, he'd been told in his tradecraft training, was to just blend in with the locals and not do anything unusual.

Approaching the food shop from a different direction he went inside past the counter and up the stairs before stopping in the shadows for a few minutes and listening, his hand again on his flick-knife.

Confident only Aboud and Wazir were inside he opened the door and entered.

"Salam aleikum, brothers," Hammond whispered, "Are we alone?"

"Wa aleikum as salaam," they replied, nodding. "We are pleased to see you again, Mr Green."

"This will be the last time we meet here, brothers," Hammond said, "There is too much risk we will be compromised. Here take these. They are unregistered. Only use them to call me - my number is already stored," he added as he handed over two pre-paid burner cell phones.

"Are you ready to join the cause, brothers? Are you willing to fight to the death for Allah the compassionate?" he asked.

"We are ready, brother, Allahu Akbar, Allahu Akbar, Allahu Akbar," they replied and started chanting.

"There is a test brothers. To show you are worthy. You need to kill a UK serviceman to show loyalty, to show you are a true Jihadist strong enough to fight with ISIS and to avenge the killings of Muslims. Will you do this, my brothers?" Hammond said.

Seeing them both nod and gaining their eager agreement, Hammond went on to describe what was needed.

"Brothers, others before you have done similar, as will others after. Do you remember the killing of Lee Rigby? This was completed by our heroic fighters in London. Like you, they were British born of foreign parents but discovered the true meanings of Islam. They became true Jihadists."

"But they were captured, and they're in prison." Aboud said, "I want to fight with ISIS, I don't want to be some kind of martyr locked up in some crummy British prison."

Lee Rigby, a British Army Fusilier, was walking along Woolwich High Street in London on 22nd May 2013 when he was attacked and killed by two British-born Nigerians, Michael Adebolajo and Michael Adebowale. They ran him down with a car before attacking and murdering him with knives and hacking at his neck with a cleaver. Both men stayed at the scene, boasting of what they have done, before being arrested by police. Both were tried and convicted and sentenced to life imprisonment, with a minimum term of 45 years.

"They had been instructed to kidnap him and take him elsewhere to kill him," Hammond said. "The plan was to escape and travel to Syria, but instead they panicked and chose to kill him in full view of the public and then stay and taunt the police. That will not happen with you."

Although devout in his beliefs and determined to hurt as many British and Americans as possible for what they had done to his parents, Hammond thought most of the young men who went to fight with ISIS behaved as if they were playing a sick video game. He still couldn't understand how someone born and brought up in a civilised western country such as Great Britain could hack off the head of a fellow person like a butcher carving meat, and then stand around boasting about it. He had no problem with killing; in fact, he enjoyed it if the targets were British or American, but he considered trying to hack off someone's head as barbaric.

"Brothers, there will be this test and then one other activity in a short while before you will fly to Turkey and join our brothers in their fight. Perform these well, and you will be hailed as heroes, brothers. You will sit by the hand of Caliph Abu Bakr himself, Insha' Allah."

Eager with excitement, Aboud and Wazir listened as Hammond continued.

"RAF Marham in Norfolk is home to four squadrons of Tornado bombers flying missions against the Islamic State. You will accomplish what Adebolajo and Adebowale failed to do. You will kidnap one of their pilots and behead him live on video," he said.

# Chapter 23

The following morning each carrying a small rucksack Aboud and Wazir left early and headed towards Bradford centre. As expected the main supermarkets were all busy. Walking through the car park, they spied a dark coloured Ford Mondeo being parked. Within moments of the female occupant leaving Aboud had popped open the driver's door using a 'slim jim' as Wazir handed him a slide-hammer. Seconds later the steering lock was removed, and the simple insertion and twisting of a broad headed screwdriver into the now empty slot was enough to start the engine. Driving slowly out of the car park so as not to draw attention they headed south towards the airport confident of at least an hour or so before the alarm would be raised.

At the airport, they drove into the long-term parking area and traversed five lanes before they found another dark coloured Ford Mondeo of similar age. Parking nearby they quickly swapped number plates across both vehicles before leaving again in the same car they had arrived in, all within the fifteen minutes 'free parking' time on their ticket. With the double cut-out between both cars the chances of them being traced through a number plate inspection were now infinitesimally small.

The journey to RAF Marham took over four hours as they could only make slow progress along the country roads. They stopped once for fuel, paying with cash Mr Green had given them the previous evening. He'd also given them an old, but fully working, 9mm Browning automatic pistol rescued from the Argentinian Army in the Falklands War of 1982, which Wazir kept playing with.

Arriving near the airbase, they drove past it a couple of times but didn't want to attract attention before driving off again twenty or so miles away and finding an overnight truck stop near the A10. Eating sandwiches and drinking Pepsi they stayed in the vehicle venturing outside only to use the toilet building. Although there were other drivers in some of the trucks, they deliberately chose not to speak with anyone.

Arriving back early the following morning they saw a lone jogger wearing RAF 'Blues'. Aboud made the snap decision to kidnap him, and they followed at a distance until the jogger turned down a quiet lane. Quietly parking the car close by, Aboud jumped the RAF jogger who, wearing earphones, didn't hear his approach. Aiming the Browning, Wazir shouted at him to get down on the ground. They'd both, however, underestimated the fitness and quick reactions of the jogger. With speed and strength stronger than Aboud expected, the jogger managed to wrestle him to the ground after first head butting him before knocking Wazir aside then leaping a gate and running off in the other direction.

Terrified they'd be caught Wazir and Aboud panicked and raced back to the car. Trying to remain calm Aboud drove as fast as he could trying not to draw attention to themselves while shouting obscenities at Wazir. Realising they'd screwed up big time and with the alarm raised and any chance of grabbing anyone now gone they headed back towards Bradford.

"Fuck, fuck, fuck, we're dead," Wazir said.

"Maybe, brother, maybe, you useless cunt. Why didn't you shoot him?"

"I couldn't. I just froze. What are we going to do?" Wazir cried.

Picking up one of the burner cell phones Aboud speed-dialled the only number stored.

"Mr Green, we failed," he said, "The person we tried to grab fought back and escaped. We failed. What are we going to do?"

"Were you seen? Was the car seen? And where are you now?" Hammond said.

"No, Mr Green. It was on a quiet road. He was jogging, and we approached from the rear. He was so quick he pushed me off and ran away. I don't think he even saw us properly."

"Where are you now?"

"Heading back to Bradford," Aboud said.

"No! Drive to Birmingham. Park the car in the McDonalds car park in Castle Vale. Wipe the vehicle clean of fingerprints first and leave it unlocked. It will soon be taken. I will meet you there at three," Hammond said before disconnecting the call.

Walking into the fast-food outlet a few minutes late, Wazir spotted Hammond sitting at a central isle table, eating. He didn't make eye contact, so Aboud and Wazir bought a meal each and sat close.

"You think you are warriors? You think you deserve to fight with our brave brothers against the infidels yet you can't even capture one man?" Hammond whispered venomously.

"What went wrong?"

Explaining and apologising profusely, and after begging for forgiveness, Hammond instructed them to go home and wait for his call, should he decide to give them another chance.

"But how are we to get home, Mr Green. We don't have a car now," Wazir said.

"That, my friends, is your fucking problem," Hammond whispered.

Driving off, Hammond watched them leave and walk towards the train station to head back to Bradford.

# Chapter 24

## Al Raqqa - Syria

The journey to Al Raqqa for Saif Kahn and Faisel Husseni was relatively easy going being most of the land between the two cities was still under ISIS occupation. The trip with their guards took them along Route 1 from Mosul through the towns of Sinjar and Wardiya where they stopped overnight. The following morning, before dawn, they headed further west before taking one of the many camel tracks up into the hills. Much of the fenced border between Iraq and Syria had already been damaged, and those guarding it were armed and vigilant. Over a dozen times they were stopped at gunpoint and checked, but their paperwork allowed them quick passage. They kept to the quieter backroads due to random attacks by U.S. Forces to vehicles travelling on the main ISIS controlled highways and once inside Syria found they could increase their speed.

On arrival in Al Raqqa late afternoon, they were taken directly to the building of Sleiman Daoud al-Afari. There the chemical and biological weapons specialist, al-Afari, greeted them warmly. Initially working for Saddam Hussein's regime developing and producing various nerve agents, including mustard agent and chlorine gas for use against their own people, al-Afari had supported al-Qaeda and then its successor, ISIS, after the fall of the Iraq leader.

Setting up a laboratory under Abu Malik in ISIS-occupied Mosul, the lab was moved to Al Raqqa after Abu Malik's untimely death from a U.S. drone strike two years before. Since then, al-Afari and his team had been working hard in trying to find other nerve agents to modify and further weaponise.

Excited by what Faisel Husseini had achieved, al-Afari had been instructed by Caliph Abu Bakr himself to offer every aid and support to help Husseini modify and produce the 200 litres of VX Agent with its unique polymer coating within ten days.

Husseini started immediately. He explained in great detail to the al-Afari's team his exact process for coating the molecules of VX Agent and between them they set up the equipment in the laboratories overnight as per his instructions.

The following morning al-Afari received delivery of two large yellow plastic drums both bearing a black skull-and-crossbones logo, which had been kept away from Raqqa and stored under armed guard.

Dressed entirely in full hazmat protective clothing, Husseini and his colleagues started distilling the contents from the drums into various glass containers and commenced the process, all under the watchful eye of al-Afari.

Within hours, the first few drops of the polymer-coated VX Agent slowly dripped into the waiting glass container.

# Chapter 25

## Al Qayarah Airbase - Iraq

Deacon received an urgent message to attend the secure video communications room at 18:00 hours local. Sitting down in front of the monitor Deacon could see Admiral Carter, Mitch Stringer, Shem Tov and Shane Walker, as well as others he didn't recognise on the call.

Admiral Carter again confirmed his and the President's pleasure at the rescue of the hostages then spoke for ten or so minutes reading from the mission report Deacon had sent.

"You did well, Lieutenant. We could monitor what was going on, but your report fills in the missing blanks. Well done again," he said before moving the conversation on to the recording Deacon had made. Asked if he thought he would recognise the people he saw, Deacon confirmed he believed he would, especially the one he'd seen up close as he'd spent quite a few minutes watching them.

"Lieutenant, the recording was quiet and all in Arabic except the last sentence, so we have a translation," the Admiral continued, "The technicians have also improved the sound quality and reduced the background scratchiness and noise."

Each part of the message was played as an original with text on the screen showing the translation. It read:

Voice 1: " - makes it much more deadly. Even washing it off the normal way with bleach and water won't help initially as the coating smears it onto the skin."

Voice 2: "How much delay does the coating provide?"

Voice 1: "Somewhere between 6 and 8 hours unless absorbed through eyes or mouth. Then the coating breaks down quicker and might only give an hour or so."

Voice 2: "And the cure? Is there one?"

Voice 1: "The standard mixture of atropine and pralidoxime if given in time. I haven't altered the actual chemical base of it, merely the coating which delays its effect, but not its potency. It's just as deadly as before, but delayed in its effect, which suits us perfectly."

Voice 2: "Are you sure there will be enough?"

Voice 1: "My dear Saif, I will have over 200 litres available within 10 days or so. We already moved all the chemicals from the al-Safira site well before the army retook possession. We also stripped the Palmyra site clean. True, some of Saddam's stash is still within the control of the Government, but we rescued more than enough. I know we have it stored somewhere very secure up in the mountains north of Raqqa, but even I do not know where. We have lots. All different types, as well. Colleagues have already moved some of what I need to the lab - 10 litres will be enough for the British and about 200 litres for Ameri — What was that? Did you hear something?"

Sounds of scratching and movement…

Voice 2: "Fuck. He's white!" in English with a slight American accent.

"Lieutenant, voice one is Faisal Husseini. We're still not a hundred percent sure who voice two belongs to, but intelligence believes it to be the person known as 'Saif the Palestinian.'

"Saif the Palestinian? Isn't that the bastard we came up against in the Canaries? This guy was dark complexion and maybe early to mid-fifties. Is that him?" Deacon said.

"Correct Lieutenant. And succinctly put. We know very little about this Saif fellow - he's almost a ghost. We were given his name after the Canaries attempt, but we never got anywhere with it. Never even found out his full name. He just disappeared. As you seem to be the only person who's seen him we need you to work remotely with the FBI facial artist's team to draw him."

"Understood, sir. What of the actual message? Doesn't sound good, does it, sir?"

"No Lieutenant, no it doesn't sound good at all. The FBI artist will be in touch," the Admiral said before cutting the video feed and calling his old friend, Colonel Brandon McAlistair, on the conference phone. Over the next twenty minutes, McAlistair confirmed the details within the message most likely referred to VX Agent and how deadly it is.

Shortly after, a visibly shaken Admiral Carter made an urgent call to Lieutenant General Warwick Dreiberg - Director of National Intelligence and senior advisor to the President.

# Chapter 26

## The Pentagon - Washington

Admiral Carter, Mitch Stringer and Colonel Brandon McAlistair from CDC in Atlanta, Georgia, met with Lt. Gen Warwick Dreiberg in the Admiral's office. Asked to provide an overview of Iraqi and Syrian involvement with chemical and biological weapons, Colonel McAlistair took the floor.

"Gentlemen, prior to the original Gulf War in the early '90s, Iraq produced large quantities of Sarin, Mustard and Chlorine Gas, Tabun and VX Agent at their al-Muthanna mega-facility approximately 60 miles north of Baghdad. It started back in the early '80s and was called Project 922 - codename for Iraq's third and most successful attempt to produce chemical and biological weapons. Early developed weapons were successfully used against Iran, and by 1984 Iraq had started producing its first nerve agents of Tabun and Sarin. In 1986, Iraq commenced a five-year program that ultimately led to biological weapons production. By 1988, Iraq had started producing VX Agent. The program reached its peak in the late 1980s during the final stages of the Iran–Iraq war. From August '83 to July '88 Iran was subjected to extensive Iraqi chemical attacks. Between '81 and '91, Iraq produced over 3,800 tons of chemical weapons agents. After the first Gulf War in '91, the UN Security Council sent inspectors to ensure that Iraq disclosed and destroyed its entire chemical, biological and planned nuclear weapons programs. Iraq repeatedly reported that it had done so, while the Clinton and Bush administrations claimed it was still hiding pre-'91 weaponry. Iraq originally stated that it had 412.5 tons of chemical weapon agents remaining. Four hundred eleven tons were destroyed under UNSCOM supervision up to '02; but one-and-a-half tons of the chemical weapon agents, including VX Agent, still remains unaccounted for," McAlistair said.

"One and a half tons? Missing? Holy shit!" Lt. Gen Dreiberg said. "How come this is the first I've heard of this?"

"Well, subsequent administrations have tried to downplay it. Don't want to cause unnecessary panic among the public," he said.

"Prior to the '03 invasion," McAlistair continued, "we know Saddam had moved all his remaining agent-based weapons and lots of other items and arms to Syria to stop them being captured by us. He always did have some WMD's but not anywhere near as many as the press and public were led to believe. In my opinion, the numbers were always exaggerated to support Bush's call for war. There's no record of exactly what was shipped to Syria before the March invasion but we know Iraq's possessions including WMDs. Once shipped, they were kept in tunnels dug under the town of al-Baida near the city of Hama in northern Syria, in tunnels near the village of Tal Sinan, at Syrian Army bases north of the town of Salamija and al-Safira, and in the city of Al-Qusayr on the Syrian-Lebanon border south of the city of Homs. It was all just stored for over two years before being utilised by the Syrian Government. Most chemicals were moved to various research labs around the country before being worked on. Some weapons were, and still currently are, being used by Syrian Forces against insurgents. A lot of the chemical weapons the Syrian Amy are currently using in East Aleppo are originally from Iraq. Unfortunately, ISIS also has or previously had access to some of the Iraqi weaponry and chemical agents. Much of northern Syria fell to ISIS in mid-2012, before some being retaken by the Syrian Army in November '13. This allowed ample time for ISIS to remove items they were interested in. Mustard and Chlorine Gas was mainly shipped to other ISIS strongholds around al-Safira, and Homs; with, we suspect, VX Agent being sent to Raqqa. If this is what they're working with, and all the evidence points to it being VX Agent, we've got problems," he said.

"Are you sure it's VX, not something else?" Dreiberg said.

"It's possible but extremely unlikely. Atropine and pralidoxime are the cure for VX, and they do refer to it being just as deadly as before, so I would say it is VX with a modified protective coating," McAlistair said.

The meeting continued for another thirty minutes, with McAlistair showing slides and discussing implications. In the end, a very worried Warwick Dreiberg agreed to call an urgent meeting with all parties concerned including the President.

# Chapter 27

## Yorkshire Dales - England

The Yorkshire Dales is an upland area of the Pennines in Northern England in the historical and beautiful county of Yorkshire. Comprising of almost 700sq miles this area is famed for its scenery, its remoteness and its breathtakingly peaceful atmosphere. Sparsely populated, it is a keen tourist attraction and a hill-walkers delight.

William Hammond stood waiting at the rear of his car. His was the only vehicle in the gravel car park a half-mile from the quiet road. Having decided to use Aboud and Wazir again, he'd called them the previous evening and directed them to meet him here. He needed somewhere remote, well away from prying eyes, and this was the perfect spot.

The faint distant purr of the Suzuki GW250 engine increased slightly, along with a dust cloud as Wazir, with Aboud as passenger, drove his motorbike into the parking area and switched off the engine. As the dust cloud settled and the silence enveloped him again, Hammond walked towards them, smiling.

"Salam aleikum, brothers," Hammond said, "Good, you are on time."

"Wa aleikum as salaam," Aboud replied. "We thank Allah for this second chance. We will do whatever you ask, Mr Green. Insha' Allah."

Opening the trunk of his car, he opened one of two large cardboard boxes.

"This, my friends, is a GS-15 agricultural aerial drone. It has six rotors, is fully rechargeable, folds down as you can see to a small footprint, and can carry a 5-litre load. It has terrain following software built-in and can fly for over 30 minutes on a full charge at almost 25 mph. It has a built-in fluid tank with variable pump and nozzle jets and comes complete with GPS enabled flight routes. There is one each. Today you will learn to fly them," Hammond said.

"Wow," Wazir said, "Where did you get them from?"

"That doesn't matter, " Hammond said, not wanting to disclose he'd used a fake credit card with delivery to an address in Luton of an old lady he paid £50 a month to as a retainer.

Making them wear latex gloves he'd bought from a DIY store in Birmingham to ensure there would be no fingerprints or DNA transfer, he gave them a box each to carry and ordered them to follow him along a track through the trees.

After a ten-minute walk, they came out into a large clearing. Hammond finished unboxing the drones, fitted the batteries, and let Wazir and Aboud play and fly with them as much as they liked. The controls were simple. The controller device had two joysticks, a number of switches and a smartphone screen. One joystick controlled the rotors speed, thereby controlling its height, as well as controlling its left or right rotation. The other joystick was for 'pitch' and 'roll' - left & right and front & back movement. Within a few minutes, both had mastered the controls, and they practised making them fly various manoeurvres including in straight lines, curved lines, and circles. Filling the fluid tank with water from a canteen, Hammond then showed them the relevant screen mode to choose the variable pump rate and nozzle spray patterns available. Finally, using the inbuilt GPS, they programmed them to fly specific routes with distinct spray patterns.

Stopping a few times to return to the car and recharge the batteries, Aboud asked what their mission was. Hammond merely stated that all would be disclosed later.

By mid-afternoon and two hours of flying each, both manually and in setting the auto flight routes, Hammond was pleased with how quickly they'd mastered flying them when suddenly he noticed a lone hill walker coming over to greet them.

After polite conversation first about the drones and how smart all this new technology can be and how he'd been watching them for over twenty minutes, Hammond finally managed to ask if the hiker was alone and where he was heading. After hearing that he was indeed on his own, liking the solitude of the Dales, he wasn't expected anywhere and lived on his own, Hammond bade him goodbye. As the hiker turned to walk away, Hammond quickly pulled out and opened his flick-knife, yanked the hiker's head back by the hair and drew the razor sharp blade deeply across his throat slicing open his windpipe and jugular.

With a gasp of expelled air, the walker collapsed to his knees, his hands feebly trying to stem the blood flow. Hammond and Aboud looked on without compassion, but Wazir went pale. Ordering Aboud to go back to the car and get the shovel from the trunk, Hammond turned on Wazir and slapped him hard across the face.

"You feel sick? You're upset? THIS IS WAR. Us against them. You want to fight with your brothers? Man up, you coward," Hammond hissed. "Check his pockets. Take anything identifying him. Do it! NOW!"

Hammond stood there watching Wazir slowly go through the corpse's pockets, taking his watch, wallet and cell phone before making both Aboud and Wazir dig a grave and bury the body. As Aboud grabbed the feet and Wazir the shoulders to move the body into the grave, the

112

nearly severed head fell back exposing the innards of the neck to Wazir who promptly dropped the body and vomited. Looking on with disdain, Hammond and Aboud half dragged, half kicked the corpse's body into the shallow grave.

Later back at the car park Hammond gave them £5,000 cash telling them to buy a run-down old van similar to a Ford Transit that Aboud would be able to sleep in. They were not to give names, and he was relying on Aboud to ensure it was roadworthy. He wanted it to be low quality - the sort owned by students, but mechanically reliable and with no distinct markings that would draw attention to it. Just an old nondescript van. It was to be stored at Aboud's uncle's garage. They are only to ever touch the insides while wearing latex gloves so that it would be full of old DNA but not theirs. Finally, he ordered Wazir to obtain a rucksack of a particular size and to get a false number plate for his bike.

# Chapter 28

## The White House - Washington

The meeting began on time in the situation room underneath the White House. Representatives from half the U.S. Intelligence Services were there. Sitting around the conference table were Mitch Stringer, Admiral Douglas Carter – Chief of Naval Operations, the Chairman of the National Intelligence Council, Lt-Lt-GenGeneral Warwick Dreiberg - the Director of National Intelligence, the Director of the CIA, Head of Homeland Security, Simon Clark - Director of the FBI, the Head of Special Operations Command, Colonel Brandon McAlistair from CDC - Centre for Disease Control, and finally, the President.

"Mr President, I requested this meeting after discussing with Admiral Carter and Colonel Brandon McAlistair about an intercepted message recorded last week in Mosul during the operation to free the hostages. It looks like ISIS has stepped up VX Agent production," Dreiberg said.

"OK Warwick, but before we continue someone give me the full idiot-level guide to this VX Agent. I want to know what it is, what it does and how can we stop it," the President said.

"Mr President," McAlistair said, rising from the desk, "I can provide you with that information. VX Agent, or Venomous Agent X, to give it its full name is one mean sonofabitch. It was first invented by the British back in the '50s. The British chemical company ICI was investigating a class of organophosphate compounds to use as

114

pesticides when they added a bit too much of this with a bit too much of that and VX Agent was formed. It was rapidly seen to be deadly, and samples were sent to Porton Down, the UK Government's chemical research centre. Once they realised what they had, their Government quickly classified it, along with some similar venomous, or 'V' discoveries as a WMD. VX Agent itself is the best-known and most efficient of the V-series of nerve agents and is considered an area denial weapon due to its physical properties. It is far more powerful than Sarin, another well-known nerve agent toxin, but works in a similar way. VX has the texture and feel of thin motor oil. This makes it especially dangerous as it has a high persistence in the environment. It is odourless and tasteless and can be distributed as a liquid or as an aerosol. As standard, it works within seconds. You can be exposed through skin contact, eating something with it on, drinking, or even breathing spray in. It attacks the enzymes in the body that normally switch off muscles, etc. With the enzymes blocked, molecules constantly stimulate the muscles, and they leak. As the muscles spasm, they tire and leak more. Death is caused by asphyxiation on your own body fluids and heart failure. It's an extremely painful way to die."

"How can it be stopped?" the President asked.

"There are a couple of answers to that, Mr President. If detected before contact and exposure, it can be neutralised by the use of large amounts of strong bleach and chlorine. It can also be diluted in extremely large amounts of water, but we are talking enormous amounts. A cupful of VX poured into a water reservoir would still be potent enough to kill everyone who drinks it. Two hundred litres of VX, and that's the amount we are talking about here, sir, in Lake Superior ... well, I wouldn't want to go swimming in it after."

"Jesus, it's that potent?"

"Yes sir, it's one of the deadliest weapons ever built. If a person is exposed to it, it all depends on timing. The effects start almost immediately, certainly within ten seconds or so. Then the only cure is large injections of a mixture of atropine and pralidoxime. That stops the agent making things worse, but of course, doesn't repair the damage already done. If you can administer Nerve Agent Pre-Treatment Set (NAPS) tablets before exposure, then you block the risk of infection, but this treatment has a shelf life within the body of only five days. After that time, you are at risk of infection again. Once infected if you administer the atropine and pralidoxime antidote in a quick enough time, you've got a 50:50 chance of saving the patient. Even then, they may be hospital bound for the remainder of their lives," McAlistair said.

"OK, that's what it is and what it does. So who's got it and how?"

"Sir, back in the '70s and early '80s, when Iraq was still our friend, they - with assistance from us and other Western countries - produced enormous quantities of chemical weapons during their eight-year war with Iran. Syria had also been developing and producing chemical weapons agents, including Mustard Gas and Sarin, and possibly VX nerve agent, but wasn't so advanced. We also know Saddam's weapons are now in Syria due to certain military deals that were made going as far back as the late '80s. A safeguard agreement that in the event either country was threatened with being overrun by an enemy nation was put in place. By the late '90s, Saddam knew that the U.S. was eventually going to come for his weapons and we weren't going to just let this go like we had in the original Gulf War. He knew that he had lied about having WMDs for so many years and wanted to maintain legitimacy with the pan-Arab nationalists. He

116

also wanted to embarrass the West, and this was the perfect opportunity to do so. After Saddam denied he had such weapons why would he use them or leave them readily available to be found? That would only have legitimised President Bush, whom he had a personal grudge against. What we witnessed soon after the 2003 invasion were many who opposed the war to begin with, rallied around Saddam saying we overthrew a sovereign leader based on a lie about WMD. This was exactly what Saddam wanted and predicted," McAlistair said.

"We also confirmed from some of the interrogations of former Iraqi officials," McAlistair continued, "that a lot of material went to Syria before the war, including some components of Saddam's WMD program. Precisely what went to Syria, and what has happened to it, is an unknown that still needs to be resolved. We have some information but not all. Satellite imagery at the time picked up activity on the Iraq-Syria border before and during the invasion. Satellites tracked a large number of vehicles, mostly military trucks, moving from Iraq into Syria. Reports found after the invasion strongly suggest it was all planned and organised by the Iraqi Revolutionary Guards to eliminate Hussein's WMD threat. Reports from Israeli intelligence also confirmed this."

"We know ISIS has taken control of a number of Syrian chemical weapon production sites and has actively been manufacturing and using Mustard Gas in both Syria and Iraq. They also had their own active chemical weapons research team, headed by Abu Malik who was killed in a drone strike earlier this year. Reporting directly to him was Sleiman Daoud al-Afari, who specialised in chemical and biological weapons, along with Faisel Husseini, a brilliant and upcoming student. His is voice number one on the recordings. We believe he has found a

117

way to coat VX agent to delay its effects," McAlistair said, before playing the recording a number of times.

After listening to the recordings in silence, the President had one more question to ask.

"Gentlemen, if this nerve agent is so deadly, and I've no reason to doubt you, wouldn't any attacker need to be a chemical expert to not infect themselves?" the President asked.

"Unfortunately not, Mr President," McAlistair answered. "All you need to do is wear protection. Anyone with $500 or so can buy a perfectly suitable, perfectly secure 100% safe Hazmat suit from eBay. The best makes are German ones. I've heard they are even cheaper if you buy them with Bitcoin off the dark web."

Taking the floor again, Dreiberg said, "So we know about a possible VX Agent attack on both the UK and the USA but what we don't know is where and when but have to assume it's imminent."

The discussion grew more heated with fingers being pointed at who should know what and when. Finally, it was agreed to inform the UK of a potential imminent attack on UK soil and to distribute Deacon's photofit picture to all agencies worldwide, including the British.

# Chapter 29

## Otosan - Turkey

In the early pre-dawn light at the Ford Otosan assembly plant on the outskirts of Gölcük, Turkey, the master assembly line program manager, Temel Kervan, walked slowly to work with his rucksack over one shoulder. A 53-year-old devout Sunni Muslim, he loved the early mornings and believed Allah had made this time of the day especially beautiful. He couldn't believe how anyone but his God could have created anything as wonderful each morning as a new dawn.

He lived a simple life and followed his religion strictly, making his wife and daughters adhere as closely to Sharia Law as possible. Utopia for him would be the expansion of ISIS throughout the region and the strict adherence to Allah's ways it delivered. He firmly believed the country was becoming too westernised. A few years previously he had visited Bodrum during the summer, its beaches full of scantily glad western women. Whores and prostitutes, he believed, shameful in the eyes of Allah. He'd been embarrassed as he'd felt himself become aroused as he looked at them. Since then, he'd become even more devout to the stricter teachings of Islam, and his wife and daughters had suffered accordingly.

Since 2013, all Ford Transit vans for Europe were produced and assembled at the Otosan plant in Turkey. A new order would come in from a Ford Dealership garage anywhere in Europe for a particular model. Sent in through the Ford Automated Product and Spares Ordering Systems, or 'FAPSOS' for short, the Otosan assembly plant operated on a 'Just-in-Time' principle. Each order would be assigned a production number, supplied from stock if already built or planned to be built if specialised. It would then be shipped, along with hundreds of others, to the relevant country before being delivered to the particular Ford Dealership garage for onward delivery to the customer.

Having received the message yesterday, he knew what he needed to do.

Temel Kervan knew to wait for one particular new order from the UK Leeds-based garage, Braithwaite Autos.

# Chapter 30

## Mosul - Iraq

In the sterile confines of the secret laboratory and under flickering fluorescent lamps, Faisel Husseini, wearing a Tychem 10000 TK Level A hazmat suit, sealed the cap of the second of two 5-litre standard oil containers - the sort that can be purchased from any fuel forecourt worldwide - with a quick-setting glue compound. He washed them down first with a strong bleach mixture, then with a powerful chlorine-based solution. Both containers were brand new purchased locally and emptied and cleansed of their original contents. Both were standard worldwide well-known brand names. After drying the outside of the containers, he put two horizontal lines through the labels with an ultraviolet ink pen. Invisible in daylight they would only show when subjected to ultraviolet black light. He then moved to the shower room and showered in a strong bleach mixture before exiting the inner then outer laboratory rooms while removing the self-contained breathing apparatus.

Placing the oil containers on the floor, he said, "That is the UK ones completed; now we ship them to our friend."

"Is that it? Is it safe?" Saif asked.

"Perfectly, brother, do you think I would touch it if it weren't? These containers are virtually indestructible. The outside has been cleaned, and the caps are locked on with glue. Unless you puncture this or open it, it's perfectly safe," Husseini replied.

Standing there looking at the containers Saif considered the havoc he could wreak with them, the sheers numbers of deaths he could make happen and be responsible for.

"You can wear gloves if you wish, but believe me, it's safe," Husseini continued.

Placing both of them within larger containers wrapped in black plastic sheeting, Saif passed them on to two of the senior and most trusted ISIS fighters.

# Chapter 31

## Otosan - Turkey

The border between northern Syria and Turkey is long. Although guarded by both Turkey and ISIS in parts to stop refugee's leaving Syria, as with many boundaries it is porous. The towns of Akcakale and Tell Abiad actually sit on either side of the border just fifty miles north of Mosul. Each day vast quantities of goods pass in both directions, many legally, some not. As always in a war zone, some people will find a way to make money. Here, people smuggling was the golden goose. Those wanting to head from Turkey to join in the fight with ISIS would pay a $90 or $100 premium to be helped across quietly. Rich Syrians trying to escape would pay many times more. Placing two new 5-litre oil containers with a well-trusted courier was child's play.

Two days later the courier delivered at night to the home of Temel Kervan. No words were said. None were needed. Both men knew what was required of them.

The following morning Temel, along with his brother, carried one container each within their rucksacks. Security was meant to check everything entering or leaving the plant, but this was Turkey and Temel had worked there many years and held a quite senior role. A simple smile and hand wave and they were in.

By lunchtime, the two containers were hidden in the webbing and springs under the drivers and passengers seats where they were completely hidden from view to the casual eye. By two o'clock Temel had completed the relevant paperwork and the Transit van, reference

123

number GG-5549DE34UK, was moved onward for shipment.

In seventeen days, it would be unloaded onto the Western Dock in Southampton to await customs clearance before being transported, along with many others, up country until finally arriving at the forecourt of Braithwaite Autos in Leeds.

# Chapter 32

## London

With the U.S. based CDC alerted and the British Prime Minister called personally by the U.S. President, the UK immediately raised its status level to hospitals and health authorities country-wide. The Prime Minister called for an emergency COBRA meeting with all senior cabinet staff, COBRA standing for Cabinet Office Briefing Room A. Also present were the Security Service (MI5), responsible for protecting the UK against threats to national security; the National Counter Terrorism Security Office (NaCTSO), who coordinate the government's strategy against terrorism; the Counter Terrorism Command (CTC), who assume initial control and response in the case of a terrorist incident; and Dr Gerald Lassiter, the Head of Defence CBRN Centre, the chemical, biological, radiological and nuclear events warfare group for the UK armed forces.

Although the origins of the threat had been explained and an audio copy of the voice recording made available, the threat was still unsubstantiated. There was also some doubt amongst some of the Cabinet Ministers whether VX Agent was the actual threat, considering the name hadn't actually been used. However, Dr Lassiter agreed with CDC's findings.

After another hour or so of back-and-forth arguing, the Prime Minister eventually took the floor.

"Gentlemen, gentlemen. Ok, having listened to you all let me finish with my conclusion and bring the meeting to an end. Although we have no idea of where or what may be attacked here, and by whom, or even when, it is good intel from our American cousins. We do NOT want to release this to the public, so we will leave the overall threat level currently as is, but keep the raised status levels at hospitals and health centres countrywide to report anything suspicious to their local Health Protection Team (HPT)," he said.

"We will also put all Chief Constables on notice of this possible threat, and I want the Joint CBRN Regiment on full alert, along with the Defence CBRN Centre," he added.

Within the hour the alert had gone out to the 43 Chief Constables as well as to the Joint CBRN Regiment, based at RAF Honington, Suffolk and to the Defence CBRN Centre at Winterbourne Gunner, Salisbury, South Wiltshire, to be put on full alert with all non-essential leave cancelled.

# Chapter 33

## Florida

Rolling over in bed, Elias Shirani switched off the bleating alarm clock. Not sure why six hours of sleep never seemed enough, he stumbled to the bathroom and got into his regular wash, shower and shave routine. By the time he was dressed in his uniform, he could smell the strong odour of fresh coffee wafting up to him. Walking into the kitchen, he leant over and kissed his wife good morning. Married for what seemed forever he still welcomed and enjoyed seeing her every day.

"Eggs will be ready in five, baby. Juice?" she said.

Nodding his reply, he sat at the table.

"Do you want to take lunch, hon?"

"Nah! Zane and I'll stop at a Taco Bell," he said as he started to eat breakfast.

Born in the U.S. fifty-six years ago to Lebanese Christian parents who'd emigrated in the '50s, he'd been married for thirty-two years and had a single twenty-three-year-old son. Zane.

Elias worked for Orange County Public Works in Florida. Originally, he'd opened up his own business, but after a short while he'd sold up and had been with Orange County almost 28 years now. Two years previously Zane, having finished college, was unemployed. Joining as Elias's assistant was a surprise and initially a worry for Elias. Zane had always been a bit of a dreamer. A rainbow chaser Elias had once called him. All he seemed to want to do was laze around the pool or mess on his computer in his room. Zane had finished High School and then College but with only average grades. Worried that he might not find a decent career to follow, Elias had been concerned when Zane first joined him in case he'd been expecting an easy time, but he'd been pleasantly surprised at how hard he'd worked.

Zane wasn't a particularly good-looking boy. At school, he'd always been a bit 'geeky'. Always picked last for the football teams and ignored by the girls he had the hots for. He'd had a few dates, but they'd all ended unsuccessfully after his fumbled attempts to get his hands up inside their tops usually in the back of his Dad's truck. Feeling left out and spurned he, like many others, turned to watching porn on his laptop. Even that had bored him after a while, and so he'd begun to try other websites. Eventually, he found he wasn't alone. There was a whole bunch of like-minded individuals out there; people like him who didn't really fit into society. People like him who the girls laughed at or ignored. People like him who didn't really have many prospects and felt exploited by the rich in the West. People like him who were easily swayed.

The first email he'd received had been very simple. It just asked him if he felt left out, marginalised, ignored. But to Zane, it was as if it had been written just for him. He was quickly hooked. Over a period of several months, he became more and more involved. He watched their videos and read their corrupt messages. He began to believe.

He even changed his religion. But in private. He came to follow and believe in the ways of Islam. Not the usual peaceful views of Islam recited and enjoyed by many, but the narrow-minded, twisted and dangerous views of the radical.

He became recruit number one-hundred-and-ninety-four on Saif's ever-growing list.

The following week he told his parents he was taking a few days off, was going camping with a friend and wanted to borrow his father's Ford Super Duty truck. Not wanting to pry, his parents said they were pleased for him to spend time with someone else, and of course, he could use the truck as long as he drove safely. Early the next morning, throwing a rucksack in the back, he muttered a quick goodbye and headed off.

The journey would take him almost two days. It was a long and tedious drive along a road interspersed with potholes and with large trucks whose drivers seemed to believe they ruled the road. Stopping a couple of times for food and gas before overnighting at a cheap motel near Rocky Mount and then again just outside Newark, he followed the road north through Daytona, then up Interstate 95 directly to New York.

# Chapter 34

## Eastern Turkish Airspace

The pilot of the Qatar registered Gulfstream G650ER en route from Baku, Azerbaijan, to New York slowly reduced height over Lake Van in eastern Turkey until the aircraft disappeared from Turkish air traffic control radar at 19:23 UTC.

With his finger on the ident transponder switch, the Captain flicked it gently to 'Off', turned his head slightly and said to Saif, "We are now flying dark."

"Continue as planned," Saif murmured back.

Dropping down to a height of two hundred feet above the lake surface, they were still flying at an altitude of almost 5,600 feet above sea level. The Captain donned night-vision goggles while the co-pilot switched the navigation system over to follow the pre-programmed GPS coordinates. Through his goggles, the Captain could see the green ghostly images of the hills surrounding the southern and western banks of the lake rising a further 3,000 feet, but the darkened path of a valley slowly opened up in front of him. With the autopilot and navigation system turning and banking the aircraft automatically as each coordinate was reached, the Captain was redundant. However, he kept his hands lightly on the controls as he stared out through the cockpit windows, ready in an instant to pull back on the yoke and climb back up to safety if need be. As the terrain below began to drop away slightly, the Captain glanced briefly at the navigation screen and breathed a sigh of relief as they approached and flew over the small town of Sirvan with almost a 300-foot height clearance.

Changing the frequency to a particular setting, the Captain clicked his radio transmission key and said the single word of "Işıklar". Suddenly in the distance, the runways lights illuminated at the small deserted airport at Siirt, near the tiny village of Pinarca. The Captain slowed the aircraft as much as he could and aligned it for a quick landing on the 6,000 foot-long north-east to south-west facing runway.

With a gentle thump the wheels touched down, and the Captain immediately applied as much reverse thrust as he could, quickly slowing the aircraft, before turning it around and taxiing back along its length. As they neared the north-eastern end of the runway, a canvas covered truck approached.

Turning the aircraft again ready for take-off, the Captain applied the brakes and pressed the switch to open the rear cargo doors. The driver and his mate from the truck quickly transferred two 100 litre rectangular-shaped plastic fuel containers and two holdalls into the aircraft hold and strapped them down. As the truck pulled away, the Captain closed the cargo doors and began to increase the engine revs while holding the aircraft on its brakes until the door open light went out. As the light blinked off, the Captain released the brakes and pushed the throttle levers to their stops. The aircraft had been on the ground less than four minutes.

Within seconds, the two Rolls-Royce BR725 A1-12 engines, each producing almost 17,000 lbs of thrust, hurled the Gulfstream along the runway before quickly taking it back up to 41,000 feet. As they passed through 10,000 feet the Captain switched the ident transponder back on and called Turkish ATC.

"This is Qatar Royal flight en route Baku to New York," he radioed. "Request royal clearance for flight duration."

Explaining the short time period offline as a technical issue, now fixed, the Captain settled back for the remaining non-stop flight to New York.

In the luxuriously furnished cabin, Prince Ahmed Jabir Kalifa bin Mohammed al-Thani, 3rd cousin to the Emir of Qatar, turned to his three bodyguards and Saif and asked why they had landed. Saif merely smiled and said there had been a small navigation problem that had now been resolved and that there was nothing to worry about.

Smiling, the Prince beckoned one of the two extremely attractive, dark haired hostesses to bring him another drink.

# Chapter 35

## Al Qayarah Airbase - Iraq

The last week had been spent exercising, training and planning. The Iraqi Army had been heavily building up strength at Al Qayarah airfield, about 65 km south of Mosul, for the past three weeks. The intention was for a September or October attack on Mosul itself with a hopeful retaking of the city by the end of the year. That was what the Iraqi Prime Minister, Haider al-Abadi, wanted. Deacon, however, didn't think it likely.

He knew from intelligence reports and reconnaissance photographs that ISIS was pretty firmly entrenched and had been building their defences for over two years. Their fighters were also quite prepared to die for their beliefs, which made any attacking force more cautious. Typically an enemy will fight until they realise they cannot win and then often surrender. Any enemy that is willing to die fighting is a tough opposition, as the Americans found out against the Japanese in the Pacific in WWII. In those cases, only overwhelming force wins the day.

Deacon knew that although the build-up was going well, the ratio wasn't yet at the 'overwhelming' level. He also couldn't understand al-Abadi's desire to keep informing ISIS of when and where the attacks would commence. The media were regularly being told of the impending attack. The Iraqi air force had even been dropping pamphlets over Mosul telling of the expected battle, urging the civilians to leave. You don't tell an enemy where and when you are going to punch them, you creep up and hit them when they least expect it, he thought. At least this fight didn't involve the US, though. We are only here to support and advise. Not that this attack would finally destroy ISIS. They were too strong and too big, but retaking Mosul was a good step in the right direction, he thought. And Arabs had been fighting Arabs for centuries and would likely continue to do so, but who knows … maybe sometime they'll see sense, he mused.

The plan now for the next few weeks was for quiet probing raids towards Mosul itself. Just far enough to check their defences and find their weak spots. Satellite imagery was good, but you still couldn't beat actual boots on the ground and physically getting 'up close and personal'. Sometimes you had to get close up to see the booby traps and minefields.

Tonight Deacon and his team, along with a group of Iraqi Special Forces, moved quietly along the desert keeping almost parallel with the edges of Route 1, south of the Adhba hills near a small village called Alepeshmanh. All were wearing night vision goggles and were heavily armed. The SEALs also had a live video feed from a Predator drone circling far above them. Looking through the greenish glow of his goggles Deacon could easily make out the folds and bends in the landscape. It was barren with the odd gully and Wadi showing. There was also a large number of small stone built walls protecting areas that had been turned over to crop growing, although nothing much seemed to be growing currently.

Although the daytime temperatures were hitting more than 120 degrees Fahrenheit overnight they dropped to the mid-fifties. But Deacon and his men were still sweating dressed as they were in full camouflage BDU's and wearing ceramic body armour. Tonight was moonless with a faint thin cloud cover and therefore extremely dark. Some evenings the stars were so bright out in the desert and far from any light radiation sources Deacon would sit and just stare upwards, mesmerised by the sheer amount of planets he could see. But not tonight. Tonight was a mission into enemy territory, and you didn't take unnecessary chances. The road they were walking parallel to had heated up in the daytime sun. In fact, it had got so hot it would blister any bare skin touching it. But it also cooled much slower than the surrounding desert. It was still close to human body temperature even at this time of night which also meant that anyone looking in their general direction using infrared heat goggles would only see the bright heat source of the road and not the shapes of Deacon and his colleagues walking close to it.

Checking the drone video feed, it showed multiple heat sources of a small group of four or five people huddled down behind a distant wall near a wadi and Deacon led his people quietly towards it, their soft-soled rubber boots moving silently over the dusty gravel and stones. Four hundred yards away from the wall, Deacon split the team to encircle the target, directing them silently with hand movements observable through their NVGs. Meanwhile, he quietly crawled forward the last two hundred yards over the rough and broken ground before lying down as low as he could behind a small clump of rocks and waited. He switched his goggles down to low power to ensure there was no chance of any leakage of green light from them.

Four weeks, he thought while he waited, four more weeks then a month's leave. Already approved unless a major event needed him, he had a wedding in San Diego to attend. His long-time friend and colleague, Bryant Schaefer, had died in a roadside IED explosion in Afghanistan four years ago. They'd enrolled in the SEALs together, gone through BUDs training on the same team, and completed numerous successful missions together. Deacon had been promoted faster than Bryant, but they'd remained close friends. He'd even been Bryant's best man at his wedding to Alex.

She was beautiful — a typical Californian blonde. Bryant had met her on a blind date, and they'd just clicked. When Deacon had been introduced to her, he could already see the love in their eyes. The three of them had spent as much time together as possible, and he thought of Bryant and Alex as family.

The IED explosion that had killed Bryant also killed two other SEALs that day. Deacon had been devastated and had sworn revenge, happily managing to take it just five days later.

Bryant had died a father-to-be and their first child, a son named Bryant David, had been born soon after. Deacon had become the child's godfather, and he still loved Alex like a sister and the boy like his own. Around the same time, he'd also met Rachel Sanchez, a Geologist working for the U.S. Geological Survey Department in Menlo Park, San Francisco, and the two of them had stayed close. Finally, after three of years of staying single, Alex had started dating again, much to Deacon's relief. He'd been saying for well over a year Bryant wouldn't have wanted her to keep mourning and she needed to live her life again. Tentatively at first, she went on a few dates. She was an attractive, cheerful woman, and soon she'd met Warren Peterson, and they just clicked. Peterson was a few years older than her, owned and ran a small garden centre business and was divorced.

Deacon had met him numerous times, sometimes just for a beer, but also as a foursome with Alex and Rachel and they all got on well together. When Peterson had asked Alex to marry him, Deacon couldn't have been happier. The wedding date was in four weeks' time and fitted in perfectly with the leave Deacon had booked.

Eight minutes later, after receiving confirmation his men were in place, he pulled his phone out of his pocket and, turning the volume to full, he selected Wagner's 'Ride of the Valkyries' and waited. Suddenly a voice shouted out in Arabic stating they were Iraqi Forces and demanding immediate surrender. Deacon pressed 'Play' and kept his head down. As the music blared out over the still desert night, five heads popped up over the Wadi wall and started firing towards him and the source of the music. Smiling, he listened to their rounds hitting the clump of rocks he was hiding behind and waited until he heard their firing cease and Martock's voice come over the radio.

"All done, skipper. Four down and a takeaway to go," Martock said.

Standing and stretching, before brushing the dust and gravel off his clothes, he switched his goggles back up to standard power and then began jogging over to the battle scene. Looking over the small wall, he could see the Iraqi Special Forces checking the dead for paperwork while cable tying the remaining wounded ISIS fighter's arms behind his back. He'd been shot twice, once in the shoulder and again in the thigh. Neither injury was life-threatening, and Deacon felt no sympathy for him as he was hauled to his feet and dragged back to the airbase for interrogation. Although Deacon never got involved directly with the interrogations, he knew from the screams he'd heard that this injured terrorist would likely be praying for his own death soon. But, Deacon thought, they'd been given a chance to surrender. None ever had, though. They'd all chosen to fight, and few ever survived.

"Ride of the Valkyries this time, skipper. Nice," Martock said, slapping Deacon on the back.

"Yeah, well … I was fed up with 'Born in the USA," Deacon laughed back as they turned and headed back to base.

# Chapter 36

## New York

Just 12 miles from midtown Manhattan, Teterboro Airport is considered a general aviation reliever airport. Operated by the Port Authority of New York and New Jersey, it's home to more private jets and aviation charter companies than any other airport in the world. As a reliever airport, it doesn't offer scheduled airline services, nor does it permit operations of any aircraft in excess of 100,000 pounds in weight on any airport surface, however it still handles almost 500 flights a day. Its goal is to offer exceptional services to the burgeoning private sector.

"This is Qatar Royal flight en route Baku to New York. Request royal clearance for landing," the Captain of Gulfstream G650ER radioed.

"Roger, Qatar Royal flight. You are cleared for approach and landing on runway 1-19 L," the tower replied.

The Captain piloted the Gulfstream down to landing with barely a bump, taxied to the VIP area and finally shut the engines down after the ten-hour trans-Atlantic flight.

US Customs, frequently slow and meticulous with the public, performed sharper and quicker with the royal flight. With royal diplomatic status the questioning was brief and the paperwork minimal. The aircraft was classified as property of the Al-Thani Qatari royal family so under diplomatic rules was deemed as Qatari soil and not able to be searched. Cleared within minutes, with Saif Khan using fake documents showing him as one of a number of personal bodyguards to the Prince, Prince Ahmed Jabir Kalifa bin Mohammed al- Thani left the aircraft and headed off, along with his security detail, to the Carlyle Hotel, Upper East Side.

In New York City for three days of meetings, the Prince was not actually in the U.S. on official royal business. Therefore he didn't warrant the attention of the U.S. State Department. However, as a senior member of the Al-Thani Qatari royal family, he did receive a team of NYPD escorts for protection. The Gulfstream was refuelled and parked in a secure area of the airport, under constant Qatari armed guard from the Qatar Consulate on Central Park South, NY, for the duration of the Prince's visit.

# Chapter 37

At seven-fifteen the following morning at the height of rush-hour Saif slipped out of one of the rear entrances to the hotel into an alley, before making his way out onto East 77th St and on towards 5th Ave. Once in Central Park, he merged with early morning commuters before hailing a cab. Crossing over to Jersey he exited his first ride and swapped cabs three more times to ensure he wasn't being followed finally hailing a new cab to take him to a Newark motel.

He gently knocked once on the room door while keeping his thumb over the spy hole. He heard movement behind the door and then it opened just a fraction. Seeing the door chain wasn't on Saif shouldered the door open grabbed the occupant by the throat jammed the barrel of his suppressed 9mm handgun up under the occupant's throat and kicked the door shut with his foot all within two seconds.

The terrified look on Zane's face said everything to Saif. Looking him straight in the eyes, and pressing harder with the gun, Saif whispered, "Are you alone?"

"W..W...Wha," Zane blubbered.

"I said are you alone? You're within half a second of having your fucking brains splattered all over the wall. Are you alone?"

"Ye..Yes, I'm alone. As..as … as instructed," Zane replied, beginning to cry.

Relaxing his grip slightly, Saif pulled Zane away from the wall, turned him around and pushed him further into the room. Seeing the room was empty apart from the two of them, Saif began to relax slightly. Turning around, Saif slipped the chain onto the door, grabbed a chair and placed it at an angle under the door handle. Grabbing a box of tissues of the dresser he tossed them towards Zane.

"Dry your eyes, boy. This is man's work now. Where's your truck?"

"Out...outside sir. It's the red one parked by the wall."

"So you're Zane Shirani. We've got a lot to do. You will call me sir. Nothing more, nothing less. Understood?"

"Yea..yes sir," Zane replied.

"Have you paid for everything in cash, as instructed?"

"Yes sir,"

"OK. Give me the keys to the truck. Pack your bag then go and return the room key and meet me outside."

A few minutes later Saif pulled the truck around near the entrance. He made sure his face was sitting in the shadow of the door and couldn't be seen easily from outside. Zane exited the motel lobby, climbed into the passenger seat, and they drove off together.

Saif apologised a little to Zane, explaining that this was serious work and he'd had to make sure Zane hadn't been compromised. He said, "Zane, this work is too serious to risk being caught, but you've done well so far. My real name's Charlie Baxter, just call me Charlie. Ok?"

Driving along Frank E Rodgers Boulevard, he told Zane to put the radio on and just act normal. Turning along Highway 17 before approaching the airfield down Malcolm Ave, they stopped at the gate before showing false documents to the guard to gain access back into Teterboro airport.

Nodding to the aircraft guard, Saif opened the rear cargo hold before removing both plastic fuel containers and holdalls and sliding them into the lockable load department in the rear of the truck. Closing the cargo hold he then climbed into the aircraft cockpit and retrieved another holdall containing a number of handguns, automatic rifles and grenades from a hidden compartment under the cockpit floor, which joined the other items in their truck.

Again nodding to the aircraft guard, who would swear no one had visited the aircraft, Saif climbed back into the truck's passenger seat and told Zane to drive out of the airport and join the I-80 Expressway and then turn onto the I-95 south.

When Prince al-Thani left in three days' time, there would be another Qatari member of staff acting as a personal bodyguard using the same false documents Saif had used to gain entry to the U.S. Paperwork would show the same number of passengers leaving as had arrived.

# Chapter 38

The skyline of Manhattan showed clearly against the eastern pale blue morning sky with the One World Trade Centre or Freedom Tower as it was nicknamed standing as a proud testament to the American way of life.

"It was a great day, you know?" Saif said, looking over towards it.

"What was?"

"9/11. I was in Kabul that day. It was magnificent. There was so much rejoicing in the streets. I wasn't involved in the actual planning but had offered ideas and suggestions on how to get through security. It was easy then. America was so 'open'. You could just walk on board carrying almost anything."

"I was only eight. I remember all the shock about it, but I was out playing hoops with my friends. I remember my parents saying they thought it would change things for them," Zane said.

"It did. Especially for me. It was a beautiful day. The shock on American faces. We watched it live on CNN. Didn't actually expect the towers to collapse. That was a bonus. America was brought to its knees, and suddenly they realised they weren't invincible. Four 'planes and almost 3,000 dead and suddenly everyone in the world knew the mighty US of A was vulnerable. Shame about the last 'plane. That was aiming for the White House. That really would have been the icing on the cake, but what the hell … ." Saif said.

"But you're American. Don't you feel any guilt about it?" Zane said.

"Do you feel guilty about what we're about to do?" Saif said.

"Well, I don't really know what we're going to do. I know it's going to be big, but that's all."

"Son, it's gonna be great. It'll be 10 … no, 20 … no 30 times bigger and no American will ever feel safe stepping outside their house again. Anyway, enough for now. Just drive," Saif said.

The traffic was heavy heading through New York, even on the Interstate and it took them over an hour to get clear of Newark and Jersey City, but gradually the traffic thinned. They stopped for gas and sandwiches near Trenton and swapped driving, but otherwise the journey was uneventful.

Between the two of them, they could have driven all night, but Saif said there was more chance of being stopped late at night, so they looked for a cheap motel just south of Fredericksburg, Virginia; famous for various bloody battles during the four-year American Civil War between 1861 and 1865.

During that period, Fredericksburg gained strategic importance due to its location midway between Washington and Richmond, the opposing capitals of the Union and the Confederacy. During the first Battle of Fredericksburg between December 11–15, 1862, the town sustained significant damage from bombardment and looting by the Union forces. Almost 200,000 Union and Confederate troops fought a sustained and bloody battle, resulting in nearly 20,000 casualties - the largest number of armed men that ever confronted each other for combat during the Civil War.

The Second Battle of Fredericksburg, also known as the Second Battle of Marye's Heights, was fought in and around the town on May 3, 1863. The Union Army finally defeated the Confederates and took control of the town and surrounding countryside.

Checking in, the old guy on reception didn't bat an eye. Saif passed over cash and paid for a rear-facing, ground floor, twin-bedded room at the far end of the building. With their age differences, anyone would assume they were father and son. Next to the motel was a truckers bar serving food. They ordered steaks and fries and a couple of Cokes and sat quietly. After eating, Zane went up to the bar to order two more drinks when a scruffily dressed older guy sat at the bar turned towards him.

"Hey boy. What'cha doing with an old guy like that? You like older guys?" the drunk said.

Ignoring him, Zane took his drinks and turned to leave when the drunk grabbed his arm.

"Boy, I was talking to you. You a faggot? You one of them homi sexuals, boy? You queer?"

Before Zane could answer, Saif reached over between them and grabbed the drunk's wrist and squeezed. Zane hadn't even seen him move.

"Hey, old timer, why don'tcha mind your business?" Saif said, as the drunk's fingers opened and let go of Zane's shirt.

"Wh … who you calling old timer, ya punk," the drunk slurred as he tried to throw a punch at Saif's head, who merely sidestepped.

The force the drunk had put into the swing caused him to spin around and knock a waitress over carrying a tray of drinks which smashed on the floor.

Used to trouble from the sort of clientele who drank there, the barman had the local police on speed dial. A few minutes later the pulsing red and blue lights of a police cruiser showed up in the car park. Saif grabbed

Zane's arm and whispered not to panic and to let him lead.

Officer Brad Millar strode rapidly into the bar, one hand holding his nightstick ready for action, the other hand holding his radio to his mouth ready to call for backup if needed.

By this time, the drunk was sat on the floor, and Zane and Saif were back at their table. The barman explained to Millar what had happened, but he still wanted to check id's. Zane showed his Florida driver's licence, and Saif pulled out a fake one made out to a Pennsylvania address. When asked why they were there and where they were heading, Saif said they had been delivering building supplies and were now heading back to the Miami office, but no harm was done and no, they didn't want to press charges against someone who'd just had a few too many.

Grabbing the drunk by the collar and handcuffing him, Officer Millar bade them goodnight and took the drunk away to sleep it off in the cells.

The following morning after a quick breakfast, they continued their journey south before arriving in Florida early evening.

# Chapter 39

## Al Qayarah Airbase - Iraq

The key to an effective fighting force is leadership and training, Deacon still firmly believed. That was something he'd been taught when he first joined the U.S. Navy and applied to join the SEALs. A good leader inspires his men, builds confidence and takes charge. This is true whether in the military or civilian life. People will always follow a good leader. But beyond leadership is training. Training builds confidence. In a fighting force training builds confidence in the men to carry out the task, and in the leaders that their decisions are correct.

The U.S. Military knew the one thing missing from this Iraqi Army preparing to retake Mosul was confidence. Too many of them had come up against ISIS and lost. That was why the US had agreed to send an additional 500 personnel, in addition to the 400 plus already deployed, to support, train and advise the Iraqi's.

Deacon had come across the Iraqi's lack of confidence first hand in the combined Special Forces attack recently near Alepeshmanh. Although Deacon and his men had set up the attack, their group leader, Captain Anwar Suleiman, had seemed reluctant to engage the enemy until commanded by Deacon and his team. So with agreement from his superiors, Deacon set about a rapid training program.

First, he commandeered two of the outer buildings at the airfield and stationed himself and his men inside. The plan was then for Captain Suleiman and his people to plan and organise an attack to re-take the two buildings.

All live ammunition was replaced with rubber bullets which were an effective training tool as they would hurt and bruise when hit by them but were not fatal. To make the situation as lifelike as possible, there would be a number of different scenarios, including daylight versus night attack, with and without smoke, and with and without hostages. The orders for everyone were the same. If you were hit in the arms or legs, you could keep on fighting. If you were hit in the body mass, you had to lay your weapon down and lie on the floor. To keep it fair both sides had access to the same weapons, goggles, masks and night-vision equipment.

For the first attack, Deacon split his team into two and placed them at strategic positions throughout the two buildings. Unknown to Suleiman, two of Deacon's team also had cross-fire positions across both buildings.

It was a disaster, Deacon mused. And these were meant to be the elite Special Forces, he thought. His team quickly picked off the attackers as they came through doorways and windows. Two were shot as they crept along one wall by crossfire from Deacon's people located in the other building. Only a couple managed to return any fire at all before being 'killed', and none of Deacon's people was hit.

For the second attempt, they tried again but this time with the building filled with smoke. This proved harder for both teams due to limited visibility, but again Deacon's team won easily, although they did suffer from one hit in a leg.

The third attempt, this time with both smoke and hostages, also became a disaster. Some of the Iraqi's bruised and battered by a number of hits from rubber bullets tried to limit their exposure by hiding around doorways and merely blind shooting into rooms. Not only were none of Deacon's people hit, but all the hostages — other off-duty soldiers wearing civilian clothes and body protection — were all hit numerous times.

"Your men are nervous, Captain," Deacon said at the debrief. "When they fire blind they become easy targets."

Suleiman wasn't happy. His men had appeared amateurish when put up against the elite SEALs. "Many have been badly bruised by the bullets from your team," he said. "They don't consider themselves capable, my friend. They look at you and your men in awe. They need to see what you do and realise they can also do this, Insha' Allah."

To show an example that evening Deacon swapped roles. Captain Suleiman and his people would defend the building while Deacon, and his team would attack and secure it. To make it harder, not only was it smoke-filled and containing the hostages, but it would be totally dark.

Deacon's team split into two and attacked simultaneously. Although the Iraqi's were also wearing NVGs, Deacon's team threw flash-bang grenades in through the doorways and windows, waited two seconds and then rushed in firing. The intense flash of light would temporarily blind anyone, even worse if wearing NVGs and the deafening explosions in a small concrete structure totally disoriented the Iraqi's as the sound reverberated around. Within moments, it was all over with every Iraqi hit with a body shot, all the hostages rescued and none of Deacon's team hit.

Sitting around outside during the debrief, the Iraqi's relaxed and smoked while rubbing their painful bruises from the rubber bullet impacts. However, they all agreed that the Americans were not Superman, and the difference was down to training and practice.

The following morning, after Captain Suleiman had a long talk to them in Arabic, with a lot of fist-into-hand slapping, shouting and other inspiring gestures, they tried again. Same setup, same scenario — a daytime attack against Deacon and his team who were holding the buildings. This time Deacon was pleased to see, and in the subsequent attempts with smoke and then with smoke and hostages, the Iraqi's had improved. Although the Iraqi's still suffered casualties, it wasn't as many as before, and some of Deacon's team had also been hit.

Over the next two days, both teams continually trained together and Deacon was encouraged to see the slow but steady improvements the Iraqi's were making. Captain Suleiman expressed his thanks to Deacon, and his men, in being able to lead a more determined and better-coordinated fighting force.

# Chapter 40

## England

The Port of Southampton, on the south coast of the UK, is the country's busiest cruise terminal and second largest container port, partly due to the port's 'double tides'. These allow the largest container and cruise ships access to the port for up to 80 percent of the time. This 'double tides' effect is the result of tidal flow through the English Channel: high tide at one end of the Channel (Dover) occurs at the same time as low tide at the other end (Land's End). Southampton, being approximately near the centre has one high water as the tidal swell goes from east to west and another as it then changes and goes from west to east. The position of the Isle of Wight also assists in funnelling water towards Southampton. Due to its location and road and rail links, Southampton is the UK's leading port for vehicle imports and exports.

The Ford Transit van, reference number GG-5549DE34UK, started on the first turn of the ignition key, and the offload driver drove it quickly down the access ramp to be parked in its allocated slot in the Western Dock of Southampton. UK Customs clearance became merely a formality as this was just one of 403 other Ford Transit vans all arriving at once on the Wallenius Wilhelmsen owned vessel, the M/V Ofduna, along with almost 2,000 other vehicles.

Two days later it started again, as it, along with seven other vehicles, was loaded onto a standard vehicle transporter to begin its journey north. Later that same day it was finally driven back off the transporter and parked in the workshop carpark of Braithwaite Autos, a long-established Ford dealership in Leeds. Here it would await its full makeover of the removal of its protective polythene sheeting and protective wax, before being polished and given a regular pre-delivery inspection, ready for delivery to its new customer.

The following morning Aboud phoned one of the trainee mechanics at Braithwaite Autos. They knew each other from school and mechanics college evening classes. Before he left that evening, the trainee mechanic quietly went into the supervisor's office, opened the wall cupboard and removed the keys for the vehicle. He met Aboud in the local pub and passed the keys over in exchange for a small plastic bag containing a dozen Ecstasy tablets and asking no questions.

At 10:20 that evening Aboud and Wazir crept past the other vehicles before unlocking the Transit van's front doors. Thirty seconds later he pressed the remote to re-lock the doors as he and Wazir easily each carried a container from beneath the driver and passenger seats, leaving the keys under the front wheel arch, where they would be picked up and returned the following morning.

# Chapter 41

## England - Thursday

William Hammond, aka Mr Green, arrived late in the evening at the seemingly deserted garage belonging to Aboud's uncle. Walking silently around the back of the darkened building, he spotted the two of them in the shadows. Pulling a handgun from his jacket pocket, he quietly crept to within six feet of them before stopping and listening.

Hammond had been living in the UK since he was fourteen and although he had slightly darker skin, he would easily pass as a local. He was completely fluent in English and even had a London accent. When he was nineteen, it was arranged for him to visit one of the training camps in Pakistan. To reduce suspicion and keep below the radar of the security services, he'd told friends he was touring around Europe for a year. Having travelled to Paris on his UK passport, he was met by a similar looking colleague who took his phone and gave him a replacement passport of Pakistani origin. He flew to Pakistan and spent ten months undergoing intensive weapons, bomb-making and general terrorist training while his phone visited all the major places in Europe and regularly updated his Facebook page. Eventually, after a circuitous route back to Prague, he re-joined his phone and using his UK passport again returned to the UK. He didn't even make a blip on the UK's security services computers.

After almost fifteen minutes watching Aboud and Wazir talking, one of them pulled out a cell phone and checked for messages, with the glow from the phone illuminating their faces. Silently moving the last few feet towards them, Hammond raised his weapon.

"Bang. Bang, you're dead," he whispered.

To them, Hammond's quiet voice was as loud as a whip crack, and they both jumped.

"What the fuck? You scared me, man," Wazir blurted, "What the fuck you doing creeping up on us?"

"Just showing you how a real soldier of Allah does it. Now keep quiet and let's go inside," Hammond said.

After checking the two containers removed from the Transit van, Hammond ordered them to open the garage doors for him to bring his car in, but to leave the lights off. He went and retrieved his car from a few streets away and after reversing in instructed Aboud to close the main garage doors again.

Opening the trunk of his vehicle, he pulled out a holdall and the boxes containing the two GS-15 drones. From the holdall, he pulled out a dark red and grey coloured suit that he began to put on.

"What's that?" Wazir said.

"This, son, is a Drager Team Master Pro Et Chemical protective suit," Hammond replied.

"Wow. How did you get it?"

"That's not important, but let's just say I have ways," Hammond said.

He'd actually purchased it completely legally through various means from eBay on the excuse of antifouling the hulls of pleasure boats. Under current EEU rulings on the use of potentially dangerous chemicals applied to the removal and painting of yacht hulls with copper antifouling, a person is expected to wear suitable protective clothing. Hammond had merely ordered it on a fake credit card and address through eBay Germany for this use. No licence or paperwork was required.

Walking back outside the rear of the garage to the empty, quiet alley behind he took both drones and both containers. He instructed the boys to stay upwind and at least twenty foot away before turning on a small torch. In the glow from the flashlight, they watched him carefully empty the contents of each plastic container into the two drones' spray fluid tanks. Securing the top caps on the tanks, he poured a strong bleach mixture over them, the plastic containers,  and his hands and arms, before removing his facemask.

Beckoning the boys to follow, he picked up the drones and carried them back inside the garage, before going back outside and throwing the empty containers into the large rubbish bins. Walking back into the garage he sat and removed the Drager protective suit before putting it back in his holdall and into his car.

"The batteries are fully charged. All you will need to do is to loosen the air bleed valve on the spray tanks before launching. Now they're loaded, they're perfectly safe. You must wear latex gloves when you touch them. Partly, that's so your fingerprints don't get on them, but also to protect you from any contamination. But as long as you don't open them you will be perfectly safe just wearing gloves. Here …," Hammond said as he handed over a half dozen pairs he'd purchased from a hardware store in Birmingham that morning.

Hammond then spent the next four hours going over the plan again and again in great detail. Finally, all three of them prayed to Allah the Salat al-'isha late evening prayer and prayed for sunshine and warm winds for Saturday.

Later that same morning Aboud set out on his mission in the van, while Wazir left soon after on his bike towards London.

# Chapter 42

## England - Friday

Jamal Aboud was so tense and excited he had trouble concentrating. This was it! This was the final test before he would become a fully-fledged jihadist. This was what he'd wanted ever since he'd first been in discussions with his local Imam, back when they had talked about the aggressions the West had against Islam, about how there was only one true God and about how every good Muslim must follow the true teachings of Allah. He would do this and not fail. Amjad Wazir would also complete his mission, and then the two of them would journey to the land of his forefathers and join his holy brothers in their fight. God is Great, he thought, God truly is Great!

The journey took him over five hours, first onto the M62 motorway past Manchester, before turning south onto the M6 and later the M5 passed Birmingham and Gloucester, eventually exiting at junction 23 about 28 miles south of Bristol. The van was running OK but was somewhat old, he thought. He didn't believe that it had been serviced particularly well, but he'd had a quick check of the engine, had made a few adjustments, replaced the oil, and was sure it would outlast this current job.

He was now on the A39 heading towards the small town called Street and decided to stop for a break and a sandwich in a quiet pull-off on the road. There were plenty of hitchhikers making their way as well, most of them were heavily laden down with camping kit and rucksacks. Seeing a trio of three young girls all walking along together, he beckoned them over.

"I'm going there as well. Do you want a lift?" he said.

Five minutes later, with their gear stowed in the back and three attractive girls sat on the bench seat next to him, he drove on, taking the A361 through Glastonbury. Smiling to himself, he again thought God is truly Great. Allahu Akbar.

A few miles further on and after passing the town of West Pennard, he took a right turn down a narrow road, before stopping at a gate. Three minutes later, after helping the girls out and giving them back their gear, he was showing his ticket at the Orange gate and answering the various security questions to an inquisitive guard. Shortly after, he drove on through the gate to find his allocated camping space in Campervan West, at the Glastonbury Music Festival 2016.

# Chapter 43

## Glastonbury Festival - UK

Now named after the local town of Glastonbury, the first Glastonbury Music Festival was held in September 1970, a year after its American counterpart, Woodstock. Originally called the Pilton Pop Festival after its location at Worthy Farm, Pilton, the following year its date was changed to the days immediately after the summer solstice of mid-June. Intermittently staged from 1971 to '81, and renamed to the Glastonbury Festival, it has now become the largest greenfield music and performing arts festival in the world and is a template for many of the festivals that have come after it.

Still located on the original site of Worthy Farm, it has now grown in size to a five-day event spread over 900 acres of land. The beautiful surrounding area of Glastonbury, known as the Vale of Avalon, is a region steeped in symbolism, mythology and religious traditions dating back many hundreds of years. It is where legendary King Arthur may be buried, where Joseph of Arimathea is said to have walked, and where ley lines converge.

This year numbers attending were expected to exceed 150,000 each day, with a peak of almost 175,000 on the final days of Saturday and Sunday. Over 2,000 acts were expected across the 100+ stages.

Very much a party and celebration event and mainly attracting the young to middle-aged, overuse of alcohol and drugs is prevalent, as is a small amount of violence and quite a significant amount of pick-pocket theft.

Security is strong but mainly to stop unauthorised access as ticket prices have grown to almost US$300 for the five-day event.

Kevin Hughes took his job seriously. He'd applied to join the local Police Force. He'd been interviewed but failed the assessment tests. He tried then to join as a PCSO - a Police Community Support Officer. PCSOs do not have the same powers as regular police officers; however, they still carry a lot of responsibility and are a critical part of the police service. He'd initially been accepted but struggled with the one-on-one role-playing and been deemed too aggressive. Disappointed, but still determined, he then joined a private security firm. Had a Psychologist analysed him, he would have discovered Kevin had suffered throughout his early life with an aggressive and bullying father, along with an Auntie who sexually molested him when he was seven.

During his teen years, he'd been constantly bullied at school and had left with few qualifications. The only subject he'd enjoyed had been biology, especially the dissecting of frogs and rodents. Unemployed for two years and living off government benefits, he spent most of his days playing more and more aggressive war games on his X-Box and toured the local streets at night trying to capture cats. Any he seized by offering them treats were soon dispatched with a broken neck and dumped in various waste bins. Had he not been accepted at the security company, he would likely have applied to the Army.

Security at this year's event was tighter than usual. In 2015, a large number of non-paying revellers had gate-crashed, climbed over the twelve-foot surrounding wall and gained entry. This year security had vowed it wouldn't happen again, with more guards patrolling the eight and half-mile circumference of the event. Kevin was armed with a two-way radio, cell phone, cable ties, and a U.S. style collapsible baton. He also carried an illegal pepper spray and was just hoping someone would give him cause to use it. His company had been one of a number contracted again to supply security and Kevin couldn't have been happier. He'd been covering this event for the last four years, and last year he'd been involved in quite a few scuffles and had managed to crack a few heads. The scuffles were usually down to the typical problems of too much alcohol or overuse of illegal drugs. Straightforward cannabis relaxed people, but the shit they smoked or injected nowadays really seemed to mix up their minds, he thought. Couple that with the date drugs such as Rohypnol or even Ketamine being used, and there were plenty of semi-conscious females around he could 'pretend' to help. Last year he'd had sex with three of them over the course of the five days, each time after helping the semi-conscious girls back to their tents or caravans before undressing them and quietly raping them. They were too drugged or drunk to fight him off and too confused after to complain.

This year he hoped to exceed that score.

Looking at the ticket the person in the faded van showed made him bristle. The bastard had three beautiful girls in tow, and he's just stopped and let them out, he thought. He was on his own, as well. What was he? A fucking queer? A fucking Paki queer boy? I'd shag 'em, he thought, especially that little blonde tart. Determined to keep an eye on where the three girls camped, he turned his attention to the van and its driver.

"On your own?" he asked.

"Just me," Aboud replied

"What's in the back? Booze? Drugs?"

"Nothing. Just food and clothes and things,"

"Knives? Weapons of any type,"

161

"Nope, nothing like that,"

"Get out and open up the back. I wanna see what you've got in there," the guard said.

Just as Aboud was beginning to get nervous and wondering how he could hide the drone, a more senior security guard came over.

"What's the holdup, Hughes?" he said.

"Just checking this vehicle, sir. Going to take a look in the rear," Kevin said.

"Why this one?"

"No particular reason, sir. Just being thorough, sir," Kevin said.

"Look, Hughes, there's a line of almost thirty vehicles behind him and more coming along all the time. Just get a fucking move on son, and stop pissing around. Let him through," the senior guard said.

Reluctantly Kevin Hughes gave the driver his ticket back and waved Aboud in, his eyes already following the pert rear of the little blonde as she walked away.

# Chapter 44

## Mosul - Iraq

Another day, another mission, Deacon thought as he and Martock slowly advanced on their stomachs towards a small incline. The ISIS prisoner they'd captured the other day had provided useful information to the Iraqi Forces. Deacon didn't know for sure but guessed that he'd been tortured. He'd heard the prisoner had died from his injuries although he didn't know if that was from the injuries on the battlefield or from within his cell later. However, he had an idea which.

Blisteringly hot in the daytime, Deacon had always been surprised just how cool the desert became at night, even in summer. In the winter, there would often be snow and ice on the ground. This evening, however, he was warm. Going into any sort of battle always raised the adrenaline - you never knew when a stray round might come your way, and if it had your name on it.

Martock raised a hand slightly, and they both stopped crawling. Martock could see through his night-vision goggles occasional heads moving about a hundred-and-fifty-foot away. ISIS were securing and making as many strongholds as possible. They had been planting anti-personnel and larger anti-tank mines throughout the area. They'd also dug trenches and had oil ready to flood them and set alight as well as deeper traps, which would cause the Iraqi Forces to stop and fill in before being able to continue. Deacon's other two men were over 250 yards away approaching with Iraqi Forces from the left and right.

When everyone was in position, all teams moved forward silently, into the ends of the trenches before moving quietly up behind the ISIS fighters. Using night-vision goggles and suppressed weapons, the killing of twelve ISIS combatants by the Iraqi's took moments. No chance of surrender was offered. It was simply a killing mission. Deacon and his team didn't partake. They were soldiers, not murderers, and anyway, their role was merely to advise and train. Just as silently, they all withdrew back through no-man's land and away to safety, leaving a picture card with an image of Iblis, the Devil in Islamic culture, tucked into one victim's shirt to worry remaining ISIS fighters.

# Chapter 45

## England - Saturday

Waking early on a sunny Saturday morning, Aboud smiled as he ate a simple breakfast of bread and hummus. Other campers nearby had been partying almost all night and he'd lain there listening to first their drunken singing before it turned to sexual grunts and groans. How could these women prostitute themselves like that, he'd thought. Rutting like animals. The West was full of whores, he reasoned, before eventually drifting off to sleep. But even though he'd slept little, he wasn't tired. Today was the day he'd been dreaming about his entire life. Today would be his day!

Wazir called soon after on his burner cell phone.

"Are we doing the right thing, brother?" he asked.

"Today we become men, brother. Today we become Jihadists. Just do as we've been instructed. Allah is watching over us. There is no God but God. Allahu Akbar," Aboud chanted quietly, "It is too late to stop now, brother. Carry out your mission and we will become heroes and our brothers will carry our names into battle."

Thumbing the 'off' button on his phone, Wazir glanced around the motorway services on the M3 motorway, at Fleet, certain that he was being watched. He was nervous. He'd never felt this nervous before and his skin was clammy. He'd slept badly last evening in the rear room of a small mosque in Forest Gate, London, home of one of the largest Muslim communities within the London area, after arriving yesterday afternoon. He'd eaten a frugal evening meal and the Imam had stayed with him until late, praying and reciting verses from the Quran. He'd risen early and started the drive to Bournemouth on the south coast.

Looking around again he couldn't see anyone watching him, so he refitted his helmet and adjusted the straps on his backpack before kicking the starter to life and pointlessly revving the engine before re-joining the M3.

After closing and carefully locking the rear doors of the van, Aboud walked around the events arena. The backing music had already started, with the main bands and artists starting their respective acts at 10:00 am through until after midnight. Even the people in the tents next door were stirring, their sexual pleasures spent. Some years the five-day Glastonbury Music Festival had been almost washed out due to excessive rain, but this year the weather was perfect - sunny days, little wind and warm temperatures. Wandering around through the crowds Aboud spotted the awkward guard from yesterday talking to a group of girls. Aboud had never had anyone leer at him, but the look the guard was giving the girls would seem to fit. Walking on past them he came across one of the many stalls selling food and drinks. Ordering a chicken kebab and a bottle of water, he waited and ate slowly before returning to his van around 11:30 am. Wearing double layers of latex gloves from Mr Green for extra protection, he unpacked his drone and ran it through its self-tests. Happy that all was OK, he powered it down and sat, prayed and waited.

<>< ><>

Wazir had kept the speed of his motorbike well within the
speed limit all the way from London. He couldn't chance
being stopped by Police for even the simplest reason.
He'd stopped at the services for a rest, a stretch and some
food. After a sudden attack of nerves and having second
thoughts, he'd called Aboud but was reassured by his
friend's confidence and commitment. Arriving at 12:30
pm in central Bournemouth he quickly found the
Bournemouth International Centre car park, close to the
beach. Motorbikes were able to park free in a large layby
adjacent, so Wazir locked his bike, but, keeping his helmet
on, walked up the car park steps to the roof terrace before
moving over to the southwestern corner and crouching
down behind the parked cars.

With the sun shining brightly and it being a Saturday
morning, the carpark was already almost full so there was
little movement of traffic. At 12:50 pm Wazir unpacked
his drone from his backpack, extended its rotor arms and
legs and carried out the same self-tests as Aboud had.

<>< ><>

At 12:59 Aboud climbed out of his van, carrying his
drone.

At precisely 1:00 pm, wearing Latex gloves both men
loosened the air bleed valves and powered up their
drones from the control remotes. Both had previously
entered the designated automatic flight paths using Lat
and Long coordinates before fully charging the batteries
again. At exactly 1:02 pm, both drones took off. Aboud's
climbed quickly to about 50 feet and flew slightly north to
its GPS start coordinate where the spraying commenced.

It then flew six sweeps north east to south west, moving 200 feet east on each sweep, before flying due east until it ran out of power and crashed into a field.

Wazir's drone headed southwest before dropping height over the cliffs down towards the beach. At 40 foot height, it turned sharply to 080 degrees, before it commenced spraying and flew one long pass the full length of Bournemouth and Boscombe beaches, before turning due south and heading out to sea until it also ran out of power.

At both locations, some people looked up and pointed but none noticed the fine misty spray slowly descending over them in the gentle breeze. Aboud put the remote controller back in the van before placing his blanket and yesterday's shirt on top. He removed his gloves, placed them on top of the shirt and pressed a switch on the small box below. Grabbing his jacket, he closed and locked his van again before walking a few hundred metres north to the festival bus station where he caught one of the free buses to Glastonbury town and then a connecting service on to Bristol. The small incendiary device in the van, along with two small plastic containers of lighter fluid stored next to it, would ignite at 15:30 pm, causing a small but intense and deadly fire to destroy any evidence.

Wazir, in the meantime, put the remote controller back in his backpack, walked urgently down the empty stairway, got back on his motorbike and headed out of town back onto the A338, the A31 and finally onto the M3 back towards London. Every instinct urged him to race away as fast as he could, but he managed to force himself to keep within the speed limits. Stopping eventually for fuel on the outskirts of London, Wazir slipped his now almost empty backpack off and crammed it, complete with remote controller and latex gloves, into a waste bin. Arriving back at the mosque, he hid his bike in the disused alley at the rear before going back to his bed in the quiet back room, where he silently wept, when, having listened to the news, the enormity of what he had completed hit him.

# Chapter 46

## Bournemouth - England

He was seven and it had been his birthday just a few days before. He liked school but liked playtime better. The weather so far this summer had been cool and damp but the forecast for this weekend at the end of June and for the next few weeks was sunny and warm, almost hot, so this was the first proper good sunny day there had been for weeks. For his birthday, he'd received a new bucket and spade as well as a cricket bat and stumps, and a swing-ball set. He'd pestered his parents all week to take him to the beach today.

Like most holidaymakers on the beach, he was also covered in layers of sun-cream or oil. Both offered excellent protection against the sun and both also offered extra short-term protection as barriers against the modified VX Agent spray.

His mother was walking back from the shop with an ice cream for him as Wazir's drone flew overhead. She never felt the spray on her head or body, nor saw it gently land on the creamy white ice cream. In fact, most people laying on the beach or playing didn't even hear the drone above the general noise of the crowded beach and the waves breaking on the shore. By the time the fine mist spray reached most people, it had already warmed in the sun and very few people even felt it land.

Thanking his mother, because he was a very polite little boy, he eagerly licked and ate his first ice cream of the day not knowing it would also be his last. Children

170

generally succumb quicker to exposure than adults, especially through ingestion, and within a half-hour, he was complaining he was feeling unwell. By two-thirty, he was sneezing and crying and his parents noticed some other children were also claiming to feel unwell. Thinking it was possibly food poisoning from the ice cream his parents carried him, by now crying continuously, towards the medical hut a few hundred feet along the beach, where there was a small crowd of other parents also queuing with complaining children.

Within minutes, he started convulsing before spewing dark coloured blood and convulsing again more violently than before, when, with a sudden shudder and a final gasp, young Tommy Jenkins became the first victim to die. Frantic parents and bystanders urgently called for Police and Ambulance support as more and more people, mostly children, began to convulse. By the time the first ambulance arrived two more children had died. With frantic radio messages going back and forth between the ambulance crew and the Royal Bournemouth Hospital, the doctor in charge of the emergency ward, remembering a briefing from a week or so prior, called his local Health Protection Team (HPT) emergency number notifying them of a possible epidemic outbreak.

# Chapter 47

## Glastonbury Music Festival - England

Judith Renfrew, a pretty 23-year-old, at Glastonbury with her boyfriend for the complete 5-day musical event, became the first known Glastonbury victim. For the past month, she'd been so excited she could hardly sleep. She'd been living with her boyfriend for over two years, and their relationship had grown and grown. Her parents had just come back from their annual vacation, and she'd had a tearful, but happy, reunion with them at the airport last weekend. Four weeks' ago she'd caught a heavy cold, and it had taken its time to go. It had been a common bug, with headaches, chills, coughing and sneezing but she'd also been nauseous a few mornings.

Eventually, just last week, she'd taken the test. She still couldn't believe it. Two strips of blue. She'd even sent her boyfriend out to get another tester, just to make sure. Positive! Two strips of blue meant positive. It was confirmed. Would it be a boy or a girl? She didn't care. Either would be fantastic. Together with her boyfriend, she'd told her parents as they came through the airport. What the other homecoming passengers must have thought to hear her mother shriek with excitement and then see the four of them laughing and crying together, she didn't care. She was going to be a grown up mum soon. But first, she was still going to go to Glastonbury. They'd been planning it for weeks and bought the tickets almost a year ago.

The only thing different this year was she wouldn't be drinking alcohol.

And she would die.

She'd seen the drone after it overflew her and had looked up smiling towards the sunny sky. She hadn't felt the two drops of moisture land on her lips as well as others land on her head and bare skin. Still recovering from her cold, her immune system was weaker than normal, and she'd been sneezing since soon after the drone pass and had complained to her boyfriend of not feeling too well and being short of breath, having runny eyes and a headache. She'd even joked that perhaps the baby didn't like the music.

Slowly feeling worse, by 3:00 pm she told her boyfriend she was going to go and lie down and would meet up with him again later. Walking back to their tent she suddenly broke into convulsive coughing before bending double in pain and started coughing up blood. Screaming for help, three strangers quickly responded and rushed towards her and the fine misty spray looking like sweat on her arms immediately transferred onto their hands as they helped lay her down. One of the helpers rushed off to the local St John's Ambulance tent to bring help. The onsite ambulance crew arrived a few minutes later and, assuming she had some form of stomach ulcer, started transporting her to the main hospital at Bath, over 25 miles away.

Strapped down to a stretcher, with a saline drip trying to keep her electrolytes balanced, Judith slowly drowned in agony on her own body fluids as her muscles became paralysed and her respiratory system was overwhelmed. On a sunny day in late June, with a final cough and vomit of dark black blood, Judith Renfrew, along with her unborn daughter, went into convulsive shock, seized and died, her face contorted in agony.

In the hour it took the ambulance crew to arrive at Bath Royal United Hospital with the still-warm body of

Judith on board, another fifteen people at Glastonbury had begun to succumb, slowly overwhelming the relatively small medical support staff on site.

The news of the possible epidemic in Bournemouth had already hit the National Health Intranet when the senior attending physician realised the potential of what was happening and immediately called his local Health Protection Team.

# Chapter 48

## London - England

Initially classified as a potentially contagious disease because of the already heightened alert status, by 4:00 pm it had been designated as a potential unidentified full epidemic outbreak. Sources were identified as Glastonbury and Bournemouth, with size and other possible outbreak sites unknown.

The Senior Director of the National Health Protection Team alerted the Minister of Health who escalated it immediately to the Prime Minister. The PM scrambled the Joint CBRN (Chemical, Biological, Radiological, and Nuclear) Regiment, based at RAF Honington, Suffolk.

By 5:00 pm, the number of sufferers had reached 150 in Glastonbury, with 5 dead; and 330 in Bournemouth, with 56 dead, many of them children. The UK National Threat level remained at 'Severe', with the response level remaining at 'Heightened'.

By 6:00 pm, the number had rocketed to 1,500 in Glastonbury, with 145 dead; and 2,300 in Bournemouth, with 367 dead.

The Prime Minister called a second emergency COBRA meeting at 7:00 pm on Saturday evening. The Avon & Somerset Constabulary were instructed to try to contain and hold people at the Glastonbury event, but the Chief Constable responded saying it was impossible. Over 150,000 people normally attended most camping for the duration, with 35-40,000 day visitors. Being the final weekend, it had filled to capacity with over 170,000 in attendance. Many of Saturdays' visitors had already left or were trying to leave, and panic was beginning to break out causing many more to flee. Social networking rumours of something contagious in the water were causing additional panic, and fights and skirmishes had already broken out. All the surrounding roads were heavily congested, and nothing was moving. People were beginning to ignore the police, and some officers had already been injured by the panicking crowds in their rush to escape.

The PM, in trying to contain the disaster, ordered the army to be deployed and all major roads leading to and from the area for a radius of 15 miles to be blocked. There was also to be no access to the M5 motorway from junctions 21 to 25. All personnel were to wear full bio-warfare protection and all potential sufferers were to be detained and isolated.

In Bournemouth, the beach was virtually empty by now except for health workers, ambulance crew, the police and the sick, dead or dying. And news crews. Everyone else had panicked and left either to go home or attend the Royal Bournemouth Hospital.

The arguments and discussions around the table at the London COBRA meeting were loud and heated. Finally, the PM announced what he was going to do. He agreed they needed to alert the public, but did not want to admit yet that it was a probable terrorist attack. Worried his government would look weak in their fight against terrorism, he insisted the Minister of Health put messages on radio and TV stating the Glastonbury outbreak was a particularly nasty and virulent airborne infection caused by a farm spraying pesticides a few hundred yards upwind of the Glastonbury event.

It would be the start of the end of his career and the demise of his government.

The message went out nationally on radio, and TV stating symptoms were similar to Legionnaires' disease, namely sickness, vomiting and breathing difficulties. If people thought they may have been exposed, they should remove their clothing, rapidly wash their entire body with soap and water, and get medical care as quickly as possible. Any clothing that had to be pulled over the head to be removed should be cut off the body instead, before being placed inside a plastic bag and sealed. That bag should then be placed inside another plastic bag, sealed, and stored securely. Removing and sealing the items in this way would help protect people from any chemicals that might be on their clothes.

Once clothes had been placed inside plastic bags, anyone infected, or worried they'd been, should inform the local health department or emergency personnel. Plastic bags containing contaminated items should not be touched again. If assisting other people to remove their clothing, wear gloves to avoid touching any contaminated areas, and ensure clothing is removed as quickly as possible.

People were to rinse their eyes with plain water for 10 to 15 minutes if they were burning or if vision was blurred and to contact the 0800 number that would follow the announcements.

Regarding Bournemouth, the Minister of Health stated this was an airborne contaminate from a ship on fire in the middle of the English Channel, blowing onshore. The contaminate had now dispersed but everyone along that stretch of coastline should stay indoors with windows and doors closed until otherwise instructed.

Within minutes, social media started claiming it was a government conspiracy and cover-up and that the Glastonbury outbreak was from the radioactive fallout caused by a reactor explosion at Hinkley Point nuclear power station and Bournemouth from a leaking nuclear radioactive fire on board a ship in the Channel, both from attacks by Russia.

Social media was wrong, but the rumours quickly spread.

# Chapter 49

With matters rapidly getting out of hand, the Minister of Health issued a further statement clearly emphasising there had been no attack by Russia and denied any issue at Hinkley Point, re-affirming it was an airborne pollutant from an accidental discharge of a farm pesticide that was causing the problem.

Many people were panicking, and the panic increased when the army arrived from Salisbury soon after and began blocking roads while wearing Hazmat suits and equipment. The police were pulled back, many of whom had become exposed due to close contact with the revellers, and only specialist Riot Police in full protective riot gear were being allowed near.

By 8:00 pm, the toll in Glastonbury was over 9,000 people claiming symptoms, with over 4,000 dead, including the original on-site ambulance crew. What had started as just another fun festival day had turned into an apocalyptic nightmare. With people collapsing, convulsing and dying where they fell, those not yet suffering were trying desperately to get away. Law and order had broken down rapidly, with hordes of angry, frightened and desperate individuals attacking anyone or anything in their way. Barriers were being dragged down and kicked aside, often into the paths of others also trying to escape. The riot police were being overrun and pushed aside with a number having already been injured. In addition to the deaths caused by the infection, more than a dozen people had died after being injured by the police trying, and failing, to maintain order.

Aboud's van had ignited on time at 15:30 pm as planned and the onsite fire brigade had attended, not realising at that point the seriousness of the outbreak. Not suspecting anything deliberate, the fire crew had assumed the gas valve had been left open on a camping cooker. The intense fire had destroyed the van along with 6 other adjacent trailers and caravans close by, as well as a number of tents.

Since then, other fires had started in the general mayhem and panic of people trying to escape. Scores of people had tried to break out across fields to get away from the army, now arriving.

Knowing he had to stop infected people leaving, the Prime Minister refrained from a shoot-to-kill instruction but authorised a forced hold and detention policy. The Minister of Health issued another statement asking individuals who'd already left to stay home and report their location to the local police and Health Authority by telephone, after again stating that all outer clothing must be removed and sealed as contact with the residue could spread infection, but emphasising that people themselves were not contagious.

All exit points from Glastonbury were now blocked, and the army had set up decontamination showers. Porton Down had confirmed both outbreaks were from a modified VX agent. The Joint CBRN had assumed local command, and the large numbers of remaining public were being separated into 'those exhibiting symptoms' and 'those without'. Those without were further divided into male and female queues and made to strip to underwear and then mass-showered in hot soapy water with bleach added. They were all given Nerve Agent Pre-treatment Set (NAPS) tablets to provide protection against exposure to VX, before being provided with white emergency paper clothing. All removed clothing was placed in large dumpster bins. Those displaying any symptoms were being detained in large tents where emergency doctors wearing protective clothing had started injecting people with large amounts of atropine and pralidoxime using auto-injectors. The more severe cases were being injected by Combo Pen containing atropine, P2S and avizafone.

Still, the Prime Minister failed to state the UK had suffered terrorist attacks.

By eleven o'clock, there were over 13,000 people with symptoms and over 9,000 dead at the Glastonbury event; and 6,700 showing symptoms with 4,000 dead in Bournemouth. Health services were running out of medicine, and abandoned vehicles in and around the Glastonbury event were hampering the arrival of additional water trucks and ambulances. With the lack of water meaning the cleansing showers were shorter and less effective, coupled with the shortage of medicine, and in a decision that cost many more lives, the Prime Minister allowed Dr Gerald Lassiter, the Head of Defence CBRN Centre, to authorise the issue and use of placebos to pacify angry patients.

The army, police, MI5, Defence Science and Technology Laboratory at Porton Down, the Joint CBRN and all local emergency services were by now involved.

By midnight, the death toll was standing at over 16,000 people, but the mortality rate was slowing as treatment was taking effect, although some new cases were expected from individuals who'd managed to escape the containment and get away.

<><><>

The security guard, Kevin Hughes, wasn't feeling well. He'd missed being exposed by the drone as he was upwind of it when he saw it flying over. Assuming it was from someone just wanting aerial photos, he started to follow it, hoping to find its pilot and demand they hand over the memory card, but he'd lost sight of it soon after due to the crowds. By 3:00 pm, he was back on ticket duty for the afternoon and evening crowd when he heard the urgent call for ambulance services go out over the radio. He'd even held up incoming traffic to allow the ambulance with a patient suffering from a suspected burst ulcer to leave, lights flashing and siren screaming. Since then things had slowly gone mad, he thought. Firstly, a fire had started. The onsite Fire Brigade had quickly attended, but the fire was fierce and wasn't easily extinguished. Embers and sparks had drifted to a number of adjoining tents, igniting them as well, causing panic.

Then he'd heard of more people becoming ill, and the limited amount of medical staff on-site had soon become overwhelmed. Additional ambulances from the local towns of Street and Glastonbury had arrived and quickly filled up with sick patients. Soon after, messages started arriving about people collapsing and dying.

Trouble escalated, and the panic started. Kevin had been involved in crowd control and in trying to keep order amongst the masses.

More people were complaining of being unwell, and rumours had started circulating of some form of airborne or water contamination. Panic quickly escalated further, and people were expected him to do something to help. Other fires were started, some accidently, some deliberately. By now people were experiencing blind terror, and everyone started rushing towards the exit gates and crowds built up by the turnstiles.

One young girl lay gasping on the ground vomit running down her chin. He picked her up and carried her in his arms towards one of the medical tents, groping a feel of her breasts and backside as he did. He didn't notice the sweat sheen on her skin transfer to his hands.

As the crowds became more riotous, Kevin came into his own. With nightstick extended and pepper spray in his other hand he swung and struck as many panicking revellers as he could. He heard the distinctive crack of at least one forearm snapping under his ferocious attack, and he began to grin incessantly as his striking nightstick broke noses and split skulls, blood droplets spraying everywhere.

People were tripping and falling and becoming trapped in discarded barrier gates as they were overturned in people's rush to get away. Vehicles were banging into each other as drivers tried to manoeuvre through the crowds. Wiping the speckled blood from his face, he turned just in time to see someone about to strike him with a metal bar. Ducking and kicking out, his work boot struck the attacker on the knee, breaking his kneecap. Blinded by fury, and with years of being bullied pent up inside, he finally snapped and repeatedly stamped on his assailant's head and neck.

Finally pulled off by two of his colleagues, he collapsed on the floor next to the body of his attacker.

More police were arriving and trying to maintain order, but the crowds were just too large. With the main exit gates now trampled thousands of people tried to escape. The police were soon completely overwhelmed, with some police cars being overturned and set alight. Kevin staggered away from the main scene towards some tents to try to find a drink. Bursting into a tent, he found two teenage girls trying to gather their belongings. As the one on the right turned and screamed at him, he struck her hard, once, in the throat. As she collapsed and slowly suffocated, larynx crushed, her friend tried to ran away. Kevin struck her twice on the head with his nightstick, and she collapsed unconscious next to her dying friend.

With his blind fury now morphing into unrestrained sexual urges, he ripped her clothes off and proceeded to rape her. As she began to wake up and tried to push him off, he closed his hands around her slim neck and squeezed harder and harder as he repeatedly thrust into her, before coming copiously inside her dying body.

Finally spent he climbed off her before wiping himself clean in her clothes. Leaving the tent the realisation of what he'd just done slowly becoming clear to him.

As the police fell back and the army arrived and took charge, the equivalent of martial law was imposed. Kevin wandered around in a daze. Soldiers in full biological Hazmat protection began rounding people up and shepherding them towards assessment tents and showers. Bodies of the dead and dying lay where they'd fallen. To him, the dead seemed to outnumber the living. Terrified and mentally regressing back to the time when his mother tried to protect him from his angry father, Kevin Hughes climbed on to one of the abandoned stages, lay down in the corner and went to sleep.

Within the hour, he'd started coughing up blood.

# Chapter 50

## London - Sunday

At 01:00 am, the Prime Minister finally declared a national emergency and raised the UK Threat Level to Critical, with the Response Level increased to Exceptional. In a live television broadcast, looking slightly wide-eyed and panicky, he also admitted the previously issued information about the cause of the outbreak to be inaccurate and that the infections were being treated as a determined and deliberate terrorist attack. As often occurs in politics, the blame started being laid. The first political casualties were the Minister of Health, along with the head of the Security Service (MI5), responsible for protecting the UK and its citizens against threats to national security, as well as the heads of the National Counter Terrorism Security Office, and the Counter Terrorism Command. In a knee-jerk reaction typical of a failing Prime Minister, all were immediately replaced.

The PM confirmed the current death toll stood at 16,728 with more expected. All railway stations and airports were now under maximum security rulings with most flights and trains cancelled. London Underground was closed, along with all government and public buildings and would remain so until further notice. Being a Sunday, he ordered everyone to stay indoors until more was known about whether these attacks were isolated. The civilian and Military Police were being deployed to guard all the main towns and cities, with the army guarding all airports and all government and critical buildings.

The country was now effectively on lockdown. The Glastonbury event site was closed off and temporarily under military rule. All remaining public still there were now being evacuated and either detained in medical isolation or in hospital or were being released after being screened, medically examined and interrogated.

In Bournemouth, the beach area was sealed, and in both locations, the police and various security services had already started a detailed interrogation of survivors to ascertain who saw what. A mandatory order was issued for the collection and examination of personal cameras and cell phones from both the living and the dead for any footage to be reviewed.

# Chapter 51

## The White House - Washington

With telephone lines across the Atlantic buzzing, the President called another urgent meeting in the situation room beneath the White House. Admiral Douglas Carter, the Chairman of the National Intelligence Council, Lt-Gen Warwick Dreiberg, the Director of the CIA, representatives from Homeland Security, the Head of Special Operations Command and Simon Carter - Director the FBI, joined the President and Colonel Brandon McAlistair from CDC.

Lt-Gen Warwick Dreiberg started the meeting.

"Mr President. Gentlemen. The attack on the UK is unprecedented. Latest figures confirm almost 17,000 dead out of approximately 25,000 infected. That's a 68% mortality rate. It seems there was no warning of the impending attacks and initial reports, although I need to state these are not yet confirmed, show two simultaneous attacks using aerial drones. The chemicals used have been confirmed as a type of VX nerve agent by Porton Down and samples are being dispatched, as I speak, to Colonel McAlistair's team at CDC," Dreiberg said. "In a knee-jerk reaction, their Prime Minister has sacked the head of their health ministry, along with the head of MI5, and the heads of their Counter-Terrorism Command and NaCTSO, who have all been replaced. The media over there are already calling for a change of government because of mismanagement, but their PM seems to want to go down fighting. They don't even know if the attacks are over yet, but the UK is now on their highest alert status and on virtual lockdown."

"Has anyone yet claimed responsibility?" the President asked.

"No sir, not yet," Dreiberg continued, "But anything this big has been well organised. At this stage, and until we learn differently, we have to assume this is directly tied to the information Admiral Carter brought to us recently."

"What about intel? We had no forewarning?" the President asked.

"No sir, nothing. Chatter is at normal levels. This was kept extremely quiet," Dreiberg said.

"Mr President, General Dreiberg is correct, sir. We've been pushing our informants for any whisper, anything at all. But nothing, sir. Even our assets in place haven't come up with anything," the CIA Director said.

"Goddam it," the President snapped. "We spend billions of dollars on satellites, technology and manpower and monitor almost every fucking phone in the world. I can hear Putin fart before he does and you're telling me no-one heard a fucking thing?"

"No sir, I mean yes sir, Mr President, sir. Nada,"

"So do we believe this is the modified VX Agent we heard about, Colonel?"

"Highly likely, sir. Won't know for sure until we get the samples analysed, but the data we have so far confirms every indication, including the time delay between the actual contamination and when the effects were being felt," Colonel McAlistair said.

"So, Gentlemen, where does that leave us?" the President asked.

"Well, sir, we have no idea if the information Admiral Carter's people found is still correct, but as it referred to both the UK and U.S. attacks, we have to assume it is. The

UK attacks were at an annual rock music event held out in the country and at a popular beach on the UK's south coast. The music event is generally just known as Glastonbury, named after the local town near there. It's a bit like a Woodstock - most attendees are in the 16 to 40 age group. It started small but has grown in popularity each year. It's well organised and efficiently run, with most attendees camping out and usually, being England, it rains. This year the weather has been fine. They get quite large stars playing, and I guess it's the biggest outdoor music event they hold," the CIA Director said.

"As to the beach," he continued, "that's one of the most popular beaches on their south coast. There are other beaches closer to London, but those are pebbles and shale. The Bournemouth beach is favourite because it is all sand. It's only a ninety minute or so drive from London, and many people are living close to it, so in good weather, in the summer it's always very busy. They were both easy, soft targets and, although I don't know if this is relevant, only about 50 miles apart."

"OK, Gentlemen. Let me confirm: The UK was hit unexpectedly at two sites. They now have almost 17,000 dead from what we believe to be the nerve agent being manufactured in Iraq or Syria. The attackers remain at large. There were no warnings, there was nothing from the NSA or any of our assets, they chose two soft targets, and we're likely to be next. Do I understand it correctly?" the President said.

"Yes sir, that's about it."

"And it's 4th July weekend next week, and we have no idea if, where and when these bastards will strike again," the President said.

"Yes, sir."

The President sat there thinking for almost five minutes, fingers steepled together in front of his face, almost touching his nose. He picked up a glass of water, sipped and then placed it down.

"OK Gentlemen, this is what we're gonna do. I want every security department put on high alert, and I want the National Guard put on stand-by. But quietly. As you may have noticed, it's election year, and I'm not going to be remembered as the President that cancelled the 4th July celebrations. There will be enough news coverage about the UK attacks on CNN etc. and I do not want the American people to overly panic. This administration has been accused of being weak and having to cancel these celebrations would be the deathblow. I want the Department of Defence chemical, biological, radiological, and nuclear (CBRN) division on full alert and ready to deploy at a moment's notice, under the command of General McAlistair of the CDC. I want everything as tight as possible, but the message to the American people is business as usual. I will also sign an Executive Order banning all civilians from flying drones, no matter what. Anyone caught doing so will face an immediate two-year prison sentence," the President said.

"In the meantime, use every means possible, and I mean every means, to confirm the whereabouts of this guy Husseini who's building this fucking stuff and his colleague, Saif. It's paramount we discover their next target in time," he continued.

"And if we do find Husseini or Saif?" Dreiberg asked.

"Do you need to ask?" the President said, "It's like these people want to die. They have no fear of death at all. Their sole aim is to kill as many people as they can. If they die in the process, they get to have their 72 virgins all the quicker. Like the Japanese in World War 2, for them, it's an honour to die in battle. If you can, finish the bastard and do it hard. Would be nice to get them to Gitmo and see what else they know, but most of them seem to prefer to die than talk. Remember, they've got to get their stuff into the country, so every cargo and shipment needs to be checked, and every person entering the country double-checked. All leave is cancelled, and it's double shifts for everyone, starting now. We will not be caught like the UK has been. Agreed?"

Seeing Dreiberg's face, the President said, "Warren, you disagree?"

"Mr President, sir. I don't disagree with you, sir, but I think we all need a reality check. We don't know how many teams are out there preparing to hit us next week. Do we close down all the borders? Do we perform complete person-by-person, vehicle-by-vehicle searches for everything coming down from Canada and up from Mexico? All we'd end up doing is clogging up the airports and seaports, and for what? The bastards might already be here. Maybe they've been here for years and are working at McDonald's. There is absolutely no way security like that would go unnoticed by both the Press and the public. It would cause mass panic, and then when the truth got out, and we all know it would 'cus Washington's like a friggin' sieve, we'd have even more mass panic on our hands."

"So what do you suggest? We just sit back and wait?' the President said angrily.

"No sir, we do everything you've suggested and more. But, we have to accept there is a high probability that this VX Agent is already in the country along with the bastards that are going to use it. Sir, I suggest in addition to what you have proposed, you announce heightened preventative security due to the UK attack, and we get Homeland on checking back this past month all arrivals into the US. That way if the Press pick up on extra work patterns we're already covered."

Agreeing to this, the President then turned to Admiral Carter and suggested he get Deacon re-stationed to the Pentagon where he could monitor a direct image feed of all people entering the US, as well as reviewing the last months' worth.

# Chapter 52

## England - Sunday

At 08:30 on Sunday morning, Mr Green, aka Hammond, received a call from Wazir from his burner cell phone he'd given him.

"Mr Green, I'm worried. What shall I do?" he asked

"Where are you?"

"I'm still in London, Mr Green. What do you want me to do?"

"Stay there until the travel ban is lifted. The Imam will look after you. Stay indoors. Do not go out for any reason. Any! Understood? You are one of the two most wanted enemies of the UK now, but you have done well, brother. You have struck a mighty blow. You are a true Jihadist, my friend. Soon you will receive the rewards you have earned. Just stay there a little longer and don't panic," Green said.

"But we killed so many. What if I'm found? I'm worried," Wazir said.

"My brother, you have done well and have nothing to fear. The Imam is trustworthy. Put your original number plate back on your bike and give the false one to the Imam to destroy. Once the travel ban is lifted, just drive home as normal. Do not speed. Just drive as normal and become lost in the crowds. Then act normally and attend work as usual. Do not speak of what you have done with anyone. Anyone. Do you understand? Not your parents, your friends, no-one. Your brothers abroad are proud of you. Soon you will be fighting with them for freedom in Syria, but for now, you must do as I say. I will get back to you when things cool down a little. Don't contact me again, I will contact you," Hammond said before hanging up.

Hammond sat thinking for a few minutes. Wazir was panicking quicker than he'd expected. He knew that if Wazir were caught, he'd fold in minutes and tell everything he knew. He was glad now the message from Abu Bakr al-Baghdadi had been clear.

Waiting a while longer while he thought things through, he then contacted Aboud with a similar message to the one he'd given Wazir.

# Chapter 53

That Sunday, with the country effectively on lockdown, and with most of the public observing the orders to stay indoors, the towns and cities remained empty. Even looters who would usually use this time to their own advantage stayed away, worried that they too could be attacked by this unseen deadly enemy.

The police, forensics, and the army were kept busy examining both the Glastonbury site and Bournemouth beach for clues as to who was responsible. All were wearing full biological warfare hazmat suits after Porton Down had verified the potency of the contaminate and confirmed it was modified VX Agent with a 'shelf life', under standard conditions, of two to three weeks, meaning the area would be highly dangerous during that time frame. After that period, average rain and plant growth would disperse the chemicals and likely make the area safe again, although any plants would contain the residue for many more months thereby making the whole Glastonbury event area non-farmable.

Based on eyewitness descriptions and the activity log of the Fire Brigade at the Glastonbury site, they ascertained where the first fire had started. Detailed forensic examination of the burnt-out van showed an initial heat source as well as confirming an accelerant had been used. Nothing conclusive was found due to the intensity of the fire, but some electronic parts were uncovered. A surviving witness who'd camped in one of the nearby tents mentioned seeing a young man of tanned appearance, but with a Yorkshire accent, who had arrived on the Friday evening. They hadn't spoken apart from a brief 'Hello', and he hadn't seen him during Saturday, but he seemed very quiet, and he'd kept to himself, which had appeared to be a little strange considering the type of music event they were all enjoying. The cell phone belonging to this witness was examined, and a partial facial image of the person who had driven the van was found, having been taken at a party the night before the incident.

Having checked the faces of the bodies of those who'd died locally and not found a definite match, police issued a grainy photo and associated photofit of a person of interest they wished to speak with who might have information useful to their investigation.

In Bournemouth, the police scoured the area for any signs of evidence but with spring tides around the solstice just a few days previously, most of the beach was being covered by the sea at high tide twice a day, and any evidence had been washed away.

# Chapter 54

Late on Sunday night, following advice from the police and security forces, and with no more attacks reported, the Prime Minister announced the slight relaxation of the alert rule. With all transport effectively stopped, there were the beginnings of a public outcry. Businesses were also calling the Governments' hotline, questioning what to tell their employees and who would cover the salary bills of staff ordered to stay at home and of subsequent lost business.

All indications were that the attacks were now over so the travel restrictions would remain in place until 05:00 Monday morning, but then businesses could open as usual. Government and public buildings would remain closed at least one further day, but London Underground would be allowed to operate a limited service, as would the railways and airports. The security level would remain at red until further notice, meaning the public should expect extensive travel delays and frequent bag searches, etc. An emergency bill was being passed to allow the police unlimited stop-and-search capabilities of individuals, vehicles and even the right to search properties without warrants.

The police and MI5 started making inroads into the investigation. The current death tolls stood at 11,469 from Glastonbury and 5,742 from Bournemouth, with almost 3,000 being children. There was also a small number more, in the few dozens, expected imminently from people who had managed to get home and had subsequently collapsed but had yet to be discovered. Longer-term deaths were estimated likely to grow by another 4 - 5,000 over the following six months due to long-term damage caused to respiratory systems. Over the next twenty years, directly related deaths would rise to a total of nearer 37 - 40,000 from the incident, depending upon the exposure rate and the delay from any initial exposure to treatment. Patients' symptoms would vary from mild to severe and would require lifelong medical support with shortened life expectancy caused by increased cancers and lung disease.

In Glastonbury in particular many of the infections and deaths had been caused by people panicking and pushing past each other trying to leave, and in doing so transferring droplets onto skin and clothes from people already exposed. Once infected this way, they also only had a maximum of 8 - 9 hours before the symptoms started. Luckily, by the time this showed for many, the army had already set up the examination tents and decontamination showers and had also started the early treatment with effective drugs.

Twenty bodies had also been found not directly affected by the infections. A number were related to beatings, possibly by the police or army, but two had looked to have died from drugs overdoses as syringes and needles had been found close by. Two girls' bodies had been discovered in a tent. One had her throat crushed from what looked like a beating, while the other had been found almost naked. She had been raped and had what looked to be strangulation marks around her throat. Police had been alerted and would be starting criminal investigations.

With no group identified and no arrests imminent, the media were clamouring for a full public investigation while demanding the PM come clean. At the same time, senior members of the opposition parties were calling for a vote of no confidence in the Government and, in particular, of the Prime Minister.

# Chapter 55

## London - Monday

Britain and the British Police are often portrayed as slow and bumbling. Nothing could be further from the truth. Both can move extremely quickly when needed. The MI5 Security Service took charge of the primary investigation, but do not have powers of arrest within the UK, so were working closely with senior police detectives and staff at the Counter Terrorism Command.

The Prime Minister called a further COBRA meeting at 08:00 am demanding updates. The acting head of MI5 took to the floor and confirmed they had now discovered how the nerve agent had been released.

"It seems, Prime Minister, that it was contained within commercially available crop-spraying drones. Eyewitness reports show one drone was used at each location. The drone used at Glastonbury has been found. It crashed into a field about 3 miles away to the east when its batteries died and was recovered overnight by the army. It's been sent to forensics, and we are waiting to hear if any DNA or prints have been found. Reports are that the one used at Bournemouth headed out to sea, so the Coast Guard and the Navy have been put on alert to find it, but we're not so hopeful due to its size, or lack of it to be exact," he said.

"You can buy these damn things over the internet. The one recovered is less than 4 feet in diameter with 6 rotors. It can fly for almost 30 minutes and is designed to spray crops in rough or unfriendly terrain. You can pre-programme it to fly any route you want and it will even auto-adjust and stay at the same height above the ground. Hill farmers in places such as Thailand and Vietnam use them quite extensively, so I am informed, and the model found is of Chinese origin," he continued.

"So do we think China was behind this?" the PM asked.

"No sir, there is no indication of their involvement. In fact, there's no indication of who was responsible. No terrorist group has yet owned up, and there was no increase in chatter prior to the event. Since then it's increased, but what we've intercepted hasn't pointed a finger. As to Glastonbury, as you know, Prime Minister, there were a number of fires started. The first was in an old Ford Transit van that had only arrived the previous evening. Some witness reports have stated the drone took off from near this van. In total, there were over a dozen fires, some accidentally started in the panic and chaos, but some were started deliberately, as in any riot situation. This first one has forensics interested. It started inside the van and used a high-grade accelerant, something similar to paint thinners or lighter fluid, and pretty much destroyed everything within. The fire spread to other vans and tents close by but wasn't as hot. The Fire Brigade onsite managed to extinguish it as most people hadn't started falling ill by then. Forensics has found what they believe to be parts of the electronic controller device and antenna used to control the drone in the vans ashes, so this looks to be a deliberate action to destroy and hide evidence."

"What of the driver? Has he been detained or even identified?" the PM asked.

"No sir, not yet. One of the witnesses camping nearby took photos on his phone, and we believe he captured a partial image of the suspected van driver. The techies have improved the image as much as possible, but it's still grainy. However, the witness has confirmed he thinks it looks to be the driver, but can't be sure. It seems he was smoking marijuana most of Friday afternoon and evening so isn't really sure about anything. The photo has been issued as a person of interest to all ports and airports country-wide, and we've been inundated with possibilities, but, so far, all are turning out useless, bar one. However, on a positive note, a bus driver on the Glastonbury to Bristol route contacted the hotline. Detectives have already been to see him. He remembers a similar looking person getting on his bus early afternoon on Saturday. The only reason he noticed was that everyone was still heading towards the event and this person had obviously left because he still had his entry sticker on his jacket. He didn't appear to have been acting suspiciously or anything, the driver just thought it odd that he hadn't stayed. Cameras outside the bus station in Bristol and more cameras at Bristol Temple Meads train station show the same person, or someone closely resembling him, heading north. Correlation of the timecode from the images, against tickets purchased, shows a similar looking person bought a one-way ticket to Bradford Interchange via Birmingham and Sheffield, changing Leeds, catching the 18:30 out of Bristol. We've interviewed the ticket sales person who served him. By what she could remember she said she thought he looked a little nervous, but couldn't really be sure."

"Could she identify him in a lineup?" the PM asked.

"Possibly, sir. The station cameras at Leeds show him arriving at 22:02, departing again at 22:35 and walking around looking nervous. He appears to be agitated and constantly looking at anyone close to him. Bradford Interchange cameras show him arriving 22:56, but their cameras lose sight of him when he leaves the station, but we got the local police focussing on investigations in that area and checking with all taxi cab drivers who were working at that time. Obviously, he could be a complete innocent; we just need to find him to be certain. Five ten, Asian or Middle Eastern skin colouring, black hair, and a small and well-trimmed beard. Wearing jeans, dark T-shirt, and dark jacket, possibly leather," the head of MI5 said.

"What about facial recognition? Why hasn't he been identified? He must be on some watch list somewhere?"

"Possibly, Prime Minister, but facial recognition isn't one hundred percent accurate, especially if the image is degraded, as it is here. You can see, sir, it's slightly blurred. The cameras at the train stations are not particularly high quality. We are doing our best, sir."

"Well if he's on a watch list and being watched, why wasn't he stopped from going there?"

"There is a difference, Prime Minister, between being on a watch list, if in fact he was, and being watched. The watch list merely places him as a person who might be considered a possible threat."

"Well why wasn't he being watched?" the Prime Minster asked.

"Sir, at any one time we have literally thousands of Asians on our watch lists. Many are British born. Anyone visiting a relative, however distant, in Syria, Iraq, Iran, Pakistan and a number of other countries is enough to get them placed on the list. Any social media support of terrorism, or posting on suspected websites gets them on it as well. But we just don't have the manpower and resources to actually watch and trail every name on the watch list even part-time, let alone to offer full-time surveillance."

Realising it was an argument he couldn't win, the PM didn't respond and just sat there in silence.

"As to the drones," the acting head of MI5 continued after a few more seconds waiting, "we have traced their journey from the company in China shipped to an address in Luton. Police raided the address but just found a house with an old lady who receives cash each month from a Mr Green to take in packages. She calls a mobile number when anything arrives for him, and he turns up a day or so later. We have a trace on the phone, but it's not showing any activity. However, we will know as soon as it's turned on. It's a burner, so no luck tracing the owner. She can't give much of a description apart from she thinks he's maybe twenty to thirty and he's tall. She said he could be Arabic, or Indian, or Pakistani. She even thought he might be Spanish or Italian, but with an English accent, so not much help there. However, she did say a smaller parcel arrived a few days before these latest packages which he picked up, but she can't remember if there was any label on the package."

"What about going public with this. To get the public to help, I mean. The Press are all over this. We need to be doing something, man," the PM said.

"Yes sir, we are asking the public for help. The picture of the possible van driver is being shown nationally and especially on the local news and papers in and around the Leeds and Bradford areas, but we don't know for sure whether he's our number one suspect or just a witness."

"Until he can prove otherwise, I want him classified as our number one suspect. Understood?" the PM replied angrily.

Around that time in the morning, Wazir put his helmet on, kick started the bike to life and headed out of London going west on the North Circular Road before joining the

M1 motorway heading north. The roads were almost as busy as usual. Whether it was the same spirit as immediately after the July 5, 2005, London bombings when Londoner's still travelled as normal and wouldn't be beaten. Or whether it was just people needing to be where they had to be because otherwise they wouldn't get paid, traffic was almost as much as any standard Monday morning, and Wazir soon disappeared in with the crowds.

He exited the M1 near Northampton and stopped for fuel before re-joining the motorway, careful to keep within speed limits.

Four hours later, a sweating and very frightened Wazir finally arrived home.

# Chapter 56

## London - Monday

After a few minutes break for refreshments, the acting head of MI5 again took to the floor and addressed the group.

"Regarding the van at Glastonbury forensics has found a significant number of fingerprints over its exterior. Those close to the heat source have all been damaged, but some useable ones have been found near the front and are being analysed. The plates on the van were false, but we traced the owner from the VIN to a Rajiv Singh of Birmingham. CTSF (Counter Terrorist Specialist Firearms) battered the door down much to the surprise of Mr & Mrs Singh who were enjoying their evening meal last night. We took them in, but Mr Singh claimed to have sold the van about ten days ago to a young chap that fits the van driver's photo. No receipt, but his wife confirmed it. Said the guy seemed to have a northern accent. Didn't give his name and paid cash. Appeared to know what he was doing as he gave the van a good check over, examined the engine, etc. The Singh's are shit scared, sir. Gave us all they could. We'll hold them another day or so, but I don't think they know anything more," he said.

"So where are we now?" the PM demanded, his face turning red with anger.

"This driver is still our best lead currently for the Glastonbury attack. We're still examining the footage from cell phones, and a few have shown the drone flying, but none conclusively show where it took off."

"How do they get their funds? Who's paying them?" the PM asked, changing tacks slightly.

"Well sir, we don't know for sure. A lot of their funding comes from the Middle East, with Saudi and Qatar being the primary benefactors. As to how they actually get the money, they often use Hawala. International bank transactions are too easy to trace, and most countries have transfer limits which raise flags when a value threshold has been exceeded. Not so with Hawala. Illegal in many countries, it's an informal money transfer system. In countries where it is accepted, there are rules and regulations such as recording the identity of the customer and the value of the transaction. Unfortunately, Hawala is popular in countries where formal banking is too expensive, heavily regulated, or even non-existent. It's been around for centuries."

"So how does it work," the PM asked.

"Simple example, sir. A Pakistani taxi driver here in London wants to send money to his family in a village in Pakistan. He goes into a Pakistani shop here and hands over his Sterling cash to a broker. Within a couple of hours, his brother in the wilds of Pakistan can go into a local broker shop in his village and collect the equivalent amount, minus the broker's commission, in Pakistani Rupees. All done without any paperwork and impossible to trace. The brokers, a select group often of local businesses, communicate either by phone or nowadays usually by text. It's all done on a trust system. The Middle East still runs extensively on it. Places like Dubai welcome it, in fact. All the lowly paid migrant workers in Dubai, Saudi or Kuwait need to send money home. The banks there don't want to be inundated with poor migrant workers wanting to send small amounts to various back-of-beyond countries. Most don't even have bank accounts, preferring to be paid cash, so this works perfectly for them. But being all word-of-mouth, it's very hard to police and trace, sir. In fact, we believe the London attack in July 2005 was funded this way. Never been able to prove it, though. I think it's highly likely this attack was funded the same way."

"As to the Bournemouth attack," he continued, "we have witness reports and CCTV footage of a motorcyclist wearing a backpack walking up to the roof level of the main car park close to the beach. He kept his helmet on so we don't have a view of his face, but he appears male from his body shape, about 5 foot 10, and slight build, which just about covers a third of the population. He was out of sight on the roof floor, but CCTV shows him descending the stairs again very soon after we believe the attack took place at 1:00 pm. He's still wearing his backpack, but the shape looks different, less rigid. His bike was parked in the free parking section outside the range of the cameras, but we have a similar motorcyclist heading through three junctions minutes later out toward the motorway. We also have him joining the motorway and heading east. Earlier footage has him arriving around 12:25 am from the A338. Number plate cameras pick him up arriving in West London along the Chertsey by-pass and joining the Hammersmith flyover heading into the city at 15:20 pm. There is nothing distinct about his leathers, helmet or bike, although it has been identified as a Suzuki GW250 and he appears to have ditched the backpack. We tracked him through the city and out onto the Romford Road, but then we lost him. We've issued descriptions, and we're waiting for a break. We've confirmed the number plate is fake, and he was there at the right time, so at this stage, he's our prime suspect. We've instructed traffic to check every fuel station on that route and to check their waste bins for his backpack. Those are the two main lines of enquiry we're following."

Slamming his cup down and spilling tea over the table, the Prime Minister's face was red with rage.

"17,000 dead! I've got to face Parliament, and the public, let alone the fucking media that are circling like bastard vultures and you're telling me you've exhausted the leads? They're dead. 17,000 people are dead, over 3,000 of them kids and you don't have any fucking leads? My job's on the line here. I want answers, and I want those fucking bastards caught," he screamed, white frothy spittle gathering at the corners of his mouth and spraying in all directions from his lips.

# Chapter 57

## Northern England

Jamal Aboud and Amjad Wazir had met up late on Monday evening at Aboud's uncle's garage. Aboud had strutted around in the dark boasting of their achievements.

"Brother, we have done as asked. We have slain many disbelievers. We are real Jihadists. There is no God, but God. Allahu Akbar, Allahu Akbar," he'd chanted.

Wazir, however, was not as excited.

"Why do I feel we've done wrong, brother? They were innocents, man. Men, women and children, but not soldiers. They were like our neighbours. Just people having fun. And so many of them. Why do I not feel like you?" Wazir said.

"You're weak. You think like the disbelievers. You're wrong. I am Muslim, and I want this country to become a Muslim country. ISIS can bring this about and, Insha' Allah, they will one day. The mighty Allah has sent us to rid the Earth of disbelievers. There is no God, but God," Aboud had replied, punching Wazir hard around the head.

"You want to be a man, but you're weak. You're nothing! You couldn't even shoot that airman. You should go back to your Mama," Aboud said, with a look of disgust on his face.

"Fuck off! I've done as much as you, asshole. Mr Green said he's proud of me. Proud of both of us," Wazir said, smacking Aboud back.

After a few more half-hearted smacks at each other, they both eventually settled down and managed to sleep in the small, cramped office at the rear.

At 08:30 am the next morning, Aboud's pre-paid burner phone rang. William Hammond, aka Mr Green, contacted them and told them to bring their bags and their passports and meet him on the bridge by the duck pond in Horton Park in two hours. He then disconnected the call, and unbeknown to Aboud and Wazir removed the sim card from his phone and snapped it in two, before dropping both pieces into a roadside drain. He carried the phone itself to another public waste bin before stamping on it with his heel and dropping the broken remnants deep in amongst the garbage.

Hammond was already sat on a park bench with views of the duck pond bridge when Aboud and Wazir arrived. They were both carrying backpacks. Hammond stood and walked towards them from behind. He carried on directly past them murmuring, "Follow me 100 yards behind," before heading towards the car park.

After looking around to make sure they weren't being observed, he opened the trunk and told them to put their bags in then get in the car. As soon as they were all in, he started the engine and drove away, careful to keep within the speed limit.

"Mr Green, we're so pleased to see you. Where are you taking us?" Wazir asked.

"Today my young Jihadist's, you travel to our great homeland. I have money and flights booked for you from Newcastle to Amsterdam, then on to Ankara in Turkey where you will meet ISIS representatives who will take you safely across the border into Syria. There you will meet our great leader, Caliph Ibrahim, commander of the faithful, or Abu Bakr al-Baghdadi, as he is better known to his supporters. He is very proud of what you have

211

done. He has planned a big feast for when you arrive, and you will sit, as honoured guests, at his feet," Hammond said.

"But Mr Green, we've killed thousands the news says. We'll be hunted down. Aboud's picture is all over the news. We'll be caught. I don't want to be in jail all my life," Wazir said, starting to cry.

"Brothers, brothers. Relax! You have both done well. Our masters are pleased with what you have achieved. It is a mighty blow against the UK, and you will become famous. But first, we need to get you out of the country to Syria to join ISIS and fight for the cause. As two of our mighty warriors do you think our great leader, Caliph Abu Bakr, would let you get caught? Of course not. He is waiting to meet and pray with you," Hammond said. "He issued instructions for a private charter to fly you to Amsterdam. You will not go through the main airport or through security. I will drive you straight to your 'plane. You are safe, brothers. Now sit back and relax."

The warm June sunshine streamed in through the car windows as Hammond drove north through Keighley towards Skipton and on through the Yorkshire Dales National Park towards Newcastle, as both Aboud and Wazir drifted off to sleep.

Waking with a jolt as the car hit a pothole, Aboud came fully awake and said, "Where are we?"

"We're heading through the National Park. The police aren't likely to be stopping traffic here, they're doing that on some main roads, but we're safer this way," Hammond said.

"I'm hungry. And thirsty. When can we stop for food?" Aboud said, looking around and seeing the quiet small road they were driving on.

"Brothers, I have food and drinks in the back. We can't risk your face being seen, so I brought everything with me. I will find somewhere quiet, and we can stop."

A few miles further on, having not seen anyone or any other traffic for a while, they came to a small dirt track off to the right heading up towards some trees.

"Let's check this place out," Hammond said turning onto the track, as the jolting and bumping brought Wazir fully awake.

The gravel track led up and behind a thick grouping of trees to a small parking area beyond. Seeing the place was empty, Hammond swung the car around in a half-circle, facing the front back down the track the way they'd come, before applying the brake and stopping.

Getting out, all three stretched and looked around. The place was deserted with the only sounds being birds singing. Hammond popped open the trunk and said to Aboud to get the bag out containing the food and refreshments.

"Why the polythene, Mr Green?" Aboud asked as he stretched right into the trunk.

"To keep my car clean," Hammond replied as he pulled out a suppressed 9mm and shot him twice quickly in the back of his head.

Hearing the soft pops, Wazir spun round, saw the dead body of his friend hanging out the trunk and tried to run away. He'd only gone five feet when Hammond fired again, and Wazir gasped and fell face down, his pelvis shattered. Wazir cried and tried to crawl, but Hammond walked up to him and, using his foot under Wazir's shoulder, flipped him over onto his back.

"But why, Mr Green. We've done everything you ordered?" he gasped through pain-clenched teeth.

"You certainly have my little Jihadist. Maybe too well. You're right. You will be hunted down. With so many

213

dead, the government won't let it rest until you're caught. And you would lead them straight back to me, and we can't allow that," Hammond said as he shot him again, this time straight in the forehead.

Dragging the body by the feet back to the car, Hammond bent and lifted Wazir's body and bundled it on top of Aboud's in the trunk and slammed the lid closed. Walking around the area, he scuffed the loose gravel over any drops of blood, confident there was nothing left to find.

Stopping to eat a sandwich and downing a bottle of water, he stood looking around at the beautiful views and listened to the birds singing. Finally, he drove off and headed toward a deserted farm he'd found a few weeks previously, before parking up until nightfall.

Later that evening he rolled the now swelling and smelling bodies out of the trunk, pulled out a shovel and using the sharpened edge of it like an axe, cut off their hands at the wrists, and then hammered the shovel into their mouths to destroy their teeth. The bodies were then rolled in the polythene before being buried. He destroyed their two phones after wiping them clean of prints and removing and snapping the SIM cards into pieces. He threw the broken phones into a stream then buried the severed hands separately at four locations, and then walking back to the car he cleaned and stowed the shovel. During the long drive home to Reading, he disposed of the broken SIM cards out of the window.

# Chapter 58

## The Pentagon - Washington

The flight from Al Qayarah airfield to Bahrain was by C130 Hercules turboprop with Deacon changing to a C-5 Galaxy for the onward flight to Washington, but it was still a long and slow journey. However, Deacon was happy with the change. The seats on the Hercules had been canvas with aluminium framing, but at least the Galaxy had standard seating and he'd managed to sleep.

Landing at Joint Base Andrews, formally known as Andrews AFB, he was surprised to find a staff car waiting to take him the short journey to the Pentagon.

The Pentagon is one of the most secure buildings in the USA. The complete structure is shaped like a pentagon, hence its name. With 17.5 miles of corridors and a floor space of over 6.6 million square feet, housing over 23,000 workers each day, it's one of the largest offices in the world. There are five floors above ground and two floors below. It's made up of five concentric rings labelled A through E from inside to out. Only the 'E' ring offices have windows. Built during WWII when steel was in short supply for much-needed weaponry, there are no elevators in the building, only ramps, stairs and escalators. The layout was designed for maximum efficiency, and it only takes a maximum of seven minutes to walk between any two points within the building. The central plaza was informally known as 'ground zero,' a nickname originating during the Cold War on the presumption that it would be targeted by the Soviet Union at the outbreak of nuclear war. One rumour that had never been confirmed or denied was of a small nuclear device being located deep underground beneath the central core, powering the entire building.

After clearing the various levels of security and dropping his screened luggage off at a secure room, he looked up to see his old friend Mitchell Stringer waiting for him.

"John, it's good to see you again. How was the flight?" Mitch said.

"Mitch, my man, you're a sight for sore eyes. Long and boring. So what's the plan for today?"

With that, Mitch led Deacon up to the top floor and outer ring, their footsteps echoing on the polished shiny floors. Deacon's security pass would allow him to walk to specific floors and areas in rings E and D unescorted. To gain access to the remainder of E and D rings, Deacon would need to be accompanied by Mitch. He would need an armed escort for rings C and B, and anywhere else was off-limits to him completely.

Arriving at Admiral Carter's office, Mitch said the Admiral was waiting for them, so Deacon knocked and entered. Deacon was always impressed by the Admiral's inner sanctum. It was an outer room with a long window and a view outside across the Pentagon Lagoon Yacht Basin to the Potomac River beyond, but the Admiral had clearly made the room his own. The expected photographs of the Admiral shaking hands with the various Presidents' he'd served under, adorned the wall behind his desk. Along the adjacent wall were photos of various naval aircraft in flight and of ships he'd served on. Directly opposite the Admiral's desk was a large painting of the Admiral's last sea command and the United States' first nuclear-powered aircraft carrier, the USS Enterprise. There was also a small coffee table in the corner along with four comfy chairs surrounding it, as well two more office chairs facing the desk.

Rising to his feet from behind his large wooden desk, rumoured to have been hand-built for the Admiral with reclaimed wood from the USS Maine — the U.S. battleship sunk in mysterious circumstances in Havana harbour on February 15th, 1898 — the Admiral stood as Deacon saluted and returned the salute, before taking Deacon's hand and shaking it warmly.

"Lieutenant, it's good to see you again. You did good work in rescuing the girl hostages from Mosul," he said.

"Thank you, Admiral. It was a team effort. Not just us over there on the ground, but those supporting us as well. We were all glad to bring the girls to safety."

"Well not all the girls were grateful Lieutenant, but Mitch can bring you up to speed on that later. First, to business," the Admiral said.

With that, Mitch and the Admiral began to inform Deacon of the latest developments and the current situation.

"All UK, and U.S. agencies are on full alert, and almost 17,000 have died in the UK. There have been no further UK attacks, and everything is getting back to as normal as it can after a horrific attack like that. No-one has admitted responsibility, but we are confident it's the ISIS conversation you overheard and recorded. CDC has confirmed the bastards used a modified VX Agent with a delayed action coating. This is exactly what was discussed. It slows the absorption of VX by six to eight hours once it's on the skin, but then it's just as lethal as ever. It has a mortality rate of almost 70%, and as you know from watching the news, a lot of the deaths were people on the beach, including children," Mitch said.

"The bigger worry now is according to the recording, there's twenty times the amount of VX heading here. What the fuck is the target and when?" he continued.

"Has a state of emergency been declared yet?" Deacon said.

"No it hasn't, and it's not going to be. The President wants these killers caught before they attack here, but he's not willing to cancel the 4th July celebrations. As you know, he's in the last stages of his second term, and he refuses to end his presidency being seen as a lame duck who had to cancel this year's Independence Day celebrations. He's said he isn't willing to have the military on every corner, scaring the public. So every security department's on full alert, but in the meantime, it's business as usual."

Admiral Carter opened a folder and passed copies to Deacon of the UK grainy photo and photofit picture, as well as all the other CCTV images sent over by the British of the possible suspects. Looking closely at them, Deacon had no trouble confirming these were definitely not pictures of the suspects Saif the Palestinian and Faisel Husseini he'd seen in Mosul.

"We didn't think they were the ones, Lieutenant, but as you are here it was worth checking," the Admiral said.

"The British are making every effort and are already the most surveilled nation with almost 6 million CCTV cameras keeping watch on their every move, with over half-million in London alone," the Admiral continued. "Using some of their latest facial recognition software, they are sending over copies of anyone who arrived in the UK within the last ten days and look similar to your identikit drawings of Khan and Husseni. Your job here is to examine each one and see if they match. Customs and Border Protection here also record and store all facial images of visitors to the US. Again, anything that flags up as a 60% similar match or higher in the past month is being forwarded directly here to Mitch, and the two of you need to work through them all."

"Admiral, happy to serve in any way I can," Deacon said, before he and Mitch moved to Mitch's office and sat down to examine the previously recorded images as well as the live feeds directly from the National Security Agency (NSA) in Fort Meade and from the Defence Intelligence Agency (DIA) in Bolling that Mitch received.

Later that evening, sat with his wife, Helen, in a comfy chair in their apartment in the trendy Washington district of Adams Morgan, Mitch watched Deacon finish washing the dishes.

"John, you're our guest. You don't need to do the dishes," Helen said.

"Helen, my lovely Helen. You've been working all day and still you made a great meal while this bum of a husband of yours was providing me with beer. You know my rules - you let me stay here when I'm in Washington, in return, I do the washing up. Now sit back and relax, I'm almost finished," Deacon said, as he smiled and topped up all their wine glasses with a classic Californian Chardonnay he'd picked up earlier.

Mitch Stringer and Deacon had met when both were studying at Columbia University. They'd hit it off together and had become good friends. Both had intended on joining the U.S. Navy and had enlisted after graduating, with Deacon applying to join the SEALs and Stringer applying directly to Naval Intelligence. Since then they'd regularly kept in contact with each other, often sharing information when they could.

Naval Intelligence suited Mitch perfectly. He was friendly, intelligent, and had a knack for finding needles in haystacks. He was a details guy who also had the ability to explain things clearly and succinctly and to speak easily with senior officers.

It hadn't taken long for Mitch to come to the attention of Admiral Douglas Eugene Carter, the tough ex-Carrier Battle Group Commander who occupied the Chief of Naval Operations chair in the Pentagon. Soon after he'd joined Naval Intelligence, Mitch had made a presentation to a number of senior officers, including Admiral Carter. His ability to explain a technical matter clearly, without being intimidated by the audience or condescending with his knowledge, had found a soft spot in the Admiral's tough exterior. The Admiral had a well-known reputation of not suffering fools lightly and of demanding his subordinates come to the point quickly. Promoted and moved to the Admiral's department, Mitch began working closer and closer with the Admiral until he became the Admiral's personal advisor.

Soon after moving to Washington, Mitch, a keen dinghy sailor, had met Helen. Two years after, she became his fiancée then eighteen months later, his wife. She was now a middle-level accountant in a prestigious Washington law firm.

Sitting on the balcony watching the sunset and seeing the colours of the sky bleed from pink through purple to blue, they sat, talked, reminisced and enjoyed each other's company. They also discussed the forthcoming wedding in San Diego of Alex Schaefer to Warren Peterson in less than four weeks' time at Our Lady of the Rosary Church in Little Italy, San Diego. Deacon was to give the bride away as Alex's father had died from cancer a few years back. Mitch and Helen would be there, as well as Rachel Sanchez and a large number of U.S. SEALs.

Finally, just as they were getting ready to retire and Helen had already gone indoors, Mitch took Deacon's arm and motioned for him to wait.

"I didn't want to mention this in front of Helen, but there is one problem you need to be aware of," Mitch said to his friend. "The girl you rescued, Laura Williams, has been on various TV talk shows along with the other girls. They're all grateful for the rescue, but Laura is saying that you and your colleagues went too far and murdered her boyfriend. She says that you killed him and their other guards without warning and then smacked her around in making your escape. She's also been saying that you threatened her and then when she cried out, terrified, on the boat, one of your men also threatened her. Most of the news channels are ignoring her complaints as stupid love-struck rantings and that you and your team saved them from certain death, but two of the talk-show hosts are trying to make a big deal of it and demanding answers from the Navy. It's all being ignored at the moment and I know it's come as far as Admiral Carter's desk, but he's just answered with a terse No comment on operational matters so far. But it could escalate, especially being an election year and one of the election candidates has picked up on the phrase out-of-control service men."

"Goddam it, the bastard was about to rape her when I shot him. And the other guy would have gone second," Deacon said.

"I know, John. Both the Admiral and I have read your action report, which is why he's ignoring the reporter, but we both know how sometimes these things have a life of their own. Anyway, I'm sure it'll soon be all forgotten, but I just wanted to make you aware," Mitch said, clasping Deacon on the shoulder.

Deacon tried to put it out of his mind, but that night he slept poorly.

# Chapter 59

## Florida - US

Elias Shirani was running late this morning. It was just one of those mornings when even the simplest task seemed to take twice as long as it ought to — drinking coffee, he'd coughed. Not hard, but enough to jolt his hand and spill a splash of brown down his shirt. Having changed, he couldn't find his keys or his watch. Just the sort of day he didn't need, he thought.

Also Zane had been acting strangely. Ever since he'd got back from his camping trip he seemed different, Elias thought. He'd rarely been home in the evenings, and although helping at work, he seemed to be not all there … almost like he was constantly thinking of something else. However, he'd said he had a new friend that he wanted to bring round the following evening, so maybe it's a new girlfriend, Shirani senior thought.

Today they were off to headquarters to pick up more supplies. Elias had been caught short before so now he liked to keep at least five days' worth at home in his locked garage. That way he always had stock on hand for his most demanding customers. But traffic was getting worse. The annual summer holidays for all the schools in the U.S. and Europe had started, so hotels and flights were becoming fully booked. Everyone wanted to be on vacation. On the local news last evening, they'd even announced that water consumption had almost doubled in the last few days, and would likely remain that way until early September, so expect hosepipe bans.

What with increased traffic and temperatures up and humidity off the scale for the summer months from mid-June to mid-September, Florida is not such a nice place to live, he mused.

It took them almost ninety minutes to get to the headquarters then another thirty minutes or so to grab what they needed. He took the opportunity to hand in his job sheets from the past month and also picked up new brochures. Usually, he would just rely on the post, but while he was there, he thought.

Stopping on the way back for lunch Shirani senior decided something needed to be said.

"Zane, what the fuck's the matter with you, son? You've hardly said a word all morning. In fact, you've hardly said a word since your camping trip. You mom's worried. What's up?" he said.

"Nothing," he said, "just got things on my mind, 's'all."

"Anything you want to discuss with me?"

"No way! Just drop it. Yeah? Drop it!"

Slowly eating his lunch, Elias Shirani thought that if that's the way he is with his new girlfriend, then heaven help her.

Arriving back home and unloading the stores, they then set out on three jobs together, Shirani senior trying to make conversation, Shirani junior just offering the odd grunt.

Later that evening, Elias spoke to his wife. They hoped Zane was just nervous about his new girlfriend meeting them so they agreed to make her as welcome as possible the following evening, hoping love might blossom between the new couple.

# Chapter 60

## The Pentagon - Washington

For the second day in a row, Deacon spent the day staring at a computer screen until his eyes glazed over. Eventually, he and Mitch had sat down and tried to work out a compromise.

"Hey, man, we need to find a better way with this. The UK has roughly 220,000 visitors a month, that's approximately 70,000 in the ten-day period we're interested in. Two-thirds are male, and roughly 12 percent of those are triggering a 60% facial match. That's over 5,500 images from the UK alone. Add to that the larger U.S. figures for the last month, and that's another half million pictures to review. Even flicking them through at three a second is going to take you over two thousand hours to view them all. And there's more arriving every day. Let me speak with IT," Mitch said.

Two hours later the compromise was complete. Special clearance for Deacon had been requested and authorised by the Admiral. Instead of looking at each image in turn on one screen, Mitch and Deacon were in the stand-by control room, deep underground. The sixty-foot wall was made up of multiple plasma screens that could all be linked by software to show the same image or many smaller ones. It was now displaying four images per screen across 48 screens and refreshing them every ten seconds, as that was how long Deacon needed to scan once from left to right. At a 500% increase in photos reviewed every hour, it was still a mammoth task but was now in the achievable basket.

At four o'clock Mitch received a call requesting them to attend the Admiral's office. Walking in, the Admiral introduced Deacon to Simon Clark, the FBI Director.

"Director, it's a pleasure to meet you," Deacon said.

"Well, Lieutenant, I've heard good things about you from both Lieutenant Stringer here as well as the Admiral. I was here to update the Admiral, but he asked me to wait and include you two as well. Shall I begin?" Clark said, looking towards Admiral Carter, who nodded.

"It seems like the UK security people have hit a brick wall," Clark said. "Their police believe they may have identified two suspects, a Jamal Aboud and an Amjad Wazir, both British born Pakistani's. Both seem normal youths, and neither was on a watch-list. Both have now disappeared. They'd issued photos, albeit fairly poor quality grainy ones having been taken from a train company's CCTV system, of a possible suspect or witness getting off a train in the northern town of Bradford and asked the public for help in identifying him. They've received lots of calls, but one seems to have panned out. Yesterday, an anonymous caller gave them the name Jamal Aboud. When they followed up, they found this guy was missing. He is a trainee mechanic and works at his uncle's small repair shop. When police investigated, they couldn't find him but did find a motorcycle that the uncle finally admitted belonged to one of Aboud's friends, Amjad Wazir, who's also gone missing. Neither of them has been seen since Thursday last."

"So they think these are the culprits?" Mitch said.

"It's looking good, so far. Their forensic people have examined the van at Glastonbury, and they confirmed it was deliberately set fire to with an incendiary device. The original owners who sold it a couple of weeks back have confirmed that the person who purchased it from them matches the photo of Jamal Aboud. So this Jamal Aboud is definitely a person-of-interest."

"What about the other guy?"

"He's disappeared as well. He usually works in a small supermarket, and the manager has confirmed he's not been at work since last Thursday. His motorbike matches the description of the one the police are looking for in connection with the Bournemouth attack. Homes of both Wazir and Aboud are being forensically examined, along with Wazir's motorbike, with parents and relatives taken in for questioning, but all are remaining very tight-lipped. In an interesting side issue, the supermarket manager also confirmed this guy Wazir had been off work for a couple of days three weeks previously. It may not be connected, but that was the time two men roughly matching their descriptions attacked and tried to kidnap an RAF Flight Sergeant out jogging early one morning. The Sergeant fought them off, and no one was ever caught, but it's too much of a coincidence to ignore, and I don't like coincidences," Clark said.

"You think maybe a trial run or something," Mitch said.

"Not so much a trial run, but we know these groups often have initiation ceremonies, so it's possible it was something like that. What the Brits don't yet know is how these two were contacted, how they were turned and radicalised and whether they were working alone or as part of a bigger team. They obviously had support, but whether there are more just waiting in the wings or these were the only two, they don't yet know. Quite a few of their close associates are being questioned, and all UK airports and shipping have been put on high alert to watch out for them. The problem is they don't even know if they are still in the country or have crossed the Channel. They could even be being hidden in one of the many mosques in that area. Unless their police receive collaborative proof they are in a mosque, they won't venture in because of the worry of being labelled anti-Muslim. That whole area around the middle north of the UK is a breeding ground for radical Islam and is a hotbed for racist labelling."

"Were drones definitely used and do you know which type?" Deacon asked.

"Yeah, one at each location. The one used at Glastonbury was a GS-15 agricultural model. They are assuming the same type was used at Bournemouth. They were shipped from China to a London address. We've confirmed both with the manufacturer and multiple shipping companies that none of these drones has been ordered for shipping here,"

"But they could have been brought in another way? They could already be here," Deacon said. "What about the VX Agent? How did that get from Syria to the UK?"

"That is still a mystery. Not shipped to the same London address, so their police are still checking, but if immigrants can just get into Britain through their Channel Tunnel, or hiding on the back of a truck from France, then getting ten litres of fluid into a country like the UK is child's play," Clark said.

"I've been speaking with Shane in Baghdad. Even he isn't hearing anything specific to the US. There's lots of increased Internet and phone chatter now concerning what has happened in the UK and ISIS are claiming responsibility, with their usual bluster and generic threats against us, the big Satan; but nothing specific or in more detail than the regular crap they put out," Mitch said.

"So where does that leave us?" Deacon asked.

"It's the President's choice how much the public is told," Admiral Carter said, "but for now, we carry on at the level we're on. You two get back and continue with the photos and let's meet again tomorrow at three."

Pushing his chair back and standing up, Deacon bade goodbye to the Admiral and the FBI Director, knowing he had a long evening ahead of him.

# Chapter 61

## Washington - July 1st

Deacon awoke early from a sleepless night but felt good. Quietly dressing in trainers, shorts and t-shirt, he crept downstairs and out the front door, gently closing it behind him. They'd had no success the previous day, but Deacon just felt today was going to be productive.

Jogging along Columbia Road, he swung left through the grounds of the Washington Hilton before heading back up Connecticut Avenue to the Smithsonian National Zoological Park where he ran around the perimeter twice, before heading back to Mitch and Helen's home. Both were already awake, and Helen asked him what he wanted for breakfast.

Agreeing on toast, bacon, eggs and coffee, Deacon ran back upstairs to shower, arriving back in the kitchen ten minutes later, hair slicked back and wearing clean and pressed BDU's.

"How far did you go?" Mitch asked.

"About twelve miles in total. Had to clear my mind. Don't know why, but I feel good things are going to happen today," he said.

Giving Helen a thank-you peck on the cheek as she passed him his breakfast, Deacon settled down to tuck into crispy bacon.

"You know, Helen, if you ever decide to leave this bum ..."

"Yeah, right. Like I'm worried now, pal," Mitch laughed.

The adverts on the morning news channel had just finished, and the logo for Fox News came on the TV screen.

"Coming next, are our armed services out of control? Exclusive interview with Laura Williams, recently released from Iraq," the Fox News presenter said.

Stopping eating mid-bite, Deacon, Mitch and Helen turned to watch the screen as the image of a fresh-faced, golden blonde haired girl filled the screen.

During the next few minutes, Laura Williams described a different-from-reality account of hers and her friend's kidnapping and imprisonment. According to her, their kidnappers had been compassionate and kind. No mention was made of the daily beatings from the old Arab crows, or of the limited food and poor sanitation. Instead, an image was portrayed of the five girls all happily cleaning and cooking, under the watchful eyes of the friendly guards. Her story grew even more extreme when she said she had befriended one of the guards who had provided extra food for them and was trying to help them escape. According to Laura, this guard had fallen in love with her and would do anything Laura asked. He had planned to bring them all out to safety when the Navy SEALs had attacked and murdered him in cold blood. He hadn't been armed, neither had another, and they had tried to surrender and had their arms raised, yet they'd both been murdered cruelly by the SEAL team leader. This same man had then verbally abused and threatened her, as had another SEAL, as they were all making their escape.

The news presenter then turned away from a sobbing Laura to face the camera and asked, "Is this what we expect from our armed forces? Murder is murder in any country. We need answers, and we need them today. What did this person think when he executed two harmless and unarmed Iraqi's? Does he think he's above the law? He and his team need to be brought to justice."

An open-mouthed Deacon looked at Mitch.

"What the fuck? She was about to be raped, yet I'm the bad guy?" he said.

"Hey pal, just ignore it. I'm sure it'll all blow over. C'mon, let's get to the office," Mitch said turning off the TV as he stood from the table and slapped his friend on the shoulder.

Climbing into Mitch's car a few minutes later, Deacon said, "I don't believe this. We saved her life, all of their lives, yet we're being seen as the bad guys? Where's the other side of the story about them being held and threatened with beheading and about her about to be raped? So much for balanced journalism."

Not sure of what to say, Mitch stayed silent, and the two of them rode the twenty minutes to the Pentagon in silence.

Grabbing coffees before they caught the elevator down to the stand-by control room, they entered just as the IT people were setting the screens up. Having made good progress through the images the previous day and feeling lucky, Deacon decided to have a change this morning. He asked to start with images taken from the Canadian border crossings, and within seconds the screens were filled with images from Vancouver in British Colombia, to Saint John in New Brunswick.

By noon and with no success, they stopped long enough to eat a quick sandwich when Deacon suggested changing to business airports.

At 1:37 pm, and with tired eyes and an aching neck from constantly sweeping his head left to right along the wall of screens, one particular image suddenly held his attention. His eyes fixed on it, and he looked closer and closer. Rushing to the keyboard, he pressed the Spacebar to stop the images refreshing then hit the backspace to jump back one complete set of pictures.

Staring at the screen for almost twenty seconds, he quietly said, "Got you, you bastard," before slapping his hand down hard on the desk, shouting, "Eureka!"

A startled and semi-dozing Mitch sprang to life.

"What? Eh? You sure? Is it him? Sure?" Mitch said.

"This is him, Mitch. Saif the Palestinian. I'm sure of it. This was taken at Teterboro Airport, New York, eight days ago," Deacon said, having cross-referenced the EXIF data on the photograph.

"It says here he's a Qatari security guard for Prince Ahmed Jabir Kalifa bin Mohammed al-Thani who's here in New York. C'mon, we need to go to New York and meet the bastard," Deacon continued.

"Hold fire, pal. First, this Prince likely has diplomatic immunity, and he might have left the U.S. by now anyway. Let me contact Homeland and TSA," Mitch replied.

Within ten minutes, Mitch had confirmed the Prince and his entourage had left three days later with the same number of guards they had arrived with, but photos of him leaving didn't show the guards' faces.

Speaking on the telephone with Gerald Dobson, the General Manager of the airport, Mitch asked if there were any additional cameras located there likely to show people arriving and leaving. Dobson confirmed there wasn't, saying all passengers on international flights obviously went through the regular screening of the Customs and Border Protection department, but passengers on Diplomatic flights were offered a higher level of privacy by using the VIP terminal. Asking about the Qatari flight in question, Dobson checked and confirmed that both the aircraft and its passengers had Diplomatic Status, but a local television crew had been videoing at the same location on that day because one of the Kardashians' private jets was due to arrive shortly after the Qatari's left. Cameras had been set up earlier that morning so it was possible there might be some footage recorded. He hadn't seen any of it himself but suggested Mitch contact the TV station to check.

After heading back upstairs and informing the Admiral, Mitch managed to get the CEO of the small television company on the phone. When the CEO confirmed they had some test footage that happened to show the Qatari flight boarding, but refused to part with the video without a court order, the Admiral grabbed the phone and boomed down the line, "Listen, you little prick. This is Admiral Douglas Eugene Carter, and I am the Chief of Naval Operations at the Pentagon. This is a matter of national security, and if I have to come down there with a subpoena, I'll shove it so far up your backside it'll stick out your goddam throat. Then I'll have the FBI and Homeland Security crawling so far up your ass they'll be able to read the small print. Now stop wasting my fucking time and send us the video before I get really pissed."

After a few seconds of stunned silence, the CEO quickly agreed to release it. Mitch pointed out that all they wanted was the 30-second clip taken of the Qatari's boarding the plane and the CEO said he would get his technical people to email it as soon as they could.

While they waited in the Admiral's office, Deacon reviewed the photo repeatedly, each time becoming surer that this was the man known as Saif the Palestinian.

Eventually, after waiting for almost an hour, Mitch's email pinged with a new message arrival. The video

233

clearly showed the Prince and his four security guards, along with a number of other staffers. Three of the guards looked exactly like the photos of them arriving, but one looked slightly different - slightly taller and less muscular. The similarities were close enough to pass an initial examination, but not a detailed one. The more they watched, the clearer it became to see the differences in the build and stance the fourth guard.

"Well, gentlemen, it's pretty obvious these are two different people. It would seem they are trying to play us for fools. Unfortunately, much as I'd like to grab that little fucker by the neck, we will have to go through the State Department and make a formal request for Qatar to identify the person, due to the Prince being a Royal with diplomatic immunity and Qatar being a sovereign nation," the Admiral said.

"However, get Clark on the line and let's get the arrival photo and Deacon's photofit of both men to all news channels, law enforcement and officials in the tristate area," the Admiral continued, looking at Mitch.

"Sir, with respect, I think it should go wider. We've no idea where this Saif has gone," Deacon said.

Agreeing, the Admiral instructed Mitch to request the FBI issue the images to all regions in the northeast from New Hampshire down to North Carolina.

Following a brief but urgent call with General Dreiberg, who, in turn, spoke with the President, the Department of Defence CBRN along the east coast was placed on full alert.

# Chapter 62

## Florida - US

Arriving home early as instructed on Friday evening, Elias Shirani kissed his wife hello. She'd told him in no uncertain terms this morning to make sure they were on time today, or even early. This was the evening Zane was bringing his new friend round for dinner, and she wanted to ensure everything was tidy and welcoming. She'd already marinated some chicken ready for him to grill outside later and was just finishing preparing the salad and home-made rolls. Ushering him upstairs to have a quick shower and tidy himself up, she asked where Zane was.

"He grabbed the truck and has gone to pick her up," Elias said. "Said he'd be back in an hour or so."

Standing under the warm cascading water, he thought Zane had still been quiet all day and hoped it was just down to nervousness about the coming meeting.

With the house looking immaculate and the two of them also getting a little nervous, Elias grabbed a beer from the fridge when they heard his truck pull up outside.

Elias felt his jaw drop a little when Zane walked in and introduced Saif as Charlie Baxter. Not sure what the relationship was, and whether this meant his son was gay, Elias and his wife tried to make Zane's guest welcome, but the start of the evening was very strained. Saif said little and ate his food quietly. As the night wore on the atmosphere became more and more awkward.

Eventually, the limited conversation came round to the terrorist attack in the UK. Elias turned the TV on, and they watched the latest CNN news. Trying at least to get some conversation going, he said how terrible the attack was, and the offenders must be caught and punished. Instead of agreeing, Saif was less supportive, and Zane began talking about the evil West, the fate of the struggling ISIS and how good a caliphate would be for everyone, especially the forsaken USA.

When Elias and his wife started arguing with Zane, Saif slapped his hand down on the table and took Zane's side, agreeing that the U.S. and the West were broken, full of disbelievers and against the only one true God, Allah, and deserved everything it got.

With tensions heightened Elias was just about to ask Saif to leave, thinking he would call Homeland Security the following day about this zealot when Saif pulled a suppressed 9mm from under his jacket and shot Elias Shirani straight through the forehead. His wife was momentarily stunned as his blood dripped down her face, but before she could fully register the horror of what had happened, Saif turned and shot her twice in the chest just as a scream started welling up in her throat.

Stunned by what had just happened, Zane turned on Saif and started to attack him. With a simple sidestep and twist, Saif slapped him down to the floor.

With the hot tip of the suppressor barrel jammed up under his chin, Zane began crying as he was slapped hard across the face.

"You think this is a game? You feel sorry for them? They were disbelievers. They would have informed on us. I didn't come here to be stopped by the likes of them. You better decide whose side you're on, boy. You're either with me or against me. This is what you signed up for. You decide," he snarled, grinding the gun barrel deeper.

With tears in his eyes, partly from the shock of seeing his parents executed and partly from the pain of the hot barrel, Zane pledged his allegiance to Allah and started reciting, "My parents were disbelievers. Only Allah has the true meaning. Death to America. My parents were disbelievers. Only Allah has the true meaning. Death to America."

After what seemed an age, he felt the tension pressing the barrel under his chin slowly relax.

"You fail me, boy, and you'll be next. Now dry your eyes and become a man."

Saif went to the kitchen, grabbed a towel and wrapped it around the dead father's head to keep it in one piece. He'd been staying at a cheap motel on the edge of town since arriving in Florida with Zane. Careful not to leave a paper trail, he had paid for the room upfront in cash and had only ventured outside in the evenings when there was less chance of being seen. Zane had picked him up from there earlier in the evening, and he'd brought his possessions in the truck.

Between them, they carried the bodies one at a time and placed them in the freezer in the garage. Saif then reversed Zane's truck in and removed the two 100-litre plastic containers and holdalls that he had been keeping under his bed in the motel and put them in the garage as well.

Closing the garage door, Saif put his arm around Zane's shoulders and led him back into the house, shutting the door behind them.

Zane was terrified his beating heart could be heard. His mind was racing ... How had he gotten into this mess? The emails and videos he'd watched had been adventurous - fight back against an oppressive government, help the underdog - but now this mad bastard had murdered his parents in cold blood. This wasn't what he'd signed up for. He wasn't a murderer. He hadn't wanted his parents to die. How could he get away without being killed?

Making sure he did nothing to upset Saif, Zane had a very uncomfortable night.

# Chapter 63

## Fredericksburg, Virginia

Friday night was fun night for Officer Brad Millar. It was the start of the holiday weekend, Monday being the 4th July, and he and his colleagues would be working full shifts and overtime for the next three days, what with parades and all. But not tonight. Tonight he was off duty, and it was an evening for beers, chicken wings and a few games of pool in the local bar with friends and colleagues.

On his third beer and after winning two games and losing one, he had just ordered some nachos from Trish, the barmaid, as chasers to the wings when the local news channel came on the TV above the bar. The images of the photo and two photofits flashed up behind the female newsreader. Shouting to the barman, Hank, to turn it up, Brad shouted to his colleagues for quiet so he could listen.

The newsreader was stating that police, and the FBI were looking for these 'persons of interest' in connection with immigration issues and that anyone with information as to their whereabouts should call the 1-800 number shown below.

As the screen changed to the next news item, Officer Millar sat thinking. The photo and one of the photofit pictures looked familiar, but he couldn't quite remember where. He took another swig of beer when it suddenly came to him. It looked a lot like the older one of the two guys he'd met last week when Joe, drunk as usual, had started that fight in the trucker's bar on the edge of town. The ticker tape line at the bottom of the news screen was still showing the 1-800 number, so calling to Trish to hold the nachos and look after his beer; he decided to head back to the office to call it in.

Shirley, the receptionist, looked up in surprise when Brad walked back through the door.

"What'cha forget, hon?"

"Nothing, babe, work to do, that's all," he replied, walking over to his desk. "Anything new come in recently?" he asked.

"Just these latest alerts. I've already copied them and put them on the Chief's desk. Here ya go," she said, handing them over.

Flipping through them he saw the top one was of a DUI suspect, the second was a report of a breaking and entering, and the third was a BOLO, a be-on-the-lookout notice, with the same pictures he'd seen on TV.

The contact number was for the J. Edgar Hoover Building, FBI Headquarters, in Washington.

Cursing under his breath, Officer Millar got out his notepad and picked up the phone.

# Chapter 64

## Washington - July 2nd

Mitch's phone rang at 06:20 am. The Admiral was always an early riser, and he ordered Mitch and Deacon to meet him and Simon Clark at the J. Edgar Hoover FBI building at 935 Pennsylvania Avenue at 08:00 am.

After parking, they hurried up to the main building concourse. A cute brown-haired receptionist took their names and then walked them to an elevator, reached in and pressed '5' and then left them. When the doors opened, Simon Clark was waiting for them, along with the Admiral. Sitting down in his corner office, Clark ordered coffee for them all then pulled up a screen on his wall display.

"Gentlemen, since the pictures were published last evening, we've had over 500 calls, and we are expecting more as the day goes on. Agents and local police will be following up with each and every one, but we expect the majority to end up being false. Some of that is because the public is eager to help, some down to the poor quality photo, but we hope 10 - 15% to be genuine potential sightings that need investigating. Unfortunately, we've received calls from as far afield as LA to Nova Scotia, so the effort today is in checking and ruling them out as quickly as possible," Clark said.

"So can I ask why we are here? You could have covered this by telephone?" Deacon asked.

"We break these calls down into probabilities," Clark replied. "Those from callers who seem less sure, or only saw a glance are rated lower than some others, although as I said, all will be followed up. However, when we get a call from someone like a police officer, we rate those pretty highly."

"And?"

"And we got a possible sighting from a Fredericksburg patrol cop about two hour's drive away. He called in late last evening, and he's pretty sure the photo and photofit match a person he saw just over a week ago in Fredericksburg. I was going to get one of my agents to go visit him then thought you might like to deal with it yourself," he added.

"I'm in," Deacon said. "What else did the patrol cop say?""He was called to a fight at a trucker's bar on the edge of town. A local drunk had shot his mouth off at two guys passing through. One was young; the other was possibly your guy. The drunk swung a punch and knocked over a server, spilling her drinks. The barman called in the local police, and Officer Brad Millar attended. The barman made it clear to Millar who started what and the drunk spent the night in the tank. Millar says he checked these two guys' id's and all seemed fine. One was from Orlando, Florida. The other had a Philly address. He's the one in the photos. He didn't make a note of their names as it was a clear case of too much drink, but he said he would have remembered if that guy's name had been Saif. First one was called Zach or similar. And he thought the other was called Charlie something," Clark said.

# Chapter 65

## Fredericksburg, Virginia

Thirty minutes later Deacon pulled out into traffic in a dark blue Government Issue sedan straight onto Interstate 95 South. Clark had granted him the car after agreeing for him to follow up the lead on his own. Being a Saturday, the traffic was light, and he made quick time, and 53 miles later he pulled left off the Interstate, past the shopping centre and into Fredericksburg Police Department, Cowan Blvd. Parking in a visitor's bay, he walked into reception.

The female receptionist behind the desk asked if she could help him and he explained he was there to see Officer Millar.

"I'm sorry Officer Millar is out on patrol. He's not expected back until lunchtime," she said.

"Can you contact him, please? He is expecting me. My name is Lieutenant Deacon."

She picked up the handset, and after pressing a few buttons, and speaking with Millar, she turned to Deacon and said, "Brad says he was expecting you. He's on his way back into town. He suggested you meet him at the diner just along from here in about fifteen minutes."

Thanking her, Deacon walked back outside and along to Joe's Diner, took a corner seat and ordered a large black coffee.

Twenty minutes later he saw a Highway Patrol car pull into the parking lot, and a fresh-faced officer entered the diner moments later.

"Lieutenant, I'm Brad Millar," he said, recognising Deacon in his BDUs. "Sorry to have kept you waiting."

"No problem, Officer Millar. Call me John. Can I get you a coffee?"

"I'm Brad and no need, Cheryl's already pouring one for me," he said as the server brought one over. "Cheryl, honey, put these on my tab, will ya?"

"Much appreciated. You know why I'm here?" Deacon said.

"Sure do, the FBI called me this morning and told me they were sending someone down. Didn't know it would be military, like. So ask away. What do you want to know?"

Looking at Brad Millar, Deacon thought him to be an ordinary good honest cop. He was regular height and build, not like some of the overweight ones portrayed on TV, and he appeared to be attentive.

"Brad, the person or persons we are after are here illegally. We believe they mean harm to this country and we believe they were involved in the tragedy in the UK. Not directly responsible, but involved. How sure are you this is the same person?" he asked while passing over the photos.

Millar looked carefully at the photo and then at the photofits. He passed one back saying this definitely wasn't the younger person. With the other, he stared for quite a few minutes.

"Yup, I'm ninety-nine percent sure this was him," he said.

"OK, tell me everything you can about that evening,"

"Got the call about 20:50 pm from despatch. The barman had called it in a few minutes earlier, saying trouble was brewing. Old Joe was drunk again and shouting at some customer. I was close by so they passed the call to me. I guess it was maybe five minutes later I pulled up. There were two males, possibly Hispanic having a meal. One was early twenties, the other maybe early to mid-fifties. Joe had been drinking heavily and had started verbally abusing the younger one. The older one told him to butt out when Joe swung a punch at him, missed and knocked over Patsy, the waitress. That's when we were called. Joe, by now, had passed out on the floor, so I took him to my cruiser, and he spent a night in the cells. The two persons declined to press charges. I checked their id's, just routine. All seemed OK, so I left and took Joe back to the station."

Deacon asked specific questions about the two men, whether they had accents, what their names were, and where they were headed.

Brad Millar answered as truthfully as possible but couldn't remember much more detail than he had the night before when he'd called the FBI hotline.

"John, they were just normal guys. They were both lean. Not muscled particularly, but fit looking. They both had tanned skins, could have been anything from Hispanic-Latino, Mediterranean, Arabic or even Jewish, I guess, although if I had to choose, I'd go for Hispanic-Latino's. They didn't have any particular accents either. They sounded like ordinary Americans to me. Sorry to be vague, but that's all I've got. I didn't write the incident up 'cus there were no charges laid, and we just let old Joe go after he'd sobered up some. He's a regular for us." Brad said.

Realising that he'd gathered as much information as he could, they talked for another ten minutes or so before Deacon thanked Millar for his help, and left. Turning around just before he reached the door, he walked back and asked Millar if there was an outlet clothing shop nearby.

Before re-joining the Interstate north, Deacon, following directions, drove through the town and found an Old Navy store. Having flown from Iraq to Washington, there had been a lack of places to purchase civilian clothes. With only his standard issue of BDU's and military clothing with him, he had quickly realised he needed to be able to blend in better with the locals. Purchasing three pairs of cargo pants and five polo shirts, be dropped them in the trunk before he started the drive back to Washington.

# Chapter 66

## Florida - US

Zane and Saif were praying together. They'd started with the Salat al-fajr at dawn, and were waiting for noon so they could perform the Salat al-zuhr. After this morning's praying, Saif had sat Zane down and carefully explained the plan to him, covering it in enough detail to answer Zane's questions.

Finishing their prayers, they waited long enough to eat a quick lunch before taking Elias's work truck, with Zane driving. Today was Saturday, and the plan called for a dry run in preparation for the coming Monday.

They switched on the air conditioning to try to overcome the high humidity. Florida in the summer months was never comfortable, but this year seemed worse than most, and they were suffering. They drove in silence the forty minutes it took to reach the site. Traffic was heavier than usual being the start of the 3-day holiday weekend and Zane was already nervous. Arriving at the entrance gate, Zane had to stop at the barrier and present his pass.

"Just relax and act normal. You're shaking," Saif said.

Trying to calm his nerves and shaking hands, Zane pressed his sweating fingers to the button to lower his window.

"Hi, Zane. How'ya doing?" the guard asked. "Hey, where's the old man?" he said, looking over at Saif.

"H … he's in bed with the flu. He's sick, so I got a colleague helping me today."

"Flu? In this goddam weather? Only your old man could catch flu when it's this friggin' hot. You gotta pass, pal?" he said, hand outstretched to Saif.

Handing it over, Saif smiled as the guard checked the name and photo before giving it back.

"Well, you guys have fun. Give my best to your Pop," the guard said as he pressed the button to raise the barrier.

Smiling and raising a hand in thanks, Zane accelerated and drove into the site, closing the window.

"You did well. That was the hardest part. Now relax and think of this as just another typical day," Saif said, slapping Zane on the shoulder. "Tell me again what the usual routine is."

Over the next five minutes, as they drove around the back of the secondary building and parked, Zane explained, "It's a two-day schedule. At any time, one is active, and the other is standby. When the active one is down to 5%, it automatically changes over to the other and raises a flag electronically that it needs refilling. There's enough capacity in the system to run for three days, but we generally attend every second or as soon as the flag's raised. We refill the empty one, reset the counters, flush the system, and that's about it. Takes 'bout half hour. Pretty simple, really."

Insisting they keep to the exact same routine as normal, Saif grabbed the tool bag and helped Zane carry out the work.

Forty minutes later, they drove slowly back towards the exit. They both smiled and raised their hands and waved to the guard who nodded and waved back. He'd already pressed the button to raise the barrier from within his air-conditioned gatehouse - not wanting to step out into that high humidity.

As they cleared the compound, Zane visibly relaxed.

248

"That was easy, we've done it," he said.

"No, not yet, my brother. But I agree, it was easy. My plans always are. We just need to keep cool heads and do exactly the same Monday. It will be as God wills. Allahu Akbar," he said.

The guard filled in the official contractor visitor paperwork showing their names and arrival and departure time. In the description field, he wrote 'Routine'.

What the guard would never know was the only difference today was they had not filled the drum as much as normal. This would ensure it would run low sooner and the flag would be raised early on the morning of the 4th, requiring a guaranteed visit that day.

# Chapter 67

## The Pentagon - Washington

Arriving back at the J Edgar Hoover building Deacon found Mitch waiting for him in Simon Clark's office. Opening his notebook Deacon discussed with both of them everything Officer Millar had said.

"So do you think he was your man?" Clark said.

"Yeah, highly likely. Millar was pretty damn certain. He seems a good cop, so I'll take him at his word."

"Let me bring you up to speed on what's been happening this morning," Clark said before the three of them sat down.

"We've received confirmation back from the Chinese manufacturers of this crop-spraying drone. They've sold 42 in the last six months to U.S. based companies or individuals here countrywide. They've provided addresses to all of them, but five are to PO Boxes. I got agents and local police checking them all, as we speak. From the addresses, most are over in California being used in vineyards around the hilly regions of Napa Valley. Some are being used in the Carolinas, Georgia, Alabama and Florida in the cotton growing business. They're being used to spray insecticide in awkward locations. Each is being investigated and the machines examined and confiscated. We've also increased surveillance on the terrorist watch list of known suspects in all those states," Clark said.

"But we don't know where the next attack will happen."

"No, we don't. Not even which state it'll occur in or when, but we have to assume it'll be Monday. We're getting together a list of all 4th July celebration parades, but almost every town is holding one. We don't even know where to start," Clark said. "We've also increased surveillance on the terrorist watch list and of the No Fly list from TSC of known troublemakers in all these states, and quite a number are unaccounted for so far. We are already increasing it to all 52 states, but we're running out of manpower. Security is tight everywhere, and every law enforcement department is on full alert, but unless we can narrow it down some, we're fighting a losing battle here."

The next few hours were spent discussing various ways they could attempt to narrow down the search criteria and to listening to reports coming in from the field agents and police. Officers had visited one cotton-growing site near Birmingham, Alabama, to find the building closed up. They obtained an immediate court order to enter the premises and found most of the equipment and personal possessions missing. There was no sign of the drone delivered five months previously, but speaking with the neighbours, it seemed the owners had finally gone bust and had filed for Chapter 15 Bankruptcy. As the drone location couldn't be verified, the owners were being put on a 'Wanted Persons' list and, as time was urgent, a BOLO had been issued for their immediate apprehension.

In another case, the Californian ranch owners had sold their drone after not being impressed with its efficiency. The police had followed up trying to trace the new owners but to no avail. Again, these names were added to the 'Wanted Persons' list, and an additional BOLO was issued.

In most other instances, the drones were located, and the owners questioned. All answers were checked and the equipment inspected and, in some cases, confiscated. By the end of the day, 37 out of the possible 42 drones had been accounted for, and a number of the missing people from the No Fly list found and identified.

By late afternoon, the Admiral had arrived. He was quickly brought up to speed on the current situation and the bigger problem of trying to determine the expected target. He sat there thinking for a few minutes, then stood and went to the whiteboard on the wall.

"The problem is, I believe, too much choice. Correct?" he said.

Seeing them all nod, he continued, "We have to make some assumptions. First, let's assume the person seen in Fredericksburg is the terrorist known as Saif the Palestinian. He obviously has help so there are at least two of them. They were heading south, so Washington is unlikely to be the target. That still leaves a lot of country to consider, though. If it's big cities they're after then they're spoilt for choice. Far too many to choose from. From a military perspective, there are two primary targets. Norfolk Naval Base and Fort Bragg, just outside Fayetteville. Attacks at either of these could be devastating. Even if personnel weren't actually exposed themselves, this VX Agent would cover equipment and buildings and would make the whole area uninhabitable for weeks. That would put our national security at extreme risk. Our entire Atlantic, Mediterranean and Indian Ocean fleets are based in Norfolk, and if that were out of action, even for a short while, we'd be incredibly exposed. Bragg, as you may know, is our largest army base in the world. There's over 50,000 personnel stationed there and is home to various other services including the Special Operations Group. There are other military installations around, but these two are our largest and would be my first choice if I wanted to harm the U.S."

"Holy shit, Admiral. You make a good case," Clark said, his face losing colour. "How the hell do we protect them?"

"We need a ten-mile total exclusion zone around both entire camps. No-one in or out the zones unless authorised. Full military law within those zones with full shoot-to-kill authorisation. We've seen what ten litres of VX can do in the UK. We believe the bastards are planning on using twenty times as much here. "

"Will the President authorise that, sir?" Mitch asked.

"Not a fucking chance, Mitch. He doesn't have the balls. However, I can put Norfolk on lockdown, and General Ransworthy can do the same at Bragg. We can have patrols out covering a ten-mile radius with authority to stop anyone launching drones using deadly force if necessary. We can also limit outside exposure of personnel and have any that have to be outside wearing full MOPP Level 4 gear. CBRN teams are already on standby. We can also mobilise the National Guard to assist. The President won't be happy, but he'll agree to this. He won't have a goddam choice."

"Sir, with all due respect, what if it's not a military target?" Deacon said.

"What makes you say that, Lieutenant?"

"It's just ISIS and even Al-Qaeda before always aimed at inspiring terror. The Twin Towers, the London bombings, the Paris attacks; now Glastonbury and the beach. None were military targets. They were deemed worse by the public because it hits home to them how exposed they are just going about their normal daily lives. Soldiers expect to be attacked, Joe public doesn't. So just wondering if it will be civilian, like these latest UK attacks, sir."

"Well that, Lieutenant, is where we have to take a gamble. I suggest you, Mitch and Director Clark here work on the theory that I'm wrong. You coordinate with the other agencies on the assumption that the target is civilian. I would start with the largest cities as they have the largest parades and also look at the busiest beaches, assuming this is all planned for the day after tomorrow. If I was a gambling man, and I'm not, I'd start with Jacksonville, Tampa and Miami based on the fact they were heading south, and the other guy with Saif showed a Florida licence. That licence might be fake, but they might not have been expecting to get stopped so his may have been genuine."

Leaving the others to continue their discussions, Admiral Carter left and headed back to the Pentagon to meet with General Dreiberg and General Tarrant - Secretary of Defence, to advise and brief the President.

Deacon, Mitch and Director Clark spent the rest of the afternoon listing the various cities in Florida, Alabama, Georgia and the Carolinas, in population size order. Clark then sent official warnings of potential attacks to the Governors of each state, along with alerting the Police Chiefs of the cities identified.

Back in Mitch and Helen's apartment later that evening, after yet another enjoyable meal of steamed Tilapia, salad and potatoes, Mitch opened a second chilled bottle of Pouilly-Fuissé. Pouring three glasses, he passed them around as Helen turned the TV on to get the latest headlines.

The late evening news bulletins had already played, and it was coming up towards the second advert break when the presenter announced, "Coming next, tonight's Special Report with Lynda Anderson in an exclusive interview with released hostage Laura Williams. Is our military out of control?" and then the screen went to adverts.

"Who's Lynda Anderson?" Deacon asked.

"She's one of these 'new age' reporters," Mitch said, "She's into exposing criminal activities within government agencies, the military and even the police. She's a real hard-hitter, a real mean bitch. She's won numerous journalistic awards, I think. She was based in the Middle East, but she's here in Washington now. Not someone you want to tangle with. She's one of the ones chasing your story. She's the one whose been hassling the Admiral, but he won't bend. He calls her the pit bull, but not to her face, mind you."

"Is she really that bad?"

"Unfortunately so. I would guess she's one of the most feared journalists here in Washington. She broke the story six months back or so about a stray drone in Afghanistan that crashed and killed three families. The government were trying to keep it quiet, but she went to the village where it happened and got footage of the remaining people living there. Lots of news coverage and eventually the Major who'd authorised the drone flight had to resign, and the sergeant who piloted it got demoted, although it was actually a technical fault that caused the crash. She's a bit of a painful thorn in the backside and won't take no for an answer."

With that, the adverts finished, and the news presenter came back on the screen and announced, "Now, tonight's Special Report with Lynda Anderson. Over to you, Lynda."

Lynda Anderson, intrepid reporter to some, tenacious pit bull to others then launched into her introduction and story. She repeated much of what Laura Williams had said before about how the U.S. Navy SEAL team had rescued Laura and her friends, but her version made it seem the girls hadn't really been in any danger. Although she praised the bravery of the SEALs involved, as well as praising the courage of all the U.S. Armed Services, she started to question the possible lack of authority and responsibility.

"We have some of the bravest fighters in the world, and we send them into some of the most dangerous places to do our military's bidding. We give them the best training and the latest and most powerful weapons. We provide them with the power to complete the job. But as we know, power corrupts, and absolute power corrupts absolutely. Who polices them? Who makes sure they stay within limits? And who sets those limits? We, the public, have a right to know. We, the public DEMAND to know. Are our armed services out of control? Brave though they may be, are our Special Forces killing whoever they can? We need to hold them to account."

She then introduced Laura who again repeated her story, but this time it sounded like the girls were enjoying an excellent holiday camp when the nasty U.S. Navy SEALs broke in and took them away, having killed as many of the helpful and friendly holiday camp wardens as possible.

Hardly able to believe what he was hearing, Deacon just looked at Helen and Mitch, mouth open.

"Hey pal, don't worry. The story's shit. You know it. I know it. So does the Admiral. It'll all be forgotten about by tomorrow, you'll see," Mitch said, quietly hoping this to be true. "Anyway, back to business," he urged, turning the TV off, and the discussion again centred on what they knew of the impending attack.

Picking up her empty glass, Helen went to the kitchen to get some water, leaving the boys to carry on talking.

"But what if there are, say, 20 simultaneous attacks on 20 cities or so? How do we stop that?" Mitch said.

"You have a good point, but I think it's unlikely. There are not 20 drones that are unaccounted for, and they'd need at least the same number of people to pilot them. Obviously, it's possible, but I think we are only talking about one or two attacks, the same as in the UK."

"So we're back to trying to second guess which city. OK, let's go through them again."

Over the next few minutes or so, they ran through the list they'd made earlier, comparing population size with celebration parade routes, route access, numbers of high-rise buildings, trees — every viable permutation they could think of that could affect the use of drones and spraying.

Getting nowhere, Mitch was just in the process of ripping up yet another list when Helen walked back in from the lounge and everything changed.

# Chapter 68

"It could be Jacksonville, but it could also be Orlando," Mitch said, his voice beginning to fade a little with frustration.

"You know, whenever I think of Orlando, I think of the theme parks," Helen said, walking in to top up her glass.

"What? Say that again!" Deacon said, looking up sharply.

"I just said that whenever I think of Orlando, I think of the theme parks. Why?"

"Oh fuck! What if we've been looking at this the wrong way? The Admiral's correct in that it makes sense for it to be a military target. And, if so, Norfolk or Bragg would seem likely. But we've been assuming that if it's a civilian target, and with Monday being the 4th July, then any attack would likely be at the parades. What if they flew over the parks? Even a couple of drones spraying over those crowds … and if they had multiple drones over multiple parks … . My God, it would make Glastonbury pale into insignificance," Deacon said, his voice fading at the end.

"John, you could be right. 4th July is always the busiest day of the year at the parks, second only to over the Christmas period. Summer vacation time, weather's hot, school's out, and this year it makes it a long weekend. There could be up to a half million people in total. Jeez, I think you're onto to something," Mitch replied, ashen faced.

A few minutes later Mitch called the Admiral's home line and conferenced Simon Clark into the call. Within ten minutes they'd all agreed the four of them needed to meet back at FBI headquarters within the hour.

Arriving a little early, they managed to park in the partly empty car park and waited in reception. As expected with any major security organisation, the offices never closed. Night time was usually quieter with less staff, but the current state of emergency meant everyone was working double or even triple shifts.

An agent started to escort them upstairs just as the Admiral arrived. It was 12:30 am on the morning of July 3rd.

Waiting in the main conference room were various agents and the video conferencing system was already running with quite a few heads of department connected, many of them from their homes. The screen refreshed yet again, and the situation room beneath the White House appeared with the faces of the President and his chief advisors, including Gen. Mansfield and Gen. Dreiberg.

"Gentlemen, I think we all know each other, so introductions aren't necessary. What news do you have to get us out of bed this late or early in the morning?" the President asked.

"Mr President," Admiral Carter began, "We believe, based on reasonable assumptions, that the attack or attacks are highly likely to take place tomorrow. From a political perspective, any successful attack on our 4th July would cause major embarrassment to you and this administration and offer the most gain to the perpetrators. We still cannot confirm whether the attacks will be aimed at civilians or the military and we already have Norfolk and Fort Bragg on full alert. However, if the attacks are civilian-based, Lieutenants Stringer and Deacon have come up with what I believe to be the likeliest scenario. With your permission, I'd like to hand over to Lieutenant Stringer?"

"Granted. Please proceed."

Rising to the floor in front of the conference screen, Mitch began, "Mr President. Sirs. Lieutenant Deacon and I have spent many hours going over a whole range of scenarios based on the civilian attack being aimed at one, or a number, of 4th July parades. We assumed, and I now believe wrongly, sir, that the parades would be the target. We now believe the theme parks in Orlando to be a more viable scenario."

"How do you come to that conclusion, Lieutenant?"

"Sir, the more we thought about the UK attacks, the clearer it became. The public was deliberately targeted, not the military; it was soft targets and designed to attack men, women and children equally. I think we all agree that is part of what makes it so outrageous. That's why we personally believe that it will be a civilian attack and not against the military. Secondly, the person seen with the man known as Saif had an Orlando licence that was possibly genuine. Thirdly, although an attack on a 4th July parade would be an enormous coup, attacking the 'happiest place on Earth' would be far greater. We believe the psychological damage to the American people of a major attack in Orlando would be devastating. Like Pearl Harbour in '41 and the Twin Towers attack on 9/11, the emotional damage would last far longer than the actual loss."

Raising a finger to interrupt, General Dreiberg asked, "Lieutenant. There are what, 16 or so parks down there? Which one do you think is the target?"

"That, Sir, is the sixty-four thousand dollar question. We believe if they only hit one or two parks then the largest and most famous will be first. However, we understand they have up to twenty times the amount of VX available. It's possible there could be at least one attack on each park. However, we cannot confirm this. Director Clark's people have been checking the whereabouts of all the spray drones sent to the U.S. from the Chinese manufacturer, and all but five have been accounted for, and four of those missing are in California. Also, any simultaneously timed attack would need multiple people to instigate, and there is no evidence of that."

Everyone seemed to start talking all at once, some trying to shout down Mitch.

At that stage, Admiral Carter again took to the floor.

"Mr President, Gentlemen. Please! The Lieutenant's views are based on best guesses and assumptions. They and I realise they could be wrong, and they would be the first to agree there are some holes in their logic, but it's the best guess based on knowledge, experience and knowing how evil these bastards are. I would also like to stress Lieutenant Stringer has a higher than average batting score for guesswork. He's the best I've come across for analysing raw data and making sense of it. Partner him with Lieutenant Deacon here and, well, some of you know how damn good the Lieutenant is at thinking on his feet and weighing up a situation."

Sitting back down he nodded to Mitch to continue.

"Sirs, there are many 'don't know's'. We only know of two people so far, neither of them being the two identified in the UK. We don't know what involvement or support the state of Qatar has given to this, we don't know how many drones will be used, and we don't actually know the target. I'm sorry, Mr President, it's all guesswork, but it's the best we can come to at the moment."

In the few minutes of silence that followed, Deacon raised a hand.

"Mr President, Admiral. May I address the audience, sir?"

"Go ahead, Lieutenant," the President said.

"Sirs, while Mitch was talking I was just thinking. Why bother with five, ten or twenty drones. Why not just get a crop sprayer and fly one long pass over all the parks? You'd hit all of them that way, all 400,000 people there. It's the way I'd do it."

It took almost five minutes for the uproar to quieten down before Admiral Carter finally brought the meeting back to order.

# Chapter 69

"GENTLEMEN! Gentlemen. Mr President. OK, whether the target is the parks or the military we need suggestions how to stop this. One at a time, please."

"The FAA can issue an immediate No Fly zone for all private aircraft within a twenty mile radius around Fort Bragg, Norfolk Naval Yard and Orlando, although with the airport at Orlando there would have to be safe corridors for emergencies," Secretary of Defence General Melvin Tarrant said from his home office over the conference call. "Mr President, you'd need to issue a temporary Executive Order placing those No Fly zones under military rule, and the FAA will enforce it," he continued.

"Approved. How soon can it be implemented?" the President said.

"It can begin immediately with a one-hour transition period, sir."

"Mr President. We can have agents and local police guarding every small and private airfield in and around those zones. We can make sure nothing takes to the skies," FBI Director Clark said.

"Mr President. Will you authorise the Air Force with a shoot-down policy for any aircraft breaking the No Fly zone?" Secretary of Defence Tarrant asked.

After pausing and thinking for a couple of minutes, the President answered, "Melvin, I want the Air Force patrolling those skies. Any unauthorised aircraft is to be forced to leave the zone and land. If they evade or refuse to comply, as a last resort, I will grant you the authority to authorise the selective use of deadly force. Understood?"

The President then asked what other measures could be used and couldn't the signals that control the drones be jammed. Over the next few minutes, an FBI technician stood up and explained the situation.

"Sirs, most drones work by a command from remote controller devices that transmit and operate in the 2.4 and 5.8 GHz frequency bands. If you jammed everything in the 2-3 and 5-6 GHz bands, then they wouldn't be able to be controlled remotely. However, many other devices that would also be blocked also use those frequency bands. This includes all cordless phones, Bluetooth devices, Wi-Fi, wireless routers, and even some garage openers. Within the theme parks, it would also disable all the remote EFTPOS tills, and most, if not all, of the safety systems on the rides. Finally, sirs, we believe the drones used in the UK attacks had been pre-programmed to fly a particular route. If that was the case, then jamming these frequencies is unlikely to make any difference as the drone assumes complete control using GPS and isn't transmitting or receiving on these frequencies."

"Couldn't we block the GPS signals?"

"Not in such a small area, Mr President. We'd have to switch off the coverage for the whole of the south-east, and that would effectively close that section of the country down as too many critical systems nowadays rely on GPS signals."

Admiral Carter took to the floor again. "Mr President, gentlemen. I propose I move all non-allocated SEALs from Coronado and Little Creek and deploy them to surround the theme park's perimeters, but dressed in civilian clothing to allay the public. The Marines have already been deployed to guard Norfolk. I will also put an E-2 Hawkeye early warning aircraft over Orlando for the next 48 hours starting 06:00 today. It will detect anything bigger than a trash can flying. This will remove worries of crop-dusting fixed or rotary wing aircraft flying near or over the theme parks. I will have a couple of F/A-18 Hornet fighters, one in the air and the other on two-minute standby out of Pensacola approximately 15 mins flying time away to work alongside the Air Force. There are many small unmanned airfields in Florida some formerly used for drug smuggling, but the Hawkeye will see anything that moves across all of Florida. Any drones actually seen flying either from the air or from Deacon and his men on the ground will initiate an immediate jamming of all associated frequencies between 2-3 and 5-6 GHz from an EA-18G Growler electronic warfare aircraft flying overhead. But, we will instigate the jamming only once a drone attack has been positively identified due to the extensive problems jamming these frequencies in Orlando will likely produce. I can also put another Hawkeye and 18G Growler over Virginia to cover Fort Bragg and Norfolk. Agreed sir?"

The president pondered for over five minutes, fingers clasped, as he wrestled with the suggested options, before finally concluding.

"Not the ideal solution. The easiest would be for me to cancel all 4th July events and close all the theme parks until we catch these bastards, but I am not willing to do that. I also want the National Guard on standby, and I want to address the country at 8:00 pm Eastern this evening. Approved in principle. I want this documented and on my desk by 09:00 this morning," he said.

With that, the conference call ended, and the Admiral, Deacon, Mitch and Clark all let out a collective sigh of relief.

<>< ><>

265

The following two hours were spent discussing the plan in more detail. The Admiral issued orders for the aircraft deployment and then the discussions centred on the role of Deacon and the other SEALs.

"Admiral, Mitch and I have worked out the approximate perimeters of all the parks. It's a total of just less than 90 miles," Deacon said. "I suggest we have local police patrolling the park's perimeters at half-mile intervals. That means we need around two hundred officers on the ground. In between them, we have the SEALs. We have a total of thirty-five drone rifles available, which we will disperse around the group. The rest, including the police, will be issued with shotguns with filament cartridges. Let me explain what I mean."

With that, Deacon went to the whiteboard and picked up a marker pen.

"The problem with trying to shoot down a drone is fairly obvious. Anything you fire up comes down somewhere, so solid cartridges are a no-no in a built up area. Conventional birdshot works fine, but usually, that results in the drone crashing. It also doesn't stop someone triggering an explosion. A crash of a drone could either trigger it to explode or, in the case of it carrying a bioweapon, may even cause it to spill its contents. Knowing the problems, filament cartridges were invented by our UK colleagues in the SAS. Drones are becoming an issue in the UK, flying over football matches, etc. Under pressure from the UK Government to do something, the SAS designed ammunition specifically to take them out. Drones don't fly very fast, and you merely aim and fire in its path. It's easier than clay pigeon shooting. Hundreds of thin, strong nylon filaments are deployed and tangle into the drone's propellers causing it to stall and land. It's not a perfect solution and the drone may still land heavily and break open and could still be triggered remotely to explode. However, any explosion would be localised, and it does get it down out of the sky quickly and with minimal damage. These cartridges can also be safely used in built-up areas."

He continued, "We also have the drone rifles. Unlike jamming signals over a complete area that causes all the problems we heard about earlier, a drone rifle aims high-powered radio waves in a very tight cone. The rifles have two aerials located along its barrel, and you point them as with any rifle. The two antennas completely swamp the receiving capability of the drone. It transmits very high power in the GPS and ISM bands which not only stops the device from receiving signals from the controller including any signal to detonate, it also scrambles the GPS signals the drone receives, thereby preventing it flying any pre-programmed courses. The signals are pulsed which also interferes with the rotor speed and causes the drone to land gently as long as the rifle is still pointing at it. The rifles have an effective range of up to a half-mile."

"Well that's certainly safer than blowing them out of the sky, especially if they contain VX Agent," Mitch added.

"Sir, all the SEALs will be dressed in civilian clothing, and I would suggest the police do the same. Weapons can be hidden from view, which will keep any public awareness to a minimum. Personally, I think the main and most famous parks will be the target, being these are the ones everyone knows and would have the most international publicity. The others are either smaller or just less famous," Deacon said, finally sitting down again.

FBI Director Clark agreed for Deacon to fly down to Orlando later that morning in one of their corporate jets.

The Admiral sat there for a while just thinking. Eventually, nodding slowly, he said, "Lieutenant, everything you say is based on sound logic. I agree with your conclusions, and I will add it to the report for the President. I hope you're right. If not, the results could be horrific, and we might both be looking for new jobs."

# Chapter 70

## Orlando - July 3rd

The FBI Gulfstream touched down at 07:23 am at Orlando Executive Airport, just outside the central financial district of Orlando. As the aircraft door opened and the inbuilt steps swung down a dark grey sedan pulled up. As Deacon walked down the steps, a large heavy set man stepped out and welcomed him.

"Aaron Baker, VP of theme park security. You must be Lieutenant Deacon?" he said, extending a bloated hand.

After acknowledging and returning the gesture, Deacon dropped his bag in the trunk and then climbed in the passenger seat. As they exited the airport, Baker said, "Lieutenant, you're wasting your time. Simon Clark of the FBI called me again this morning. I know he's concerned about some possible terrorist attack, but we really have everything covered here. What most people don't realise is we have hundreds of cameras throughout the parks. Most are hidden or disguised, so the public doesn't understand virtually every movement they make is being monitored. We get to see some pretty raunchy behaviour, I can tell you, especially in the water parks. Apart from that, we have over 1,000 security staff in security clothing, with another 500 or so wearing casual clothing mingling with the public. On top of all that, all the costume wearers are also instructed to be aware and report back anything suspicious. Day-to-day security is paramount at all the parks from simple things such as pick-pockets to anyone being drunk and disorderly. And everybody entering gets their bags searched. Let me tell you, no goddam Arab terrorist is gonna ruin our 4th July celebrations. We've got it pretty well sewn up down here, so I think you've made a wasted journey, son."

Realising this was an issue that he needed to address urgently, Deacon waited a few moments in silence and looked straight ahead through the windshield. Finally, he said, "Do you carry a weapon, Mr Baker?"

"Call me Aaron, son, and no I don't. Don't need one. My pappy taught me how to fight when I was ten, and I've never lost a fight since. Why do you ask?"

"Listen, you smug sonofabitch. I could reach over there and snap your neck with one hand, while steering the car with my other, and we wouldn't even cross the white lines, all while you piss your pants as you die," Deacon said in a low voice tinged with venom.

"Wha ... what the fuck?"

"Your 'pappy' may have taught you how to fight, but I'm a killer. Do you want to go a few rounds and find out?"

"W ... w ... what? What's your problem, man?" Baker spluttered, sweat beads forming on his brow.

"Listen up. You may be able to fight and might even win some, but I'm a trained killer. We're worlds apart. I know more ways to kill you than you've had hot dinners. Now we are not up against terrorists who'll turn up and stand in queues waiting to be searched by Mickey fucking Mouse. We're talking aerial attack of a chemical so deadly that just one drop on your skin will kill you. Personally, I don't give a rats ass whether you live or die, but I am worried about the other half million or so visitors who might. Do I make myself clear?" Deacon said.

He continued, "In case you've missed the news, over 17,000 people died in the UK last week after being exposed to the same shit that's likely here. But we think there's as much as twenty times more going to be used

270

here. This stuff won't come in through the front door or wait in line. It'll come from the skies, so unless you plan to give Goofy a fucking ground to air missile, I suggest we start this conversation again. Agreed?"

A visibly shaken Baker hastily agreed, so Deacon asked to be taken to the Combined Command and Control Centre, usually referred to as C4.

Arriving a short time later, Aaron Baker showed Deacon around the two-floor building. It was very similar in design, but slightly smaller, to the one at the Pentagon that Deacon had used. Instead of each theme park, or group of parks, having to rely on their own control room and staff, since 9/11 security had been stepped up and a combined approach had been taken. This provided the same level of support whether the park was large or small. The buildings' ground floor had a curved end wall and was covered with thirty-six large LCD TV screens mounted close together. Each screen was split into three or four smaller windows showing various views of the many parks. The central twenty screens showed the larger more popular parks while the nine screens on each side covered the lesser known ones, including some of the water parks.

In front of the large screens were multiple desks, each containing a computer screen and each currently manned. Around the edges of the office was a mezzanine level, looking down into the central operations area.

Realising his error earlier, Baker explained, "The supervisors are on the first floor. They each have an area of responsibility and one or more staff on this lower level report to them. We can pull up any image from any camera and enlarge and zoom in. All camera feeds are continualy recorded so we can pull and review any footage we need. All security staff including costume wearers wear two-way radios with earpiece comms. We

271

also have various pre-set code words to be used in emergencies. We're open to the public from 08:00 through to 23:00. At midnight the cleaners and maintenance staff come in. They leave at 07:00 and we do a final security walk-through before gates open again."

With the first tensions between them now gone, Deacon was interested in understanding more about the set-up. Over the following two hours he had the complete security overview and met the individual supervisors when he explained the possible aspect of the expected attacks to them in turn. They would pass the messages down to their teams and the security people and costume wearers in the field.

During the remainder of the day, Deacon oversaw the setting up of discrete road blocks. He and Mitch had worked on the theory that due to the limited flying time of the drones, the size of the parks, and the lack of roads immediately close to the perimeters, it was a reasonable assumption that the attackers would park as close as possible. The nearest locations were expected to be the car parks themselves, so additional FBI agents in plain clothes were placed in various vehicles amongst the queuing cars.

The other SEALs from Coronado and Little Creek had arrived mid-morning. Deacon knew a large number of them personally and took a fair bit of ribbing. The local Chief of Police was also present, as was the local FBI Special Agent-in-Charge (SAC), Hank Winters. Between them, they assigned specific areas of where every person would walk and guard the perimeters of all the theme parks. Deacon was still worried that they were spread too thinly. There were just too many miles of perimeter and too many car parks or places vehicles could access, he thought.

The Chief of Police issued orders for all available off-duty personnel to be dressed in plain clothes and to assist, but many were already on duty for other 4th July parades throughout the region. FBI Director Clark had re-issued the arrival photo of Saif taken at Teterboro Airport, along with Deacon's photofit of him and Officer Millar's descriptions of both suspects to all local news channels, police and officials along the entire East Coast.

Late afternoon the news broadcast finally paid dividends. A store owner from the less affluent area of Sanford called the FBI Hotline, saying he thought he saw the person in the photo in his store a few nights ago. Deacon and Hank Winters immediately drove to the Sanford store and reviewed the store footage from the security cameras. Confirming it looked like the suspect, the FBI SAC questioned the owner who said the man in question turned up twice over a few days, both times in the evening. He bought water, juice and some ready meals. He didn't talk much and paid in cash.

Winters immediately got on his phone and organised a detailed police search of hotels and motels in a ten-block radius.

At 8:00 pm EST the major TV channels switched over from their broadcasts to the White House and the Seal of the President of the United States.

A tired-looking President faced the camera and smiled. He began, "My fellow Americans ... ."

Over the next 14 minutes, he talked about the atrocities carried out in the UK the previous week and the heightened levels of security he'd placed on the law enforcement departments within the US. He stated there was no known expected attack against the U.S. and that America was 'open for business, as usual'. People should be vigilant and report anything suspicious but tomorrow was the 4th July, and everyone should enjoy it as normal.

Later that evening, Hank Winters received a call from the local police lieutenant confirming they'd found the motel the suspect had been using, but he'd checked out a couple of days ago. It was a run-down motel in the seedier part of town, and the suspect had been in room 17 for over a week. He'd stayed in his room all the time and used HBO. Yes, he'd paid cash; yes he'd shown a Philly licence ID; and no, he hadn't spoken much. The room had been cleaned since he left, but the cleaners usually only vacuumed the carpet and changed the sheets. Unfortunately, the motel often rented these rooms by the hour and at least four people had used the room since he'd left.

Winters arranged for forensics to pull the place apart but there would likely be dozens if not hundreds of prints and DNA so anything useful would be unlikely.

Heading to bed, that night Deacon was an extremely worried man. He wasn't afraid of fighting or of dying. He'd led teams into 'no-win' situations and had managed to survive. SEAL training prepared you for the worst and then some. It made you dig deep and find that inner strength and just when you thought you couldn't take anymore, it made you dig deeper again and find even more. But he was afraid of tomorrow. Had he guessed correctly? Would the attack be tomorrow or another day? Would the attack be against civilians or was a military target more likely? Were the parks the target or had he gotten it completely wrong? How many people were likely to die if he was wrong? A thousand different thoughts kept going around and around in his head before he eventually managed to drift off but his sleep was restless, and he was woken by countless nightmares.

# Chapter 71

"It's going to be a beautiful day here in sunny Orlando today," the TV weatherman said, "It will hit the low hundreds with 98% humidity by lunchtime. There is zero chance of precipitation, and we're in for a scorcher. We're already well into the eighties, and it's only 6:00 am. Happy 4th July, everybody."

Deacon flicked the channel over to CNN. Their main news was the resignation of the British Prime Minister after there had been a vote of no confidence in Parliament. Experts were expecting the replacement PM to call a General Election and the view of the public was that a complete change of government was needed. ISIS was claiming responsibility for the attack and no-one had yet been apprehended.

A car horn sounded just as Deacon exited the hotel and he looked over to see Hank Winters waiting. Deacon jogged over and slid easily into the passenger seat. The air conditioning was already on full and losing the battle against the heat and humidity. Winters asked how he'd slept.

"Not good. Not good at all. Too many worries about too many things going wrong," he said. "I've got an annoying niggle at the back of my mind, but I can't put my finger on it. I've got a feeling I've missed something, but I don't know what. Anything back from forensics?"

"Nah, our guys say you'd get less DNA from a dumpster. Loads of prints but whether any can be identified, I dunno."

Arriving at the C4 building they split up with Deacon choosing to join the site inspection teams for the larger parks while Winters chose the smaller. Arriving back in the control rooms at 08:45, nothing out of the usual had been found. Gates would open at 09:00 through to midnight today, and a bumper crowd was expected. Lines were already forming at all the gate entrances. Aaron Baker was waiting for them and offered the latest update.

"Gents. Everyone is on station already. Between all the parks we expect close on 550,000 visitors today. All staff and security have been fully briefed and instructed to raise the alarm for anything suspicious or out of the ordinary," Baker said, his attitude and demeanour entirely different from his initial meeting with Deacon yesterday. Between them, Deacon and Baker again checked and rechecked all the security measures. Everything seemed normal, just another hot, sunny, muggy July day.

"Thanks, Aaron, I'm going to check on my men," Deacon said, before taking the keys of one of their security trucks.

By 11:30 am Deacon was back. He'd driven around each of the various parks perimeters and spoken with all the SEALs on duty. Each was dressed in civilian clothes and was armed either with a shotgun with filament cartridges or with a drone rifle. They also carried SIG-Sauer 226s pistols and were in constant radio contact with the C4 command centre as well as to their own teams and Deacon.

Deacon was still worried. This was the ideal day for any attack. The international publicity of a strike against Heartland USA on Independence Day would be immense.

Turnstile counters were showing some of the parks already to be almost 85% full and over 430,000 visitors through the gates in total. At that rate, the entrance doors would have to be closed by lunchtime.

Baker was in regular contact with his staff. There had been the normally expected problems - children wandering off and parents panicking, handbags and backpacks being put down and forgotten - but so far just regular run-of-the-mill stuff. Every visitor had been searched more thoroughly than usual and all bags examined. Some of the public had become angry over this, especially in the delay it caused, but the security staff had quietly quelled any concerns, and most people remained happy.

With the temperature and humidity so high it was inevitable tempers would overheat and there were a number of scuffles breaking out in the queues for the rides.

Suddenly, with a loud squawk, the alarm sounded, and the emergency light in the ceiling flashed Red as the message 'Code Black', and the location code came over the radio, meaning an unauthorised intrusion.

# Chapter 72

In the confusion that followed, a large number of the park's security men rushed over towards the identified area. Around the perimeters, the police and SEALs stayed put eyes scanning for any other possible intrusion. The rushing of security people, some in uniform, some in casual clothes, caused a panic amongst the public. Some people managed to stand clear, but a number were knocked down in the rush. A cry then went up that there was a bomb and people started panicking even more.

Aaron Baker seemed positively gleeful as he shouted, "Got them. They can't escape now. Quick, get your men there," to Deacon.

Deacon, however, remained calm and issued orders to the SEAL teams to remain on station. He waited. Within a few minutes security arrived at the area where the alarm had been raised and discovered it had been triggered by someone seeing a hot-air balloon in the distance. A young boy had seen it, pointed it out to his father who, aware of what had happened in the UK, alerted one of the staff, stating it could be an attack. The message the young female member of staff had understood was a hot-air balloon was approaching the park, and they were under attack. New to the job, and having only recently finished her training, she was more used to the artificial world of social media and texting. Caught off guard by real people and in a situation she didn't understand, she panicked and called in a 'Code Black' - the code used for an unauthorised intrusion into the park - and started shouting at people to take cover.

The Navy E-2 Hawkeye operators flying high overhead had seen the hot-air balloon on their radars. Its automated target acquisition and ranging system (ATARS) had discounted it due its slow speed of just a few miles an hour, and of its small radar return just off the burner and gas tank. However, as it was on a direct path towards the parks, an alert operator had already manually flagged it as a possible target and alerted a police department helicopter to intercept.

The helicopter approached the balloon and circled it. The public on the ground could clearly hear the helicopter pilot addressing the balloon pilot through a loudspeaker demanding it immediately land or risk being shot down. The balloon pilot extinguished the burners, and the craft slowly descended to be met by over a dozen armed officers on the ground, who promptly arrested him and his passengers. The pilot would later be charged with ignoring the FAA grounding order, fined $5,000 and have his pilot's license revoked for six months.

Over a dozen people in the park had been hurt in the stampede, and it took the combined efforts of the security personnel as well as their costume-wearing colleagues to pacify the angry crowd, along with offering a number of free entrance passes and lunch and drink vouchers.

Baker and Deacon agreed with Winters plan to stay within the park itself in case any other problems arose.

Another hour passed and everything seemed as normal. From the C4 control room, Deacon called his teams over the radio for a status check. The reports came back that it was still all quiet and everyone was fully alert. Deacon had imposed strict radio discipline, so there was no idle chit-chat to interfere with any updates.

Baker called the ten roadblocks that were manned by his staff one by one, and the responses were similar - all quiet so far. All vehicles containing only men had been stopped and searched. Those with families were assumed to be OK, and the intentions were to not cause concern to the public wherever possible.

Deacon overheard one of the conversations.

"This is control calling section D5. Status update, Bart?" Baker said.

"All quiet here, Mr Baker. We've had four food deliveries, as scheduled, and they checked out fine. Also had the water guys. All quiet here."

Deacon's inner niggle started buzzing again as he picked up on the keyword of water.

Turning to Baker, he said, "What water guys?"

"The regular ones from Orange County. They come every two days for the water treatment. Elias and his son, Zane Shirani. Elias is off sick with the damn flu at the moment. In this heat. Can you believe it? So Zane has another colleague with him."

Baker carried on talking, but Deacon had stopped listening. The niggle in the back of his head had turned into loud alarm bells ringing.

Water? Zane? Off sick?

Grabbing Baker by the arm and pulling him along, they raced towards the vehicle compound, while shouting at Baker, "The water - tell me about the water treatment … ."

# Chapter 73

As they rushed down the stairs, Baker gasping with the sudden exercise, Deacon said again, "C'mon, dammit. Tell me about the water."

Gasping for breath, Baker managed to explain that one of the County's rulings was any industry in Central Florida had to preserve as much water as possible, so all waste water from the parks is funnelled through to a state-of-the-art treatment plant where it is processed and cleaned, before being reused.

As they rushed outside to the parking area, they were hit by the blast of heat and humidity. With Baker now red in the face and sweating and obviously in no fit state to drive, Deacon grabbed the keys off him, bundled him into the passenger seat of the truck and rushed around into the driver's seat. Cranking the engine over while turning the A/C on full, as the engine caught he slammed the selector into drive and floored the accelerator. With a cloud of black smoke coming from the spinning wheels, they sped towards the gatehouse, horn blaring.

Seeing the oncoming truck with his boss in the passenger seat and a determined looking tall guy driving racing towards him, the guard quickly raised the barrier.

"Which way?" shouted Deacon.

"W ... what?"

"Baker. Which fucking way? Left or right? C'MON. Left or right?"

"Right RIGHT!"

Finally getting an answer, he swung the wheel over, and the vehicle skidded around to the right as it accelerated away.

"C'mon, tell me more about the water. BAKER! Tell me about the water!"

Still trying to get his breath back from the rush downstairs, along with the fright of careening along the road, he fastened his seat belt as he said, "Although the water is clean enough to drink, because the treatment centre operates to a higher specification than those mandated by state and federal requirements — LEFT LEFT!"

As they skidded around another corner, Deacon could see the D5 section roadblock ahead with a row of cars waiting to drive through the coned search area. The guard looked up at the sound of their truck racing towards them and Deacon could see one of the guards reach for his radio while the other started pulling his handgun from his holster. Jamming the brakes on the truck slewed to the right before coming to a stop behind the last car in the line. By this time the guard with the radio was screaming for help, and the other was in the two-handed stance with his weapon levelled directly at Deacon.

"Baker, get out and tell Wyatt Earp there to calm down before he hurts himself, will you?" Deacon said as he thumbed the radio master override and transmitted to all concerned to stay on patrol and on guard.

It took Baker a few minutes to get both security men to calm down and to move the bollards clear for Deacon. As Baker slid back into the passenger seat, Deacon floored the accelerator again, and the truck leapt forward in another cloud of tyre smoke for the second time that day. Up ahead, the road split. Left was towards the park, while the right was out through the forest.

"RIGHT RIGHT!"

Taking the right fork, Deacon said, "Go on!"

"Well, instead of serving it back to customers to drink, although it's perfectly safe, they use it to clean and water the parks with. All the various parks' water rides are filled with this recycled water and it's used for the automatic watering system for all the thousands of plants. It's used at night for cleaning and washing down the rides and sidewalks, and it feeds the faucets in the bathroom washbasins and is also used — RIGHT, RIGHT at the end! And also used for the washing of the buses at the car parks, and all other vehicles like this one," he managed to say.

Deacon was thinking hard and almost missed Baker telling him to take the second right and then straight on for nine miles. Although some people get wet on some rides, there wasn't enough exposure for an attack this big, Deacon thought. Something was still not making sense. Some piece of the puzzle was still missing.

"What about fresh water, or drinking water? Where does that come from?" he asked.

"Well, all fresh water comes in direct from Orange County Water, the local supply company. Fresh water is fed to all the kitchens and restaurants in the parks as well as to the drinking fountains dotted around. We also use fresh water in the sprays."

"Sprays? What sprays? You mean fountains?"

"No, the big fountains use the recycled water. You know, sprays! It's really hot out there, yeah? So all the queues for the rides and all the outside doorways have giant fans running to keep visitors cool. Well in these summer months we feed water into the airstream of the fans to help keep people cool. There're hundreds of them. They just produce a fine cooling misty spray. People love 'em. They often just stand under them," Baker said.

"And these are fed with just fresh water?"

"Well yeah, once it's been through the treatment plant."

"What do you mean, treatment? This is fresh water, no?"

"Yes, but Orange County doesn't put fluoride in the water, and we like to. We're a caring company and concerned about our children's teeth, so we add fluoride and also just a little bit of chlorine, not enough to taste but just sufficient to make sure all the pipes stay clean … ."

But Deacon had tuned out and was just concentrating on driving. The bells in his head had gotten louder and louder until they suddenly stopped. He finally realised what his niggling worry had been. If he had planned these attacks, he would have hit the U.S. the same time as the UK for the surprise element. It didn't matter which one you did first, but any delay with the second allowed them to be on alert. Not only did the U.S. guess the attack was coming, they knew how. With a spray drone attack. That would allow anyone time to prepare against them, as they'd done here. It didn't make sense! You don't tell your enemy when, and how you're going to attack them, you just do it. That's what had been niggling him - they'd had too much warning.

The dates had been important. They'd had to do the UK first because of Glastonbury and July 4th was nine days later, so they'd changed the method of attack. Like the old boxing trick. Feign with your left while you hammer him with your right.

Deacon, Clark, the Admiral … all of them had been busy watching the left while they were about to get hammered by the right.

Slewing around yet another corner, he asked, "How much farther to the plant?"

"About another three miles or so. It's out in the boonies hidden amongst the trees. Not the sort of place you want the public to see."

"How's it guarded?"

"It's a water and sewage treatment plant. It's not really guarded. Most of it is automated. There's fencing all around and a gatehouse with a barrier and some CCTV, but that's all."

"Is the guard armed?"

"Nightstick and radio, I think. We've never had any trouble there before."

"There's a first time for everything," Deacon murmured, getting out his phone.

# Chapter 74

Slowing the truck down a little, Deacon thumbed through his contact list before pressing Send. After what seemed an age, he heard the connection made and the voice of Officer Brad Millar.

"Millar, it's Deacon. The name of the guy you stopped, the younger one with the Orlando licence. Could it have been Zane?"

"Zach, Zane, yeah that sounds right, Zane," he replied.

Disconnecting the call Deacon speed dialled Mitch.

"Mitch, I think it's the water treatment. I think they're going to flood the water system with it. Everyone in the parks gets sprayed with cooling water. If that's contaminated … . Get on to the Admiral and let him know. Get Winters to bring a team of six to back me up at the treatment plant, but don't pull all our other guys out yet in case I'm wrong. Yeah, I'm heading there now with the head of park security, Aaron Baker. Also, get Simon Clark at the FBI to check Guardian and TWL for anything on a Zane and Elias Shirani here in Orlando and text me any results," he said, looking to Baker for the address and directions of the treatment plant to pass to Mitch.

It was possible both Elias and Zane were in the Guardian database, Deacon thought. Or to give it its full name, the Guardian Threat Tracking Systems, or GTTS as it's known by its initials. This is a reporting system used by the FBI to track threats and other intelligence information. It was established to collect data on terrorist threats and suspicious incidents, at seaports and other locations, and to manage action on various threats and incidents. First used in 2005, it quickly grew, and in August 2007, the Department of Defence announced Guardian would take over the data collection and reporting which had been handled previously by the TALON database system. It now recorded all persons of interest, both home-grown and foreign, who had known involvement in terrorist organisations. Many of these persons would also be included on the 'No Fly List', a list created and maintained by the U.S. government's Terrorist Screening Centre (TSC) of people who are prohibited from boarding commercial aircraft for travel within, into, or out of the US. Based on this list, aircraft that do not have a start- or end-point destination within the United States are diverted away from U.S. airspace.

Turning off the main road Deacon slowed as he came to a guardhouse manned by a lone individual. At the barrier, Baker shouted to the guard to let them in. Asking if the Orange County Water people were on site, the guard confirmed they were.

"Yeah, two of them. Zane and another older guy helping, 'cus his old man's sick or something. They said they needed to check something over in the freshwater treatment building," the guard said, pointing roughly in its general direction.

Racing over they saw the Orange County Water Company vehicle parked close to an open door with a broken padlock lying in the dirt.

As Deacon stopped the truck and they silently exited, Baker looked at him and said, "They shouldn't be in here, this is a secure room. It's the main valve and pump room. They should only be working with the recycled water, not fresh. They've no right to be in here."

Telling Baker to stay outside he slipped his SIG out of its holster and quietly entered through the door into the darkened room beyond, moving sideways into the shadow so that he didn't present a silhouette target.

Peering around in the gloom, his eyes still adjusting from the intense sunlight to the sudden darkness, he couldn't see much. Moving quietly forward with his weapon in his right hand, he used his left to feel for any obstructions. Coming to another wall, he moved slowly along to the right until his hand felt the edge of a doorframe. Listening, he thought he could hear muted conversation in the room beyond.

Gently opening the inner door a fraction, he peered through the crack and could see a mass of thick pipes, each over 14 inches in diameter, running horizontally along the walls starting from about a foot off the floor and then disappearing down to a lower level. Moving into the room further, he couldn't hear any more conversation but could see the rear outline shape of a person wearing a full hazmat body suit. The person was pouring what looked to be the last few drops of liquid from a large plastic container in through the open mouth of a large metal drum attached to the wall. There was another empty plastic container already lying on the floor.

Deacon raised his weapon slightly and shouted, "Freeze. Keep your hands in view and turn around real slo −," when there was an almighty crash from behind him.

When startled, animal instinct kicks in. It makes people jump or gasp. It also makes people automatically look towards the source of the noise. It's the body's natural reaction, and it's almost impossible to stop. Deacon was superbly fit and extensively trained. But even his animal instinct was triggered. He automatically glanced sideways back towards the source of the noise. Just momentarily. But it was long enough.

As his eyes swept back towards the suspect, something heavy hit him on the back of his head, and he fell dazed to the floor his grip on his SIG loosened and it slid out of reach. As he tried to roll away and get back to his feet, a booted foot caught him under the ribs, lifting and smashing him against the pipes. As he gasped and tried to draw breath the shadow of a person loomed over him, and he heard the faint swish of something moving fast as he was struck hard again on the head.

Collapsing, he was already unconscious as his head hit the floor and he never felt the other kicks to his body.

# Chapter 75

Aaron Baker had followed Deacon in through the outer doorway and waited until he thought he could see. Creeping over towards where Deacon had gone, he tripped over in the dark, falling against some metal shelves. He heard a commotion from inside the doorway, and as he tried to get back to his feet, he found himself looking straight down the barrel of an AK-74 Assault rifle, the latest version of the mass-produced and much-loved AK-47. Originally designed in Russia by Mikhail Kalashnikov just after WWII, the AK-47 was copied, and almost 80 million were manufactured worldwide. Due to its reliability and cheapness, it quickly became the de facto rifle for soldiers and terrorists alike. The AK-74 was a newer improved model. However, to Baker, the black circle of the barrel looked as deadly as any he'd ever seen.

Frozen in terror, he couldn't move. After what seemed an age, but was merely a few seconds, a large gloved hand reached out, grasped his shirt front and yanked him forward. Stumbling and half-collapsing in through the doorway, he almost fell over the prostrate and bloodied body of Deacon, before the gun barrel was pushed hard into his stomach and he fell to his knees bent double.

"Kneel. Kneel and pray," Saif said, as he grabbed the radio and cell phone from Baker.

Keeping the rifle pointing directly at Baker, Saif moved over to the unconscious Deacon, and half pushed, half kicked him over. Taking Deacon's radio, cell phone and his fallen handgun, Saif moved back and jammed the rifle barrel into Baker's ear.

"How many of you are there?"

Gasping for breath, Baker managed to mutter, "Fuck you."

Lowering the barrel and jabbing it in Baker's groin, Saif said, "I asked you a question."

Gasping with pain, Baker managed to say, "And I said, go fuck yourself."

Saif stood there, the gun barrel still jammed into Baker's groin. Suddenly, he moved back almost a foot, changed aim and fired.

The sound of the AK-74 being fired even in single shot mode in a closed room was deafening. As the blast echoed around the walls the next sound heard was of Baker screaming as his left kneecap shattered and blood and bone fragments sprayed along the floor and walls.

Waiting for a few moments for Baker to stop screaming, Saif moved the red hot barrel over towards Baker's other knee and said, "One more knee, two elbows. Your choice. How many others?"

Gasping for air and trying to quell the blood flow, Baker finally admitted it was just the two of them for now, but others were on their way.

Looking over towards Deacon still unconscious on the floor, all Baker could see was a bloody face and blood slowly oozing from an open gash on the back of his head.

Finally, looking back towards Saif he gasped through gritted teeth, "What the fuck you done, man?"

"I have brought the mighty USA to the realisation that its actions have consequences."

Turning to Zane who had just announced he was finished, Saif pointed to the laptop.

"Start the process," Saif said as he began unfastening the outer layer of his protection suit.

With his lower leg only still attached to the upper by muscle and sinews, Baker couldn't move. The initial pain had subsided slightly, most likely as adrenaline had kicked in and dulled the pain temporarily. He gasped, "What do you mean? Consequences?"

"For too long you have sent your drones to do your dirty work, their pilots sitting in air-conditioned comfort here in America then going home for a beer like it's all just a big game, while your missiles destroy us. Your public doesn't even care. Your news on CNN and NBC show the drone strikes while you sit there eating your evening meal or discussing the weather. They boast how accurate they are while they show buildings exploding. But they don't show the heartache and suffering you put on my people, the families ripped apart by your Paveway laser-guided bombs or Hellfire air-to-ground missiles. You don't show the bodies being blown apart, the bodies of children with legs and arms missing. No, you all just live in comfort while this happens 'over there'. Well, I've brought it over here. Let's see how Americans feel when they see the evening news showing bodies lain around here for a change. Thousands of them, all dead and dying. They won't be blown apart like the pain you cause us, but they'll still be just as dead," Saif snarled, removing the last of his protective clothing.

Still gasping with pain, Baker said, "So you plan to fly drones over and kill everyone like you did in the UK?"

"Not quite, my friend. The drones worked well over there, but here was a different plan. Now it's done. And it's too late to stop it."

"You're mad! What have you done?"

"What we have done, Insha'Allah, is to replace the fluoride in this container with what you know as VX Agent. We have over-ridden the computer, and I'm changing the mixture ratio from 1 in 50,000 to 1 in 1.

When I press the enter key on this laptop, that valve up there," he said, pointing to a device near the ceiling, "will turn and the contents of this container will be pumped into the fresh water supply. Within seconds, it will be rushing through the pipes to every outlet throughout all the parks. You Americans love your comfort. You all rush to cool your bloated bodies at every chance. Within minutes, every person close to or under a spray head will be infected. Allahu Akbar, God is Great!"

With a roar like an angry bull, Baker tried to get to his feet to attack Saif, but his shattered knee wouldn't support him. Limping very badly he tried to stand, cursing as he did so," You bastards. I won't let you do thi −," as Saif merely kicked him hard on his shattered kneecap and he fell again to the ground screaming in pain.

Zane called out, "OK, I've logged in."

Moving over to the laptop, he passed the rifle to Zane.

"Kill them."

"W..what?"

"I said kill them. Do it now while I finish setting this," he said as he clicked between various screens and reset passwords.

Zane had grown up trying to be tough. He'd always wanted praise from his parents, his father in particular, and he was sickened by how easily Saif had killed them. Killing people when playing video games had been fun, but watching his father's head explode in front of him had repulsed him. Unsure now of what he had gotten mixed up in, he hesitated.

"I said kill them," Saif snarled, pulling his pistol from his pocket, "or I'll kill you."

Moving over to the bleeding body of Baker, Zane pointed the rifle at his face.

With tears streaming down his face, he muttered, "I'm sorry," as he pulled the trigger and the full-metal-jacket bullet left the barrel at over two-thousand-nine-hundred feet per second, exploding Baker's head over the wall behind with blood, hair and brain matter.

With eyes awash with tears and his ears ringing from the gun blast, he thought he would vomit inside his mask. Turning towards the wall where Deacon's body was, ready to fire again, he stopped when he saw movement and Deacon's body disappearing beneath the maze of horizontal pipes.

Terrified to admit to Saif that he'd failed, he turned back to the corpse of Baker and fired again into his chest.

Walking back to Saif with bile burning his throat, he said, "It's done."

Switching screens for the last time, Saif finally moved the cursor over the 'Start' icon and pressed the 'Enter' key before ripping out the connecting wires and throwing the laptop to the floor. Raising his silenced pistol, he fired twice at the laptop until it was just mangled plastic. He turned and looked directly at Zane.

"But I'm not undressed yet," Zane said.

"Keep it on. You're staying," he said as he shot him through the forehead.

Moving to the door, he exited slamming it closed behind him before reaching the outer door. Forcing it shut he slipped a new padlock from his pocket into place, locked it then hit it repeatedly with the butt of his rifle until he broke the key off in the lock, just as the software program initiated and the motor on the valve near the ceiling whirled slowly into life and began to move.

# Chapter 76

As the door slammed shut Deacon forced himself to move. Still groggy from the attack, he moved as quickly as he could. He'd come to from the beating and heard Saif boast about what he'd done, but wisely carried on playing unconscious. Lying there, unarmed and unable to see clearly from his left eye due to the congealed blood, he'd been in no fit state to try and take on Saif and Zane. Had he done so, he would no doubt have endured the same fate as Aaron Baker.

He'd recognised Saif from the dark alley in Mosul as soon as he'd seen him again, even through his one blood-free eye. The voice alone had identified him - basically American with a faint New York accent.

He heard Saif tell Zane to kill them and knew he had to act now or never. Reaching under the pipes, he pulled himself under them just as he heard Zane shoot Baker, and dropped down slightly to a lower ledge, completely hidden from view. When he heard the third shot and the door slam, he slid back out now from under the pipes and staggered over to the wall. Passing the body of Zane, he climbed onto one of the larger pipes and stretched upright on it. He locked his arm muscles, gritted his teeth and putting his full energy and body into it, braced and locked his hands around the valve lever to stop it moving.

The 2.5hp motor, gears grinding, did its best to complete what it had been designed to do - open the valve and allow the mixture in the tank below to join with the rushing fresh water - while Deacon's muscles and determination did their best to stop it. Neither would succumb to the other. Deacon's arm and leg muscles began to burn at a level he had never experienced before. Sweat rolling down his face, blinding him, Deacon knew he couldn't relax for even a second. The motor hummed, still trying to complete its task, balanced equally by Deacon's power and will to stop it. Fraction by fraction the motor began to win and Deacon, digging deeper than ever before into his will, into his very being, pushed harder and harder to stop it.

His concentration so intense, he slipped into a trance. Blinded first by sweat then by the immense tightening and locking of his muscles, even his hearing had faded to only a dull roar of the blood pressure in his veins. The pain in his body was immense. He'd never experienced agony like it, and every cell was screaming at him to relax. As his vision faded to a dull glow, he pushed still even harder, his muscles now as taut as polished steel.

It took almost ten minutes for additional security to arrive, but by then Deacon couldn't hear them. To him, it was a lifetime. By then he was in a coma. He didn't hear the shooting off of the padlock, nor the shouts of his rescuers. Not sure why he was trying to stop the lever from moving, but understanding his determination, two of his rescuers quickly climbed up, and after forcing the cover off the back of the motor with a large screwdriver and wrench, shorted out the contacts inside.

It took just a few moments but eventually, with a shower of sparks and a loud bang, the fuse blew, and the motor gears finally stopped grinding. Deacon's hands had to be prised off the handle, and he was laid down, unconscious, muscles still locked solid, while his arms and legs were massaged and slowly straightened. It took almost twenty minutes until he slowly came out of his trance. Trying to sit up he managed to gasp, "Did we stop it in time?"

# Chapter 77

The rescuers looked at one another before one of them said," No pal, we didn't — you did."

Admiral Carter, Col. Brandon McAlistair, Simon Clark and Mitch Stringer flew down in a U.S. Navy C-37 Gulfstream early evening that day and landed at Orlando Executive Airport, the same airport Deacon had used the previous morning. Arriving at the water treatment plant, the Admiral saluted Deacon and thanked him for what he had done.

In the six hours since the event, Deacon had been attended to by medics, the site was crawling with police, the FBI and security people, and a nationwide hunt had already commenced for Saif.

"Congratulations, Lieutenant, you've saved the day. How are you shaping up?" the Admiral said, looking at Deacon's bruises, split lip, and bandaged head.

"Head's hard as ever, sir. A couple of stitches. Be right as rain in a few days."

"Lieutenant, your extraordinary achievement of stopping the valve turning stopped any VX Agent getting into the water supply," the Admiral said, "Colonel McAlistair here has been working on figures on the flight down. Colonel?"

"Lieutenant, You did well. I'd worked out a best and worst case scenario. The best would have been 120,000 infections and 70 - 80,000 fatalities, depending on how quickly we at CDC could contain it and treat everyone. The worst case showed over 400,000 infections and close on 280,000 dead. Apocalyptic figures. The good news is the two plastic containers seem to account for the entire 200+ litres mentioned in the recording," Col McAlistair said.

"So what made you suspect it was this?" the Admiral said, looking around.

"Just a niggle, sir. It seemed too easy like we were already forewarned. I tried to put myself inside the head of this guy, Saif. If I was intent on doing this, how would I go about it? The only part that didn't add up was why would I use the same method of delivery after allowing my opponents time to prepare. It didn't seem logical, and as we found in the Canaries, this guy is good at planning. Too good to make a silly mistake. Then I overheard a radio call, and everything just clicked into place."

"Yet again, Lieutenant, your quick thinking paid off. Congratulations."

"Yet again? Something I should know about?" Col. McAlistair asked.

"Not now, Brandon, maybe over a brandy later, but not now," the Admiral replied.

"Congratulations should also go to Baker, sir," Deacon said, "He got Saif talking when I was on the floor semi-conscious. I heard him say about the pump and the valve. If Baker hadn't managed to get him talking, I wouldn't have known about the valve. Unfortunately, the bastard then went and killed him."

"Do we know where Saif is now?" Mitch asked.

Simon Clark, having liaised with SAC Hank Winters, went on to explain that after locking Deacon in the room, and jamming the padlock, Saif was observed on CCTV running towards the main building where he'd killed a

300

maintenance worker. Removing his shirt and hat and stealing his keys, he'd stolen the workers truck and driven through the exit gate as normal. His current whereabouts are unknown but there is a nationwide hunt for him, and he is on everyone's watch list. He is currently number 1 on the FBI's 'Most Wanted' list.

"The other person," Clark continued, "has been identified as Zane Shirani, 23, living at home with his parents and working with his father, Elias Shirani, at the water department at Orange County Public Works. The mother was American born, but the father, Elias, emigrated here as a child with his Lebanese parents, now both deceased, back in '53. Neither the father, Elias, nor the son, Zane, is listed on any of the terrorist watch lists or No Fly lists. Police and the FBI raided the parents' house earlier this afternoon and found both parents bodies in the freezer in the garage. Forensics will check the place over, but we're not hopeful. As to the motel, dozens of prints and DNA. It will all be checked but nothing to help us yet."

Smiling at his friend, Mitch said, "What is interesting is the FBI dusted the keyboard of the laptop in their mobile lab over there. It's identified the user as having died over 15 years ago. His name is Steve Caan, and he was a Lieutenant in the U.S. Navy. Simon Clark contacted me while we were in the air, and I pulled his file. He joined in '87, specialising in surface warfare. He was extremely good, particularly in planning and strategy for Special Forces and received fast promotions, but left in '96 after increased security clearance found he had Iranian parents living in the US. Further investigation showed his parents as possible intelligence agents working for Iran, but nothing could be proved. However, it put paid to his chances of promotion, and his security clearance was revoked. Again, nothing could be proved against him, but as you know, often it's guilt by association. Until then his record had been excellent. However he resigned, and we lost sight of him but received a report back in 2001 that he'd died in a car crash in Europe. Anyway, that's who we've been up against. We know him as Saif the Palestinian, but we have no idea why Steve Caan took that name and why he turned against the US. The FBI and CIA are checking, and we should have more info soon. He's been using the name and identity of Charlie Baxter from Pennsylvania. It's a genuine ID, and we are currently talking to the real Charlie Baxter. There doesn't seem to be any tie-up between them, and it looks a case of stolen identity."

"So this is at least twice he's tried to cause major harm to the US. I wonder what else he's been involved in and when I'll get to see him next." Deacon said.

Moving back outside and leaving the technicians to finish their work, the Admiral continued, "Mossad have confirmed Hakim Gerbali has been moved from Mosul to Raqqa and is working again with Faisel Husseni, the guy who started this. We know Husseni reports to Sleiman Daoud al-Afari, who specialises in chemical and biological weapons, who is also based in Raqqa. We are just waiting on confirmation of when these two will be together, and we have a Reaper drone over Raqqa on standby ready to target them."

"But surely sir, we know where the laboratories are. Can't we just take them out?"

"Regrettably not, Lieutenant. They are close to civilian housing, and there's too high a risk of the chemicals escaping and causing deaths to the locals. The political ramifications of us knowingly causing a deadly gas escape would be too much for this administration to handle. No, we need to wait until we get confirmation from Gerbali of these two being away from the laboratories where we can terminate them safely."

Putting his arm around Deacon's shoulders, the Admiral moved him away from the others.

"Lieutenant, I can't express how much the country owes you. Naturally, what has occurred here has to remain classified. If it ever got out to the public how close we came to a massive disaster ... well, do I need to continue? Unfortunately, as you know, that girl you rescued, Laura Williams, has been making a name for herself on social media alleging you murdered a number of innocent Iraqi's and demanding military justice. That damn journalist, Lynda Anderson, has been running with the story and making major waves. She's a bloody pit bull, and she knows her way around Washington. Unfortunately, she's good. Very good. Her last big story was on political corruption, and if you remember, the Senator accused had to resign. Her latest target is corruption within the military and in particular, the links between the military and key politicians in awarding military contracts. This story about Laura isn't her primary focus, but it's found some traction, and she's been calling for an official inquiry into it. Being an election year, the other Press have picked up on it and can all sense a story going somewhere. The President would usually quell this kind of thing as it's not in the national interest, but although he's not running again, he wants his party to win, and the opposition is gaining ground. Being he doesn't have the balls to say no, he's agreed there will now be a hearing to determine whether, in fact, you did commit unnecessary murder of those guards."

"I've nothing to hide, Admiral. They were clean shoots."

"I know that, Lieutenant. I've read your report and spoken to your colleagues. This is all bullshit. But that's

Washington for you. You, being the officer in charge, take on that responsibility. Unfortunately, if the hearing finds you guilty, you will be tried at court martial by JAG and could face demotion, expulsion from the service, or even imprisonment ... . I'm sorry, son. I will be meeting with the President in the morning. Let me come back to you ... ."

Deacon walked away in a dazed state. A hearing? Possible court case? Could his career be over?

# Chapter 78

## San Diego - Two weeks later

A soft, gentle breeze had drifted in from the sea and twirled around the bride and groom. Flowers decorated the marriage gazebo with the blue of the Pacific providing a perfect backdrop, all under a bright August sun. The wedding of Alex Schaefer and Warren Peterson had gone off without a hitch in the beautiful church of Our Lady of the Rosary in Little Italy, San Diego. Deacon had proudly walked Alex down the aisle, and 4-year-old Bryant David Schaefer had been a perfect page boy. Alex had looked beautiful in a white lace-topped dress, and little Bryant had stolen the show by sitting on the step, smiling and facing the audience, while the priest had carried out the ceremony.

Rachel had been there with Deacon, along with Mitch and Helen and many SEALs who'd served with her former husband. Alex's sisters and friends had helped make the day fantastic before the happy couple jetted off on their honeymoon to Tahiti for a week, leaving little Bryant with Alex's sister.

Bryant senior had been a great guy - a loving husband, a courageous SEAL, and a good friend to Deacon. But he was gone and time moves on, and it was right for Alex to also move on to the next stage of her life with Warren and baby Bryant David, Deacon thought.

Rachel and Deacon, along with Mitch and Helen had stopped a couple of nights in the local Hyatt, before he'd sprung his surprise on his friends. Now, sat in the cockpit he smiled to himself and thought that life couldn't get much better. Mitch was having the time of his life on the wheel, pretending to be Cap'n Bligh, waving a wooden spoon around like a cutlass and shouting out 'Ooo arrr' and 'Pieces of Eight me hearties' every few minutes, while Helen and Rachel were down below preparing lunch. They'd checked out of the Hyatt, and Deacon had driven them down to Abbot's Boatyard where they'd boarded Lazy Days, a Jeanneau 54-foot, impeccably-equipped, private charter sailboat and were now en route from San Diego to Los Angeles via Catalina Island. They had a few days left all together before Mitch and Helen flew home from LA while Deacon and Rachel gently cruised back to San Diego. Lying back and looking up, with a beer in his hand, he thought of the forthcoming result of his hearing and decided what will be will be, as he watched the masthead make lazy circles in the sky.

# Fact File

- Project 922 was the codename for Iraq's third and most successful attempt to produce chemical and biological weapons. By 1984, Iraq started producing its first nerve agents, Tabun and Sarin. By 1989 Iraq had started producing VX Agent. Between 1981 and 1991, Iraq produced over 3,857 tonnes of chemical weapons agents. UNSCOM admit 1.5 tonnes of Iraq chemical weapon agents were never accounted for.

- There is absolute proof from various sources that Saddam Hussein smuggled his remaining chemical and biological WMDs over the border into Syria before coalition forces began the Iraqi invasion in 2003. These chemical and biological weapons included sarin, mustard gas, and VX agent.

- There was a well-documented attempted kidnap of an RAF serviceman in the UK in July 2016. No offenders have been captured.

- The fight for Mosul to oust ISIS using Iraqi Forces started in May 2016 with attacks on Al Qayarah airfield. The airfield is now used as the Iraqi Forces base. The U.S. Military is assisting with support staff including U.S. Navy SEALs.

- Any internet search will show manufacturers of crop spraying drones available for purchase.

- The majority of Florida-based theme parks spray droplet water from fans to provide cooling to the public, especially in the hottest months.

# About the Author

I am the author of the John Deacon series of action adventure novels. I make my online home at www.mikeboshier.com. You can connect with me on Twitter at Twitter, on Facebook at Facebook and you can send me an email at mike@mikeboshier.com if the mood strikes you.

Currently living in New Zealand, the books I enjoy reading are from great authors such as Andy McNab, David Baldacci, Brad Thor, Vince Flynn, Chris Ryan, etc. to name just a few. I've tried to write my books in a similar style. If you like adventure/thriller novels, and you like the same authors as I do, then I hope you find mine do them justice.

If you liked reading this book, please leave feedback on whatever system you purchased this from.

http://www.mikeboshier.com

# Books & Further Details

## The Jaws of Revenge

The fate of America lies in the hands of one team of US SEALs. The US mainland is under threat as never before. Osama bin Laden is dead, and the world can relax. Or can they? Remaining leaders of Al-Qaeda want revenge, and they want it against the USA. When good fortune smiles on them and the opportunity presents itself to use stolen weapons of mass destruction, it's Game On!

Al-Qaeda leaders devise a plan so audacious if it succeeds it will wreak the USA for good. With help from Iran and from a US Navy traitor, it can't fail.

One team of US SEALs stand in their way. One team of US SEALs can save America and the West. However, time is running out. **Will they be too late?**

## High Seas Hijack - Short Story

Follow newly promoted US Navy SEAL John Deacon as he leads his team on preventing pirates attacking and seizing ships in and around the Horn of Africa in 2010. When a tanker carrying explosive gases is hijacked even Deacon and his team are pushed to the limit.

Check out my web page http://www.mikeboshier.com for details of latest books, offers and free stuff.

# VIP Reader's Mailing List

To join our VIP Readers Mailing List and receive updates about new books and freebies, please go to my web page and join my mailing list.

www.mikeboshier.com

I value your trust. Your email address will stay safe and you will never receive spam from me. You can unsubscribe at any time.
Thank you.

Made in the USA
Middletown, DE
24 April 2018